A LITTLE TOO FAR

By Lisa Desrochers

A Little Too Far

Coming Soon
A Little Too Much

A Little Too Far

LISA DESROCHERS

WILLIAM MORROW
An Imprint of HarperCollins Publishers

EPub Edition SEPTEMBER 2013 ISBN: 9780062298997
Print Edition ISBN: 9780062299017

10 9 8 7 6 5 4 3 2 1

To the brilliant Kody K.
Keep the faith . . .

Acknowledgments

LEXIE WROTE HER story over the course of thirteen days in January and took me on quite the ride in the process. But she would have wallowed on my hard drive if it weren't for the faith and hard work of many incredible people who I am privileged to have as part of my life.

First and most importantly, to readers who have taken precious time out of your lives to take the ride with my imaginary friends, thank you from the bottom of my heart. You've made it possible for me to do something I truly love for a living, and I will be forever grateful.

Huge hugs to my family, who have supported me in all aspects of my life. I couldn't ask for a better group of people in my corner. Especially huge hugs to my daughters, Michelle and Nicole, for providing constant inspiration, and to my husband, Steven, for the ear to bend and for providing sustenance to my starving children while I obsessed over my imaginary friends.

There aren't words big enough to express my deep gratitude toward my truly fabulous and tireless agent, Suzie Townsend, who, among everything else she's done for me over the years, managed to find *A Little Too Far* the perfect home at William Morrow. And speaking of William Morrow, my most heartfelt thanks go to the entire HarperCollins team. This incredible group of people has managed to put *A Little Too Far* into the world a mere nine months after the idea popped into my head, and I started writing it. Thanks especially to my amazing editor, Amanda Bergeron, for her enthusiasm, her faith in me, and for loving Lexie, Trent, and Alessandro almost as much as I do.

Thank you to Jennifer L. Armentrout for her sage advice. To my bestest writing bud, the brilliant Kody Keplinger, whose friendship and encouragement have meant more to me than I can adequately express in just a few lines, you are and always will be my hero.

Thank you also to Jessica and Giada Bertesina, and Susi Marcone for straightening out all my garbled Italian.

To all the lovely bloggers out there spreading the word and supporting me over the last few years, huge smooches. Y'all ROCK!

And because my muse is a wannabe rock star, I need to send a very special thank-you to the bands that inspired Lexie's story. This book is basically a tribute to Jason Wade, the mastermind behind Lifehouse (whose songs beg to be written into books), with a side of Rob Thomas. See if you can hear Lifehouse's "All In" as you turn the pages of the last few chapters.

and a half years turning into a cheating bastard when you aren't paying attention. Yeah. Things happen.

"Well," she drawls, flicking through a rack of cotton shorts, "everyone was shocked. We all thought you two would end up married."

So did I.

Rick and I had talked about marriage. When I came home for summer break after freshman year, he was the one who brought it up. He was the one who started talking about where we should live after we graduated from college. We'd been voted the couple most likely to make it in our senior yearbook. I'd scribbled my name on countless scraps of paper, trying to decide whether to hyphenate or just change my last name from Banks to Hamilton. So when Sam texted me she'd heard that Rick was seeing someone at school, I chalked it up to the rumor mill.

It wasn't the rumor mill. Or it was, I guess. It was a combination of my boyfriend being an asshat and the rumor mill.

When I got accepted to Notre Dame, there was no question I was going there because, 1) it's a great school, and 2) it's Catholic, which my parents insisted on. But it's also, 3) really far away. A whole bunch of our classmates, including Rick, went to San Jose State because it's so close to home. I guess Rick was too stupid to realize that you can't screw half the campus when the place is swarming with friends of your girlfriend and not have a single one of them notice. So the rumors spread.

The stupid thing? Rick gave me a promise ring for Christmas. He did the whole spiel about how I was the

Chapter One

MY EX IS a douche. A point made all the more clear when I bump into Stacey McCarran at the Forever 21 in the mall.

"Lexie," she drawls, flipping her long, bleached-blond hair over her shoulder and putting on a sympathetic pout. "I was *so* sorry to hear about you and Rick."

It's a lie, and she knows I know it. She was after Rick the whole time we were in high school, and from the knowing smirk underneath that fake pout, I'm guessing they've already done the deed. I wonder if she even waited an hour after we broke up to call him.

Sam steps away from the rack she's perusing, holding a sheer, black tank top with beading around the low V-neck. "Stacey," she sneers, stepping up next to me. Katie is next to her, glaring thorns at Stacey. I can always count on my friends to circle the wagons.

I shrug. "Things happen." Like your boyfriend of three

love of his life, and he knew we'd spend the rest of our lives together, blah, blah, blah.

The stupidest thing? I fell for it—until we were in his bed the night after Christmas. We were technically engaged to be engaged, so I felt justified reading through his texts when he got up to go to the bathroom and peel off his condom.

Yes, it was a douchey thing to do, so maybe I'm a douche too, but it wasn't just what Sam had said. People were looking at us funny when we went to a party at Rick's best friend's house the day after I got home. It was like they were all whispering behind my back, and some of my friends were shooting me sympathetic glances even though no one said anything. I was feeling super paranoid.

So I looked.

Not only were there texts from at least three different girls, but a few pictures too. The pictures were mostly of him sitting with girls in his lap, or dancing. In one, he was kissing a blonde with big boobs, but it didn't look like more than just a peck on the lips. Bad, but not totally incriminating. But the texts . . . some of those were pretty raunchy. I didn't have time to read them all, but I scanned enough of one conversation to know that the rumors were true.

My heart scrunched itself into a tiny knot, and my chest was so empty, I didn't even hurt right at that second. The hurt came later and stayed for a really long time. Just then, in Rick's bedroom, humiliation filled the empty space instead. I was sitting on the edge of his bed, holding his phone in my hand when he came back from the bathroom. "You fucked her in your chemistry lab? *Seriously?*"

His eyes went wide, and all the blood drained from his face. "It's not what you think."

Adrenaline rushed my bloodstream at his denial, and I shook with rage. "Really? That's the best you can do?"

"Lexie, she's psycho. She, like, stalks me all the time."

I turned the phone and swiped through the texts. "Which one? Becky? Gina? Or is Helena the stalker?"

He grimaced and rubbed a hand down his face. "Shit."

I hurled the phone at him, and it hit his shoulder and ricocheted off. He didn't even grab for it on its way to the floor, where it bounced off his foot onto the carpet. "You son of a bitch," I growled, yanking my clothes on.

"Lexie, wait!" he said as I pushed past him to the door.

I spun and flung his ring in his face. "Screw you!"

And that was the end of three and a half years with Rick.

He called and texted almost every day during the spring semester, but I deleted them all without looking. My friends from home were good about avoiding the topic in their texts, so it became easy to pretend Rick had never existed. I was two thousand miles away, and he couldn't just pop by and surprise me, so I felt reasonably safe. But when an opportunity to get even farther away and spend my junior year abroad in Italy came up, I jumped all over it.

By the time I got home for summer break a few months ago, I felt pretty good. I was over Rick. I'd thrown myself into my studies and was going into my junior year at Notre Dame near the top of my art history class. That had won me the scholarship for the year abroad in Rome from over thirty applicants.

Still, I wasn't thrilled with the idea of spending my summer watching Rick screw his way through our old classmates, so I've spent my days since I got home absorbed in my Rosetta Stone software and feel pretty confident I'll be able to 1) find a bathroom (Dove passo trovare il bagno?) or 2) tell someone to go to hell (Va 'al diavolo!). My friends have been cool about avoiding the parties we knew he'd be at, so I've managed to make it all summer without so much as a glimpse of him.

And now I'm two days away from heading to Rome for my junior year, with the possibility of staying the summer for an internship if they like me.

Life is good, and I'm not going to let Stacey rub my face in the parts of it that aren't.

"Yeah, well . . . see you later," I tell her as I turn for the register.

"Bitch," Sam mutters as we walk away, just loud enough for Stacey to hear, and I can't help smiling. She hands me the top and a short, black skirt she's holding. "These are a mandatory purchase. The beading around the neckline will draw attention to your best assets," she says, cupping my boob in her free hand.

"Will you please not feel me up in public?" I mutter, taking the clothes and shoving her away.

"My job, whether you like it or not, is to be sure you don't come home without experiencing all Rome has to offer," she says with raised eyebrows and a knowing smile, "and this outfit will guarantee it."

Sam and Katie are two of a revolving group of about ten of us who hung out together all through high school, but they are the ones I've kept in closest touch with after we all left for college. Sam is deceptively feminine, with long, auburn waves and ivory skin. And she's curvy in a way that turns guys' heads. What you'd never get from her appearance is she's totally kick-ass. Confidence wafts off of her like a strong scent. She's put her brown belt in karate to use teaching self-defense classes at the women's shelter for the last few years and is by far the most outspoken of the three of us. But she also isn't great at keeping confidences confidential. I love her but don't really trust her, if that makes sense.

Katie, on the other hand, has always struggled with her weight, and, therefore, her self-esteem. I think she's beautiful, but she always lets her dark hair hang and dresses a little frumpily. She's generally quieter and more reserved than Sam and tends to blend into the woodwork. I feel like I could talk to Katie, except she's best friends with Sam, and I'm not sure which loyalty would prevail if push came to shove, so I don't.

We make our purchases and head to the Applebee's for lunch. The hostess seats us at a booth near the bar.

"Here," Sam says, reaching across the table for the bags I'm trying to wrestle into my side of the booth. "I'll put some over here."

I hand the big Neiman Marcus bag over the table to

her and keep the smaller ones. She takes it and wedges it against the wall as Katie slides in next to her.

"Can I start you ladies off with something to drink?"

Suddenly, all the oxygen is sucked out of the atmosphere, and spots flash in my eyes. I can't even look at the end of the table where the waiter stands, but I hear Katie's gasp and know it's him.

Oh, God.

"Hi, Rick," Sam says, her voice dry. "Give us a minute, okay?"

There's a long pause where no one says anything, but I feel the weight of everyone's gaze. I hate that the first thing to flit through my mind is an inventory of my appearance. I showered this morning without shaving my legs, then pulled my wet, dirty blond hair back into a high ponytail with a mother-of-pearl clip—by far the nicest thing I'm wearing. I rubbed a little foundation over a few zits on my chin and threw on some mascara, not really caring too much what I looked like. My layered tanks are old and stretched, and my khaki shorts are too baggy in the butt.

I look like shit.

I don't want to care what Rick thinks. But, *damn it,* I do.

"Yeah . . . okay. I'll be back in a few," he answers after a beat.

"Damn, Lexie," Katie hisses when he's gone. "I'm so sorry. I didn't know he worked here."

I thought I had this. I thought I was past him. So why, when I glance up and see him walking away, does my heart skip a beat?

Sam grabs the bag she had just stuffed near the wall. "Let's go."

I force myself to stop chewing at the inside of my cheek and breathe a shaky breath. "No. I'm not going to let him do this to me. I'm not going to keep living like I'm the one who did something wrong."

Katie's expression is all sympathy. "Everyone knows it was him, Lexie. You don't have anything to prove."

"I'm fine," I say, glancing up to where Rick stands at the bar. "I'm not going to be able to avoid him forever."

Sam sets the bag down, giving me the skeptic's squint. "You're sure."

I nod and pick up the menu. "I had my heart set on the turkey club croissant, and I'm not going to let my dirtbag of an ex deprive me of it."

We peruse the menus, and, a few minutes later, Rick is back. I look him in the eye this time, and *damn*, he's still gorgeous. His straight blond hair is longer than when I saw him last, naked in his bedroom, and partially covers his amazing blue eyes. He looks really classy in the white button-down and thin black tie they have him in. "Are you ready for drinks?"

I clear my throat. "Iced tea with—"

"—extra lemon," he finishes for me with that sideways smile that always sets off butterflies in my stomach. "I remember."

"Diet Coke." Sam's voice lashes out like a whip, and Rick turns to her and Katie on the other side of the booth.

"Anything for you, Katie?" he asks.

"Just water."

He nods. "I'll be right back for your order."

Katie leans across the table as he walks away, and whispers, "That wasn't so bad."

"Speak for yourself," I mutter.

"I say we order a bunch of stuff a little at a time . . . you know, to make him work for it, then stiff him on the tip," Sam says, glaring at his back as he steps up to the bar.

"Nope," I say. "He's just any other waiter. I won't give him the satisfaction of knowing he even gets to me anymore." I straighten up in my seat and look at him. "Because he doesn't . . . mostly."

"It's your show, Lexie," Sam says, "but after what he did, if it were me, I'd leave scorched earth. There'd be no mercy."

I slide out of the booth. "I'm going to wash my hands. If he comes back, order me the turkey club croissant, light on the mayo."

The bathrooms are next to the bar, so I have to walk past Rick on my way. His back is to me, and a petite blond waitress is standing next to him, rubbing her arm against his.

". . . tonight if you want. I can promise you a good time," she says as her fingers curl against his thigh and squeeze.

My stomach lurches, and I take a wide berth and walk faster, but before I make it to the bathroom door, he calls my name up the hall. I'm tempted to pretend I don't hear him, but I know he's coming up behind me fast. He's close enough he'd know I'm pretending. Which means he'd know he still affects me.

"What?" I say, spinning on him.

He stops a few feet short of me and jams his hands in his pockets. "How have you been?"

"Great, Rick. I'm just fabulous," I spit. "Are we done?"

"Look, I know I was a jerk," he blurts as I spin for the bathroom.

I don't turn around. "You weren't a jerk. You were an asshole. There's a big difference."

"Fine. I was an asshole. I'm really sorry."

I start moving again. "Sorry doesn't cut it."

"I still love you, Lexie. I can't get past it."

There's a desperate hitch in his voice that claws at my heart and stops me cold.

"Those girls . . . I was a moron." I hear him moving closer as he talks, but I don't turn to look at him. "I haven't touched anyone else since winter break. I don't want anyone else, Lexie. I want you." He lays a hand on my hip, and I swear at myself when I shudder. He gently spins me and tips my face up with a finger under my chin, so I'm looking into his eyes. "I always will."

He leans in very slowly, watching me the whole way. I can't even tell you why I don't pull away from him, but as he presses my body between his and the wall, not only don't I pull away, I kiss him back.

Chapter Two

His fingers thread into my hair as his other hand grasps my hip and pulls me into the curve of his body. It feels so good. So familiar. So easy.

It was always easy with us. I want that back so badly that I let myself get lost in the feeling . . . until someone brushes past us on their way into the bathroom, snapping me out of my fantasy. Because that's what it is, a fantasy. He took what we had and threw it away. There's no way I can ever trust him again.

He leans in again, but I splay a hand on his chest before his lips reach mine. "Don't, Rick. I can't do this again."

His fingers glide down my cheek and trace my lips. "Just think about it, Lexie. Please," he says, letting me go. "I still have the ring. It and my heart will always be yours."

"But your heart wasn't always mine. You gave it away

to Helena and . . ." I throw up my hands, frustrated, when I can't remember the other girls' names, "anyone else who wanted it."

"They never had my heart. It was just sex. That's it. It didn't mean anything." His face scrunches, pleading with me to understand.

My heart climbs up my throat at his words. "How can you say sex doesn't mean anything? We lost our virginity together. I've never been with anyone but you because it means *everything*."

He purses his lips and hangs his head. "I was so stupid." His eye flick to mine again. "Tell me what to do to fix this. I'll do anything."

"I just need to think." This time, when I turn for the bathroom, he doesn't stop me.

I wash up and splash some water on my face, then stare at my shaking self in the mirror. How can I still have feelings for him after what he did? How is there any part of me that isn't totally repulsed by him?

"Hey," Sam says when I get back to the table a few minutes later. "You okay?"

"Have you ordered yet?" I ask.

Her gaze flicks across the restaurant, and I'm guessing she's looking at Rick, but I don't follow it to find out. "Prince Charming hasn't been back. I think he was waiting for you."

I throw a ten on the table to cover the drinks and grab my bags. "You were right. I can't do this. Let's go."

We collect all my stuff and head to the parking lot. Katie pushes the button on her key fob to unlock her battered, yellow Beetle, and the alarm starts blaring as all the lights flash.

"When are you going to get that thing fixed?" Sam yells, slapping her palms over her ears.

Katie clicks the key fob again, and the shrieking stops. "Sorry."

Sam looks the Beetle over with disdain. "We definitely need a new ride."

"You don't like it, you can walk," Katie says defensively, patting her car on the roof like a dog as she pulls open the driver's door. "So, what happened?" she asks me as we climb in.

I slouch into the backseat. "He says he still loves me."

"Don't do it, Lexie," Sam warns, strapping herself in shotgun.

I tip my head back into my seat and stare at the stained roof of Katie's car. "Why did he have to turn out to be such a douche?"

Sam slouches deeper into her seat. "The sad truth is, I think it's in the DNA—somewhere in that Y chromosome is the douche-bag gene."

I lean my head into the window and close my eyes, focusing on making the twenty minutes to my house without crying. I know it's over. I've known it for months, but somehow time isn't making it easier. Whoever said time heals all wounds was a big, fat liar. My heart still remembers what we had and how it felt to lose it.

When Katie drops me at home, Trent's motorcycle is in the driveway, but the house is quiet.

"If that stepbrother of yours is looking for an end-of-the-summer fling," Sam says, flicking a glance at the bike as I get out, "you know where to send him."

I roll my eyes at her.

She leans out her window. "You think I'm joking, but I'm going to jump that boy's bones sooner or later."

"He's probably out with his friends," I say, waving a hand at the house. "Go find him and jump away."

She bangs the side of the car with her palm. "Go fuck some Italian boys and forget about your dirtbag ex." She grins. "And send pictures!"

I lean in and hug her, then move around to Katie's side, where she's out of the car, waiting. "Thanks for taking me shopping," I say, looping an arm around her shoulders.

She hugs me back. "I'm so jealous."

I pull away and smile. "I'll be in touch."

She climbs back into her seat. "You better." There's a waver in her voice, and I realize she's tearing up.

"I will. And I'll see you when I'm home for winter break."

"Bring home a hot Italian!" Sam calls from across the car.

I can't help cracking a smile as I turn for the house. I slide my key into the front lock and pushed the door open, then wave at Katie and Sam. Katie gives a bleep of her horn, and they pull away from the curb. I watch until they disappear around the corner, then head upstairs.

I climb the stairs to my room two at a time and dump my bags on the floor near my closet. But what Rick said keeps cycling through my brain.

I still have the ring. It and my heart will always be yours.

I thought we'd be together forever. But then he ripped my heart out in the most humiliating way possible. I don't think I love him anymore . . . but what if I never find anyone else? What if that was my one shot at true love? We were so happy. Why did he have to fuck it all up?

"Damn you!" I grab a picture frame off my dresser—one that has a picture of me, Sam, and Katie at graduation that I put in over the top of a portrait of me and Rick at prom—and heave it at the wall between Trent's room and mine. It shatters, leaving a gash in the blue paint next to my collage of favorite sketches.

I sink into a sobbing heap on the carpet, glad I have the house to myself. I don't need an audience for my meltdown.

"Lexie?"

Trent's voice comes through the door, but I can't catch my breath to answer. So much for no audience.

The door hinges creak as he pushes it open and pokes his head through the crack. He has a minor case of bed-head—his chocolate brown curls smashed on one side—and his wrinkled gray Loyola Wrestling T-shirt and well-worn jeans look slept in. "Hey, you okay?"

"Yeah . . . great," I heave between sobs.

"That was stupid. Sorry." He comes into the room and crouches next to me, rubbing my back.

I wipe my forearm under my nose. "Sorry to wake you up."

His deep brown eyes are all concern. "No biggie. What happened?"

"Nothing." But then Rick's face when he said he still loved me flashes in my mind, and I heave another sob.

"Come here," Trent says, pulling me off the floor by a hand. He tows me to the bed and sits, pulling me down next to him. I tuck my head against his solid chest, and he wraps me in his strong arms and rocks me like a baby. He hums as he rocks me, and I know the tune instantly. My heart melts a little, remembering the first time he ever sang it to me, four years ago.

Trent's thing, like his mom's, is music. Julie teaches piano, and by the time I met Trent the summer before his freshman year, he could play almost anything. When our parents got married two years later, Julie tried to teach me, but I don't really have the patience for sitting at the piano for a half hour each day to practice, so after about a year of trying, she finally stopped forcing it on me. But Trent couldn't get enough. He taught himself guitar and started his first garage band that year. They played together all through high school. Now he's a music performance major at Loyola. With my fetish for the visual arts and his for music, between the two of us, we have the arts pretty well covered.

All my tight muscles begin to soften as his fingers knead my shoulders. This is what only he can do for me. What he's *always* done for me.

Dad and Julie started dating the summer before I started eighth grade. By the time they got married, when I was fifteen and a half and Trent had just turned sixteen, we all knew each other pretty well.

Trent and I got comfortable around each other pretty

quickly, even before we were officially a family. We'd hang out and play Warcraft when our parents were on dates, and one or the other of us would just start talking. A lot of the time it was about our parents. I'd gone through a rough patch around that time, missing the mother I never knew and blaming myself that she was dead—which the shrink said was partly because there was a new mother figure in my life and partly because of my raging hormones and my growing awareness of my own mortality. Put whatever psychobabble label you want on it, all I knew was I hurt. I'd tell Trent how I thought I killed my mom by being born and how I wondered if that made me a murderer. He said it didn't, but I always thought he only said it to make me feel better. I'd usually end up curled around him in his beanbag chair after I started crying.

Other times, he would talk about how his dad and his new wife wanted him to go live there with his twin half brothers. I begged him not to, and he said he never would. He told me how his father used to take him to his peewee baseball games on Saturdays when he was little, and how there was a "friend" that he always met there while Trent's team played. And how he'd tell Trent to stay put with the other kids while he helped his "friend" with something at her car. And how he left for work the day after Trent's seventh birthday and never came home. And how all Trent really remembered was Julie's crying all the time. And how his dad and his "friend" had the twins just a few months later and got married as soon as the divorce was final.

From there, we just started telling each other everything else. He's the only one who knows all the sordid details of my love life—things too embarrassing for even Sam and Katie. I've confided all of it to Trent, in detail. Like how, graduation night of our junior year, when Rick and I were in the backseat of his dad's car in the process of trying to lose our virginity, he couldn't figure out the condom in the dark and ended up tearing it. And how we'd done it anyway, without protection. When my period was three days late, Trent had been right there with me, sweating out each day until it came. He had gotten in Rick's face when we started dating at the end of sophomore year and gave him the standard brotherly warning about treating me right. And when Rick screwed around on me, Trent made good on his promise and decked him.

But that's just the kind of guy Trent is.

With effortless charm, classic good looks, a quick wit, and an impeccable sense of style, he's basically a six-foot, two-hundred-pound people magnet. I doubt there's anyone who's ever spent more than five minutes with him who doesn't consider him a friend.

He graduated from high school the year before me and left a wide swath of broken hearts in his wake. I'm convinced that more than half of my friends in high school were only friends with me because they hoped I'd hook them up with him. "I can't believe you're related to Trent Sorenson! He's so hot!" is all I ever heard, even from Sam and Katie. Hell, I'd even crushed on him a little when our parents first started dating.

Though he's not one to kiss and tell, I get the solid sense that the trend of endless friends and countless broken hearts has continued into his first three years in college. But what I know that no one else does is that things aren't as easy for Trent as he makes them seem.

Only I know how deep his father's leaving cut. He hated his dad so much that, when our parents got married, he wanted mine to adopt him, but his dad wouldn't let that happen. Trent feels like his father made him an accomplice in his mom's undoing. No matter how many times I tell him it wasn't his fault, he beats himself up constantly for not having seen what was going on. And he's never told anyone else, including Julie, what happened during all those peewee baseball games. He feels *that* guilty.

Only I know that the reason he's never panned out to be the college wrestler everyone thought he would be is that his heart just isn't in it. He's wanted to quit since freshman year to focus on his music, and the only reason he hasn't is because he's afraid to disappoint Dad.

Only I know that since sophomore year at Loyola, he's wanted to quit school altogether, but he knows how much that would disappoint Julie, who thinks any musician worth his salt needs classic training.

He's miserable, and only I know it.

But our *big* secret—the one we spit swore to each other we'd take to our graves? We were each other's first kiss.

It was the day after my fifteenth birthday, about five months before Dad married Julie, and it was one of my bad days. I was in Trent's lap in his beanbag, crying over how I'd killed my mother fifteen years earlier, and he wiped the tears off my face and told me everything was going to be okay. He rubbed my back and pulled me to his shoulder, and the next thing I knew, we were kissing. The kiss was tender and sweet, and it lasted for a long time. I still remember how gentle his hands felt as he hugged me closer and that his lips tasted like bubble gum. But the instant it was over, we knew it was wrong. He just looked at me for a minute, then cleared his throat, and said, "We can't do that anymore."

I nodded, we spit in our palms and shook on it, and that was that.

It's always been easy to talk to Trent. Just knowing he loves me unconditionally—that he'll never judge me, and I don't have to hide who I am from him—it makes me feel understood. And he's never stopped holding me when I'm upset. Like now.

"I'm guessing this is about Rick," he says, and I hear the edge to his voice.

I hiccup and nod.

"What me to kick his ass again?"

I snivel. "Would you?"

"Anything for you, Lexie," he says with a squeeze of my shoulders. "Tell me the whole sad story."

I love how my name sounds when he says it. When he sings, his voice gets a little gravelly when he gets to the really emotional parts, and he says my name like that, with just a hint of gravel.

I breathe deep to get my thoughts straight. "Sam, Katie, and I went to the Applebee's at the mall. I didn't know he was working there this summer."

"Hmm . . ." With my cheek pressed against his muscled chest, I feel Trent's hmm more than I hear it. "Let me guess: He's sorry and he wants you back."

"He still has the ring."

He combs his fingers gently through my hair, and goose bumps prickle my scalp. "And you're thinking about it."

"Does that make me totally sick?"

"Yes. I think it does."

I shove away from him but then see the smile in his eyes. "I miss being with him . . . the feeling like we belong together. I miss being that close to someone."

"You still have me," he says with a wink.

I narrow my eyes at him. "And I miss the sex."

His eyebrows go up. "He was that good?"

I shrug. "I don't have anything to compare him with, but when we were together, I knew he loved me. I guess that's what I miss."

He pulls me back into his strong arms. "Love pretty much blows, but, for what it's worth, I think you'll regret it if you take him back."

"What if it was just a mistake? He says he won't do it again." Part of me is desperate to believe it, but as I say it, I realize I don't.

"Can't teach an old dog new tricks."

I pull away and look at him. "Have you ever cheated on anyone?"

He contemplates that for a second. "I'm not going to say I haven't pissed a lot of girls off, but I prefer to do it honorably. If it's just a hookup, I make sure they know that before anything happens, and if I'm with someone and I want to hook up with someone new, I break up with the one I'm with first."

I roll my eyes. "So chivalrous."

"Say what you will, but I've never been anything less than straight up with any girl I've ever been with. I've never lied or gone behind anyone's back. Ever."

As much as it sounds like it would suck to be one of his many hookups or dumpees, it's hard to argue his point.

He pulls away from me, and I shiver, suddenly cold. "Wait here. I'll be right back." He stands and moves to the door, then gives me his signature lazy smile before disappearing into the hall.

I grab a tissue from the box on my nightstand, blotting my eyes and smearing off my ruined mascara, and a few minutes later Trent is back with two tumblers, each with about an inch of dark amber liquid in it.

"Drowning sorrows this big calls for a double shot of Randy's scotch," he says, handing me a glass. "Good thing your dad springs for the good stuff."

We both knock it back, and my face pinches involuntarily. But once I'm past the initial burn, I feel my insides start to warm.

"Warcraft?" he asks with a nod at my TV.

"Yeah, sure."

"Nothing like a good troll slaughter to help you forget all your shit." He gets the game all queued up, and, by the time he hands me my remote, I'm starting to feel all warm and gooey inside from the scotch. I slide back and lean into the stack of pillows on the headboard.

Our first quest involves more blood than usual. My

avatar, Galidrod the elf, powers through a troll barrage easily. I imagine Rick's face on each one as I shoot them, and they explode in a shower of purple guts. It's totally therapeutic. But then Trent's avatar, who he for some reason made human and named Jethro, is wounded as he takes out the last orc, and Galidrod, who, through my unparalleled Warcraft prowess, has accumulated massive healing powers, has to save him.

"So, what should I do?" I ask once Jethro is up to full strength again.

"Run like hell."

"But I miss him."

Trent shakes his head and pauses the game. "You don't miss him. You miss the *idea* of him."

I set my remote on the nightstand and turn on my hip, facing him. "What does that even mean?"

He lifts my legs and loops them over his, rubbing his palm against the grain of the three-day stubble on my calf. "You were together for a long time. You thought you'd be together forever. It was what you knew, and now you're out of your comfort zone. It's easy to want to go back to the safety net."

He just so totally hit it on the head. I want the safety net. But the problem is, the safety net has a huge freaking hole in it now. It'll dump me on my head if I trust it.

But it still hurts.

"You're right. I miss the idea of him."

"It sucks," he says with a small nod.

I sigh and shift deeper into the pillows. "But what if he was supposed to be The One?"

"He wasn't."

"How do you know?"

His hand pauses on my leg, midstroke. "Because he never deserved you."

"What if I never find anyone else?"

He stares into my eyes for what has to be a full minute before saying, "You will."

An electric tingle zings through my insides, and the next thing I know, his lips are pressing against mine. I don't even know who made the move.

But it doesn't stop there.

Kissing Trent is like sticking my toe in the ocean and suddenly being in over my head. I'm drowning in him. I don't know whether it's him or the scotch, but as his tongue edges my mouth and slips through my lips, desperation like I've never felt before swells inside me. Years of suppressed desire rear up, and, suddenly, I'm starving for him. The only thing I know for sure is, if I don't have him right now, I'll die.

My heart gallops in my chest as I slide down on the bed and pull him down with me.

"Shit, Lexie," he breathes between kisses. "What are we doing?"

I grab fistfuls of his thick brown curls and pull him to me, smothering the question on his lips with another kiss.

He doesn't resist when I pull off his shirt, then mine. He doesn't try to stop me when I wiggle out of my shorts and thong and kick them to the floor. He moans deep in his throat as my fingers trail over his cut abs and pop the button of his jeans. And when my hand slides in under his waistband and finds his erection, he stops breathing altogether.

Never during any of it, even once we're both naked on my bed, does any part of me feel like we shouldn't be doing this. All of a sudden, he isn't my stepbrother. He's everything I've ever needed.

Chapter Three

His touch is gentle, but I can feel the same desperation in it as fills me. I've never wanted anything so much.

And he wants me too.

My fingers trace the lines of his defined biceps and pecs, down his abs, and through the tuft of dark hair to his erection. He moans my name again when I squeeze hard and rub, and his hand trails slowly across my hip to the inside of my thigh. I gasp, and all the muscles in my groin tighten around his fingers as they slip inside me. He withdraws a wet fingertip and strokes my clit, and when he presses, fireworks explode inside, and I moan. I have just a second to think that he's way more experienced than me before I can't think at all. His finger flicks, and I let out another gasp and arch up as he takes my left breast into his mouth. He rolls his tongue over my nipple, and goose bumps skitter over my entire body. His hot breath scorches my skin as his mouth and tongue explore, turning my whole body into one throbbing nerve ending.

His tongue finds my belly button on his way lower, and he brushes his fingertips up the inside of my thigh. They slide inside me again as he trails his lips and tongue along the sensitive skin there, then his mouth is on me. His tongue swirls over my clit and sends a series of pulsing shock waves through me. I hear my moan as it escalates into a mewl, but there's nothing I can do to stop it. When he twists his fingers deep inside me and sucks my clit, my head spins, and I think for sure that I must be dying.

"Oh, God," I gasp when he sucks again, harder. All I can feel is Trent and the magic he works with his fingers and mouth, bringing me higher and higher. The sounds rolling out of the deepest part of me don't even sound human anymore as I hit the peak of this excruciating ecstasy somewhere around Jupiter. I'm panting for breath, and stars flash in my eyes from lack of oxygen. He gives one last suck, and I scream as I'm plummeted off the precipice and free-fall back to Earth.

I have a few condoms in the drawer of my nightstand, and I have just enough presence of mind to pull one out and tear it open.

"Here," I breathe, as he kisses his way back to my mouth.

Heat pulses through me with the rhythm of the throbbing ache between my legs. The lights are on, and I can see every detail as he rolls the condom on, including how much bigger he is than Rick. I never realized until this second that men's packages came in such different sizes.

When he's ready, he rolls on top of me and looks down at me with a question in his eyes. I feel his firmness pressing against the inside of my thigh and align my hips with his. His moan when my fingers sweep down his back and pull him tighter against me sends fire through my veins. The very tip of his thickness enters me, and I'm so ready for the rest of him that I let out a whimper when he stops. For a second, he doesn't move, every muscle in his body taut as he fights with himself. His tortured gaze holds mine. "God, Lexie," he says, but it's strangled. "God," he breathes again, squeezing his eyes shut.

Before he can change his mind, I rock my hips against his, taking him all the way into me. His face pinches as he sucks in a sharp breath, then lets out an agonized groan.

He fills me completely, stretching me in a way that heightens every sensation, so when he finally gives in and grasps my hips, thrusting himself deep inside me, I cry out in the most sublime pain I've ever experienced. I rock against him as he pumps, at first excruciatingly slowly, but then harder and faster. His muscles ripple under smooth skin with the motion, and my hands glide over them, memorizing every detail. Pressure in my groin builds like a brewing volcano with each thrust until I feel sure I'm going to erupt.

I flip us so I'm on top and sit up, straddling him. I trace a finger along the lines of the tattoo over his heart—the kanji symbol for knowledge—as he grasps my thighs and rolls his hips underneath me. I helped him pick out the pattern for his ink when he turned eighteen. I got a matching one seven months later, when I turned eighteen.

His hips roll under mine, and his pecs flex under my fingers as his hands slide up to my hips, pulling me harder against him. I trail my fingers down his chest to his cut abs. He was buff in high school, but I remember his saying when he started college that scholarship athletes spend more time training and in the gym than they do in class. The results are spectacular.

As I ride him, his thumb finds my clit and rubs circles. He's soft and slow at first, but he rubs harder and faster as my moans escalate to actual gasps of, *Oh, God!*

I'm making a lot of noise. I might even have screamed at him to fuck me harder. All I know is that he does until everything inside me explodes in a burst of pure bliss. At the same instant that he lets out an animal growl, I go limp on top of him, breathing hard. We lie here for a long time as we catch our collective breath.

As strange as it should feel to be here with Trent like this, it doesn't. I'm not totally immune to his charms, and since we first met, there's been an underlying current of sexual tension between us. Now that we've done it, released the beast, I feel more content than I remember ever feeling before. It feels right, like we fit perfectly, his body and mine—like this is where we've always belonged, in each other's arms.

Finally, he opens his eyes and looks at me. "Are you okay? I was a little . . . rough."

"I'm amazing," I say, pressing a kiss to his lips.

His tongue circles my lips, and I open wide, swirling my tongue with his and kissing him like my life depends on it. He moans softly, and when I pull back, a lazy smile creeps across his perfect lips. "So, what happens now?"

And that's when I come crashing back to Earth—and reality.

I just had totally mind-blowing sex with my stepbrother.

And I'm leaving for Rome in two days.

Which is a good thing because I just had totally mind-blowing sex with my stepbrother.

He's still inside me, and all I can think is, *Oh God. What did I do?*

I'm just about to open my mouth to say . . . I have no idea what, when his eyes widen and he dumps me on the bed and leaps off it. He's out the door in less time than it takes my racing heart to beat.

Does he know what I was thinking—that what we just did is a hot mess? But then I hear it. The garage door.

Dad and Julie.

I get up and kick Trent's clothes under my bed. The scotch glasses clank together as I toss them under too, and I'm fairly certain at least one of them breaks. I grab my clothes off the floor and yank them on, but I get my tanks on backward.

"Lexie!" Julie yells up the stairs.

"Coming!" I holler back as I spin my shirts and stick my arms through.

I cringe in the mirror over my dresser, smoothing my yes-I-just-had-mind-blowing-sex hair and unsmudging the mascara under my eyes, then rip open the door.

Julie looks up at me from the bottom of the stairs, and suddenly I go all paranoid. Can she tell? Does she know her son just fucked my brains out? But she doesn't look alarmed, or horrified, or disgusted, or any of the things I know she would if she'd heard us.

Tall and slender, she's a classic beauty. I've seen pictures of my mom, and they have some things in common—like a narrow face and long, wavy, blond hair, which Julie usually wears twisted onto the back of her head in a messy bun, as it is now. But where Julie has some of the warmest brown eyes I've ever seen (something Trent got from her), Mom had green eyes—which I inherited, along with her dirty blond hair, a-little-too-full lips, and fair skin. Even at forty-five, Julie could be a model. She's that stunning. As beautiful as both she and Trent are, though, it's obvious from Trent's strong jaw, thick brown hair, and skin that bronzes if he just thinks about the sun, that the deep end of his gene pool came from his father, whom I've only seen in pictures.

"I got you some things for Rome!" she announces. "Have you started packing?"

"Not yet," I answer with a glance back at Trent's closed door before trudging down the stairs to where she stands. "What did you get?"

"All the tour books say American food is hard to come by and very expensive there."

"Which is why I was planning on eating Italian food," I say warily.

"I just picked up a few of your favorites . . ." She waves a hand at the kitchen, where I hear Dad crashing around, unpacking groceries. "Nonperishable things that are easy to pack. Come on," she says, turning for the kitchen.

I chew the inside of my cheek with worry as I follow her into the kitchen, and she sends me back to my room a few minutes later with a grocery bag full of pretzels, Skittles, Pringles, Saltines, and a small jar of peanut butter. "Dinner will be ready in half an hour," she calls to me as I make my way up the stairs.

My stomach tightens at the thought of food . . . and at the thought of eating it at a table with Trent. I stop and turn around. "I ate a super late lunch with Sam and Katie. I think I'm just going to pack and go to bed."

Her forehead scrunches as she takes a few steps toward me. "You're not getting sick, are you?"

"No, Julie. I'm just not hungry."

She purses her lips like she wants to argue, but finally says, "Fine. But let Trent know we're eating soon."

I nod and climb the last few stairs.

Trent is picking at his acoustic guitar in a way that I know means he's writing something new. I love to watch his creative process—how it starts with a simple melody that blooms into a rich harmony, then he adds lyrics, and it's a whole, hauntingly beautiful song. I used to sit on the floor in his room with my homework or my sketchpad or whatever for hours, just listening. There is this one song he wrote when we were sixteen that he titled "Someone, Somehow." It's the tune he always hums to me when I'm sad. He says it's about how fate sent him the one person on this planet who truly understands him.

That person is me.

The chorus is what always gets to me.

You fill the hollow places life has left behind.
And now your soul is tangled into mine.
When I needed an angel you were there,
you, to all my secrets I bare.
I needed you then,
and I need you now.
Someone, somehow.

I'll never forget the first time he sat on the edge of my bed and played it for me. I cried like a baby, and he held me. We woke up curled together in a ball under my sheets the next morning, and he kissed my cheek and told me he loved me.

That was probably the best night of my life.

I yearn to go listen—to see what this melody will bloom into. But I don't. I don't knock on his door. I don't even go near it. Instead, I stand in mine and call down the hall, "Dinner's on in thirty," then close my door in case he opens his.

I toss and turn all night as I lie here listening for any sound from the room next door, torn between wanting to hear Trent tiptoeing toward my door and dreading hearing him tiptoeing toward my door. I can't explain why, but I get up in the middle of the night and fish his T-shirt out from under the bed. I tug it on, then climb back into bed. As I lie here wrapped in his scent—something warm and a little spicy that's just Trent—I fantasize about going to him.

I don't. I can't.

I wake up early, and the first thing I do is listen for him. When I don't hear anything, I crawl out of bed, hugging his T-shirt around me, and grab my iPad. I bring it back to bed with me and type, *Is it illegal to have sex with your stepbrother* into the search window.

The consensus on wiki.answers.com and answers.yahoo.com is that it's disgusting but not illegal, so at least that's something. But I can't stop thinking about it. So much so that Rick has barely crossed my mind since it happened—and then only to realize how much more Trent made me feel in twenty minutes than Rick ever did.

I pull my sketchpad off my nightstand and flip to my work in progress to settle my frazzled nerves. It has always fascinated me how much a single expression can say, and my sketchbook is full of people with expressions I could never describe in words. This one's a pregnant woman sitting on a park bench. I saw her there a few days ago when I was bored and had taken my sketchpad to the park. Her eyes were on a little boy on the jungle gym, but she was talking in hushed tones to her baby bump. She wasn't smiling, but there was something about her expression that struck me. I can't quite capture it.

I erase some of the shading around her face and start again as I listen intently through my wall for any sign of Trent. Finally, around eleven, I hear him rustling around in his room. His door clicks open a few minutes later, and I hear him stride past my door on his way to the stairs.

"Mom!" he calls, "I'm going to the gym!" Then the front door opens, and my window rattles as it slams closed.

I bunch his T-shirt up to my nose and watch out my window as he straps his duffel onto the back of his bike. He swings a leg over the seat, tugs on his helmet, then flicks the engine to life. I duck behind my window frame when his head turns in my direction, but a second later, he hits the throttle and rockets off, leaving another skid mark in the driveway. I move back to the window and listen until I can't hear the roar of his engine anymore. When he's gone, I drop onto my bed with my arm over my eyes and just lie here, remembering. I remember the feel of his hungry mouth moving on mine; the way his fingers knew my body—played it perfectly, just like it was his guitar; how he filled me to overflowing, both physically and emotionally.

Why do I feel like I'm suffocating? Is it because of what happened? Or because it can't happen again?

I jump and sit up when Julie knocks on my door. The hinges creak as she opens it and pokes her head through. "Your father and I were wondering if you want anything special for your last dinner in the US of A. We could go out or whatever you want."

I cross my arms over my chest so she hopefully won't recognize Trent's Loyola Wrestling T-shirt. "Olive Garden," I say, then crack a shaky smile.

At first she just looks at me funny, but then understanding dawns, and she smiles back. "Ah . . . Italian."

"I'm kidding. How about Outback?" It's Dad's favorite, and it may be a while before I can get an American-sized heart-attack-on-a-plate.

"I'll tell your father." She smiles as she closes the door,

and I can't help wondering what she'd think if she knew I just slept with her son . . . and maybe want to do it again.

THIS IS . . . AWKWARD.

I didn't think the whole going-out-to-dinner thing all the way through. Trent and I sit across the table from one another, totally ignoring each other's existence. I cut my steak into smaller pieces and push them around my plate.

"What time did we decide you have to leave for the airport?" Dad asks, sawing a hunk off the slab of beef on his plate and looking at me. He's got his usual disheveled-professor look happening, with messy salt-and-pepper hair, five o'clock shadow, a wrinkled white button-down open at the collar, and wire-rimmed glasses. But it works for him.

"Ten thirty. My flight's at one."

"Did you hear that, Trent?" Julie says. "You'll need to get your butt out of bed before eleven tomorrow morning."

He glances up from his food, which, now that I look at him, I see he hasn't eaten either, and I can't help but think of the last thing I saw him put in his mouth . . . which was basically me. He pushes his dark curls out of his gorgeous eyes. "I wasn't . . . I didn't know you wanted me to go."

"Of course you're going! You want to see Lexie off for her exotic trip abroad, don't you?"

"I thought . . ." His eyes slip to mine for the briefest instant. "I just thought the car would be pretty full."

"Nonsense," Julie says. She pats my hand. "So it's settled, then. We'll all be ready by ten."

I glance at Trent and catch his gaze for just a second before he looks away. I half check out as Julie and Dad go off on everything I'm going to see, recalling their anniversary trip to Rome a few years back.

Rome and Florence, which aren't too far apart, are the art capitals of Italy. The Renaissance and the Baroque Movement were born there. Raphael and Bernini. Michelangelo and Leonardo da Vinci. Their work is everywhere and has influenced the very makeup of those cities. This is an art history major's wet dream. I've been looking forward to this trip for months. I've been living for it.

So why is my heart in my throat at the thought of leaving?

After dinner, Dad drives us home. I shoot glances at Trent in the backseat next to me. We should be laughing and giving each other shit, same as always. His silence is killing me.

He glances at me and catches me looking, but this time, I don't turn my eyes away. He holds my gaze and, after a minute, mouths, "We need to talk."

I nod.

"Do you need any help with the last of your packing?" Julie asks as we push through the garage door into the kitchen.

"No. I think I'm mostly ready except for last-minute stuff."

She nods, then, out of nowhere, she goes all teary and wraps me in a hug. "I can't believe our little girl is going halfway around the world all by herself."

"I'm twenty, Julie. I'm not that little."

"Lexie Banks, world traveler," she warbles in my ear.

"We've got the international plan set up for your phone," Dad says, "so we expect to hear from you."

"You will," I say, extricating myself from Julie's grasp. "I'll call when I can."

"Remember the time difference," Dad reminds me.

"Don't worry. I won't call you at three in the morning." I give him a devious smile. "Much."

He kisses my forehead. "We love you, kiddo, and we're extremely proud of you."

"Thanks, Dad." I make my way to the stairs, and Trent follows. "See you in the morning."

When we get to the top, Trent hesitates outside my door. "Is it okay if I come in?"

He's never asked before, and I hate that he feels like he has to now. "Sure."

We step through, and I close the door behind us.

"Listen, I get how awkward this is, but you're my best friend, Lexie." He breathes deep and drops his gaze. "If I did something to screw that up, I'll never forgive myself."

I step into his arms, and they're strong around me without my even having to ask. "I don't know what happened last night . . . if it was just the scotch or . . ." I look up at him. "You're my best friend, and I don't want that to change."

He kisses my forehead. "Good. So we're agreed. Last night never happened."

I hug him tighter, never wanting to lose this. "Agreed."

"Even though it was pretty damn amazing," he murmurs into my hair.

I smile into his T-shirt. "Mind-blowing."

"I'm really going to miss you. I don't think we've ever gone more than a few months without seeing each other."

It's true. Even though Indiana is a plane ride away, I see my family pretty often. I'm always home for Thanksgiving and winter break, and they come out to Notre Dame for the USC football game because that's Dad's alma mater. Anytime one of Trent's wrestling matches is within reasonable driving distance, I buy a bus ticket, and there's spring break. But this year, I'm only coming home for three weeks at Christmas, then not again until the end of the school year in May—and maybe not even then if I get the summer internship.

"How will you survive without me?" I ask into his shirt.

"It's gonna be tough." He breathes a sigh, then pulls away and looks down at me. "So, we're okay?"

I smile up at him. "We're okay."

He backs toward the door, looking majorly relieved. "Good. Love you. See you in the morning."

"Love you too. 'Night."

He closes the door behind him, and I just stare after him for a long time. Finally, I strip to my thong and slide his Loyola T-shirt on. (Don't ask me why I didn't give it back.) I hesitate at Trent's door for a second as I pass by it to the bathroom to wash up and brush my teeth. When I finish in the bathroom, I click off the light, and pull the door open—just as Trent comes up the hall, a towel slung low on his hips.

He stops short in the door when he sees me. "Oh, sorry. I didn't know you were still in here."

"I'm done. All yours."

I start to squeeze past him in the door, but he stops me with a hand on my shoulder. "Nice shirt."

My heart kicks up a notch, and my cheeks flame. His T-shirt hangs to midthigh, but, suddenly, I feel totally exposed. How do I explain this? "It was . . . you left it—"

"It looks better on you anyway." His fingertips brush down my arm and accidentally skim the side of my left breast, and I feel my nipple harden—which is uber-obvious since I'm braless. "You should keep it."

"Thanks."

"So, I'm going to . . ." He tips his head at the shower.

"Yeah . . . okay. Well . . . 'night."

As I slip past him, his towel comes untucked. In the second before he grabs it and tucks it back around him, I catch a glimpse of his enormous erection. And, God help me, I'm dripping wet. I press my palm against him through the towel.

He closes his eyes and blows out a shaky breath. "Why can't I stop wanting you?"

In one deft motion, he spins me against the wall and slides my thong down. I kick it off and wrap my legs around his waist as he presses me between his rock-hard body and the wall. He crushes his mouth to mine, and his tongue slashes between my lips and takes possession of me. An animal groan purrs deep in his throat and totally undoes me. My pulse pounds in my ears and throbs between my legs, and any inhibitions I had evaporate like fog in a stiff breeze.

He takes my lower lip between his teeth and looks at

me with fire in his eyes, then kisses down my neck as his fingers slide inside of me, working their magic. I'm still sore from last night, but that doesn't stop sparklers from igniting deep in my belly as his fingertips stroke my most sensitive spots.

"Oh, God," I moan as he crooks his fingers inside me and works me into a total sexual frenzy. I feel like all my insides are on the outside. Every nerve ending is on fire. When I can't stand it another second, I reach for his towel and yank it off.

Chapter Four

HE'S HUGE AND hard, and I don't even care that we don't have a condom. He shifts me lower on his hips, and I feel his firmness against my thigh. I reach for him and stroke.

"Jesus Christ," he moans, and I come totally unhinged.

But just as I'm about to press myself lower on his hips, taking him inside me, there's a crash from downstairs. We both look up, startled, and I hear Julie call something to Dad. Dad and Julie's room is down there, and they almost never come up, but the reminder jars us both back to our senses.

Trent grimaces and lowers me to my feet. He reaches for his towel, wrapping it around himself. "Shit. I'm sorry."

I'm shaking as I scoop my panties off the bathroom floor. "I . . ." I bite my lip. "I'll see you in the morning." I scamper toward my room without looking back.

But I don't go to sleep.

I lie under my sheet with his T-shirt hiked up around my waist and close my eyes, picturing Trent on the other side of the wall. I touch the places he touched me, trying to re-create his movements with my less-skilled hands. I imagine him on top of me. Inside me. But my orgasm is disappointing. It's a shadow of the monster that woke inside me last night, when it was his mouth and his fingers driving me totally out of my mind.

Why can't I stop wanting you?

His words echo in my head as I finally start to doze off, and I wonder the same thing about him.

TRENT HOLDS MY hand in the backseat of Dad's car on the way to the airport, but he doesn't look at me. Going to Rome is the best thing for me right now. I need time away from him to think. Something between us is fundamentally different, and I have to decide if I want it to stay that way—if I want Trent to be something more . . . if that's even possible—or if I want to try to get back the companionship and camaraderie we've always shared. I can't decide that while we're together because my body keeps trying to override my powers of rational thought.

The only silver lining—I haven't wasted a second thinking about Rick in the last forty-eight hours.

My phone vibrates, and I pull it out of my pocket, reading Sam's text. *Miss you already, gurl. Text me when you get to Rome!*

I will, I text back.

My phone buzzes again. *Make sure to include pics of all the hot Italian boys you meet!*

I smile. *I will do my best to indulge your fantasies.*

Speaking of fantasies, I'll make sure that brother of yours doesn't get lonely while you're away.

A steel band tightens around my chest as I shoot him a glance. The muscles in his forearm ripple as his thumb drums on his knee to the music from his iPod, giving the appearance he's relaxed. But the muscle twitching in his jaw reveals how tense he actually is. I push the memory of what those hands are capable of out of my mind and ignore the pulsing ache in my belly as my thumbs type in the only words they can and not give away what I'm really thinking. *Knock yourself out.*

We get my bags checked, and Dad, Julie, and Trent walk me to security.

Julie pecks me on the cheek. "Call us when you're making your connection in New York," she says, adjusting the collar of my blouse.

"And as soon as you get to Rome," Dad adds.

I lift my eyebrows at him. "You know that's going to be at one in the morning your time, right?"

"It's fine. We won't be able to sleep unless we know you're safe." He steps up and hugs me so hard I'm surprised he doesn't dislocate a rib. "Love you, kiddo."

"Love you guys too," I say, turning to Trent.

He just looks at me for a long heartbeat, and I'm not sure how this is going to go. What am I supposed to say? He saves me the anguish of trying to figure it out when he closes the few feet between us and wraps me in his strong arms. "Love you," he whispers into my ear. He's said those words to me a thousand times, but today they feel different. They make my insides quiver. He presses a kiss to the corner of my mouth, and I want so badly to turn that fraction of an inch and kiss him properly.

When he pulls away, I ache. It's a whole-body withdrawal, and for a second, I'm not sure I can get on that plane.

Julie sniffles, and when I glance at her, she's dabbing a tissue to her face. "When your father and I met, we hoped you kids would never feel like 'steps' to one another, but you two are closer than we ever could have hoped."

I fight the wince, and I can't even look at Trent.

"You better be on your way, kiddo," Dad says, handing me my backpack.

"Arrivederci." I try to smile as I glance at Trent, but it feels more like a grimace.

As I back toward the security line, Trent's eyes are pinched, and his jaw is set. He breathes deep and closes them. I turn away and don't look back.

THE FLIGHT IS long, made longer by the fact I'm terrified of flying—which really stems from my fear of heights. Or more specifically: my fear of plummeting to my death from them. The only way I can get past it is to get an aisle seat as far from the window as possible and put in my earbuds. Sometimes, if I can convince myself I'm on a train, or a bus, or a slow-moving banana boat to China, I can actually doze off. But this time, when I finally doze off somewhere over North Dakota, I dream of Trent. He's totally invaded my subconscious, taking over and setting up base camp.

I imagine him going back to Loyola—all the girls there—and I can't deny the jealous prickle in my gut. I don't want him to be with other girls, honorable or not. Would he tell me if he was sleeping with someone else? When I was just his friend, his stepsister, he would have told me anything if I asked. Now that I'm his lover, would he still? He said he's never snuck around or lied to girls. Does that apply to me? We're not technically dating— because *hello,* he's my stepbrother—so it wouldn't be sneaking around if he hooked up with someone else. Would he see it that way? Or would he feel like he needed to tell me?

I chew all the skin off the insides of my cheeks as I go around in circles with that until I'm about to drive myself insane. Finally, I click on the TV on the seatback in front of me and try to find something to watch that will distract me from my fucked-up brother-lover issues.

I'M EXHAUSTED BY the time our flight touches down in Rome. But I'm also excited. During the endless movie marathon that I didn't really watch, I came to a decision. This is my time to reboot. Here, I can reinvent myself into whoever I want to be. I'm not going to be the girl whose boyfriend screwed around on her behind her back, or the girl who slept with her brother on the rebound. I'm going to be the new, improved Lexie. The one who has her shit together. The one who's got an entire school year ahead of her in Italy. The one who's going to blow her professors' socks off with her witty insights and observations, so she gets an invite for that summer internship.

Next summer is my last before graduation. It's the last summer I'll be home. If I play my cards right, maybe Trent and I won't be under the same roof again except for a few weeks during winter break.

If I just stay on an entirely different continent, I can't fuck up again.

I'm actually smiling as I flag down a taxi to take me to my new life.

You know those lines in the road? The dotted white ones that are supposed to divide your lane from the lane of the guy next to you? What I find out in the next hour is, in Rome, they're just a suggestion. I determine within a mile of the airport that my taxi driver is suicidal. Within a mile after that, I realize *all* taxi drivers are suicidal. As a matter of fact, everyone who drives in Rome seems to be. I wonder if it's a question on the Italian driver's test.

Are you a suicidal maniac?   ☐ Yes   ☐ No

Only the yeses pass.

We spin through roundabouts at totally unsafe speeds and power down tiny alleys hardly wide enough for the toy car I'm riding in. I swear to God, at one point we take out a fat guy with a bad comb-over whose chair is extending just a little too far into the street at a roadside café.

By the time we bump up a cobbled alleyway and stop in front of a graffitied stucco building, I'm so shell-shocked I can hardly pry my fingers off the torn vinyl seat. The driver, a short, stout, middle-aged guy with some serious BO who doesn't speak a word of English and probably won't live to see fifty, dumps me and my luggage on the narrow sidewalk. I stand for a second after paying him and watch his tin can of a taxi speed off. What I'm really waiting for is to see if I'm having an actual heart attack or just an anxiety attack. I never thought it possible for someone to scare me more than Trent, but that automotive experience approached the horror of riding on the back of his motorcycle.

Trent. *Shit.*

This is my new life. I'm not going to think about my brother-lover problems in this life. But as I grab my suitcase and tow it across the cobbles, there's no denying that the guilt is back. And mingling with the guilt is something just as deep. It's that hunger for him. I felt it the whole time we were making love, and even after, like there was no possible way to get enough of him. I haven't been gone twenty-four hours, and I already miss him so much, it hurts.

I blow out a sigh and fish through my purse for the key they mailed me. Usually, foreign exchange students stay in campus housing, but there is some big remodel that didn't get finished in time, so they put me in an apartment just across the Tiber River from campus . . . so they say. I look again at the painted wooden plaque on the side of the building to make sure it's the right tiny-cobbled-alley-which-is-really-a-road, then at the number next to the door. When I slip the key into the lock, it fits. And then it turns.

Must be the right place.

I walk into a short hallway with a padlocked door to the left and a narrow stairway ahead of me. They told me upstairs, so I'm guessing I go up.

I drag my suitcase up the stairs and get it so wedged at the corner near the top that I have to kick it to get it unstuck. But then I lose my grip on the handle, and it topples to the bottom. I decide it's not worth going back for until I know for sure I'm in the right spot. I trudge up the last few stairs to the door and stick my key in. It opens. I throw my backpack through, then retrieve my suitcase from the bottom of the stairs, careful to turn it sideways at the corner. Once I've wrestled it into the apartment and closed the door, I look around.

And it's charming.

To my right is a dark, wooden, dining-room table and four chairs, and a door on the far wall beyond it. To my left is a small, sunny, sitting room, and past that, through a doorway, a speck of a kitchen barely big enough for one person to turn around in. Next to the kitchen door is a bookshelf with a few books that I'll have to check out when I have some time, and just behind me is a worn green love seat and a small end table, all of which fill the room except for a narrow walkway to the kitchen door and three narrow stairs that lead to a window. Upon closer inspection, I realize the window is really a very small glass door onto a patio. I unlatch the window-door and swing it in, then climb through. The patio is huge—easily twice the size of my entire apartment, and I expect to find several doors opening onto it, but there aren't. Only mine.

I move to the low wall at the front of the building and lean my elbows on it, looking down at the street. I'm on the roof of the single-story building next door to my apartment. And it's all mine. It's enclosed on three sides by the walls of the two-story adjoining buildings (mine, the one behind, and the one next door), and there are windows in those walls, so it's not like I can sunbathe nude or anything, but it's nice. There's a lounge chair in the corner near some climbing vine with orange flowers, and I can already imagine myself sitting there studying.

I duck back in the window and go in search of the bedroom, which I find is through the door in the dining room, at the very front of the apartment. It's easily the biggest room in the house, spanning the whole width of the front of the building—a whopping twelve feet or so. The heavy drapes in the two large windows are looped back, and the windows let in lots of natural light. The floors are terra-cotta tile, and all the furnishings, including the carved mahogany headboard of the double bed, look antique.

I catch myself smiling at the giddy shiver of nervous excitement that courses through me. This is all mine. My first apartment.

In *Rome*! I can't believe I'm really here.

I peer out the windows overlooking the street as I tow my suitcase past the end of the bed to the huge, wooden armoire in the corner and take a minute to unpack my things. When I'm done, I spin, flopping back on the bed and pulling out my phone. It's only now that I realize I never turned it on when we landed. I hit the power button, and there are three texts and a voice mail.

I check the voice mail first.

"Call us as soon as you get this, kiddo," Dad says. "You should have landed an hour ago, and we're getting worried."

I check the time on the call, and it was an hour ago. I punch in the country code and the number and wait for what feels like forever for it to connect.

"Lexie," Julie says the instant she picks up. "Are you there? Is everything okay?"

"Sorry. I forgot to turn on my phone. But everything's great. My apartment is so cute."

"Thank God. We were hoping it was just something like that. How were your flights?"

I roll onto my stomach. "Everything went really smoothly."

"And customs?" she asks.

"They just checked my passport and my student visa. No problems."

"Wonderful, sweetie. Trent sends his love. Here's your dad."

I wait through a short pause as Julie hands the phone off. "Hey, kiddo," Dad says, "sounds like everything went according to plan?"

"No problems," I answer.

"So, you're at your apartment?"

My apartment. *My* apartment. In *Rome!* "I just got here," I answer as that giddy rush hits me again. "I love it."

"Safe neighborhood?"

I get up and go to the window, swinging it open and looking down at the passersby in the street below. "It seems fine, but I've only been here a few minutes, so . . ."

"You should get the lay of the land . . . find the best route to school and a grocery store for whatever staples you need while it's still light."

I lie back on the bed, feeling the cool cotton of the duvet calling to me. "I'm really tired. You know I can't really sleep on airplanes. I've got all day tomorrow, though. Orientation's not till Thursday."

"Okay. Well, get some rest then, and we'll talk more tomorrow."

"Okay, Dad. Sorry to keep you up."

"Not a problem. Love you, kiddo."

" 'Night."

The line goes dead, and I drop the phone and rub my eyes.

I don't realize I'm sleeping until a heavy bass rhythm shakes the bed. I open my eyes to find the midday sun that was beating down on me when I explored the patio gone. It's past dusk, just the hint of maroon on the horizon. I haul myself off the bed and go to my front window. People stroll my little street in groups and in couples, hand in hand. As I watch, many of them disappear into the door next to mine, and I realize that the single-story building next door that my patio is situated on top of must be a bar or a club or something. Music pours out the open door, and a couple dances in the street just outside.

I bring Julie's food stash with me to the kitchen and tuck my meager supply into the cupboard. I find the bathroom, a tiny thing off the corner of the sitting room, and pee, then wash up and splash my face. When I come out, I hear laughter in the street. I climb out my patio door and feel the bass rattling the floor under my feet. The summer breeze feels cool now that the beating sun is gone. I move toward the ledge and look over the edge at the gathering crowd in front of the bar below. I should find out if there's a store nearby.

"Ciao bellezza."

A skinny boy with curly black hair, probably a little younger than me, is looking up at me. He holds out his arm in my direction and smiles. "Ti amo. Vuoi essere la mia prima amante?"

His friend jabs him in the arm and smiles up at me. "Facci salire, bellezza! Vogliamo provare il tuo letto!"

I have no idea what they're saying. I shrug and smile down at them. "Sorry."

"Ah! Americana!" the second boy shouts. "My friend say you beautiful."

"Oh . . . thanks."

"You come for . . ." He mimes tipping a bottle to his lips. I shake my head. "Not tonight."

He grabs his friend's arm and drags him closer. "He turn eighteen today. He love you. He want you for his first lover."

My eyes widen, and all of a sudden I feel the need to check that my door is locked. "Sorry," I say again, backing away from the ledge, but when I look up at the balcony across the street, there is the oldest, most shriveled woman I've ever seen standing there staring at me. The road is so narrow that she's only about ten feet away, and I can see every pruny detail. Her thin white hair is pulled back in a tight bun, and I swear her wrinkles have wrinkles. She's so hunched that I bet she could kiss her belly button, which makes her look about three feet tall. Her sharp gaze shifts very deliberately to the boys down below as the English-speaking one calls, "Please, beautiful lady! Take us to your bed!" then back to me, and she tsks. I mean, seriously tsks. She sticks her finger out at me and flicks it up and down three times as some clucking noise comes out of her shriveled lips, and, if it's even possible, her face creases deeper as she narrows her eyes at me.

I duck back inside and close everything up tight, deciding there's really nothing I need out there that can't wait until tomorrow. When I'm satisfied no one is getting in, I strip my clothes off into a heap on the floor and fall into bed. The sheets feel rough against my skin—so Italians aren't big on fabric softener, apparently. But I know what *is* soft. I get up and dig through my things in the armoire for Trent's shirt, which I admittedly stole. I slip it on and crawl back into bed, and I'm out before my head hits the pillow.

And, once again, I dream of Trent.

THE SUN IS bright in my window when I wake up, and it's obvious that early morning is long gone. I roll on my side and grab my phone, looking at the clock. Eleven.

And then I notice I have a text. It's from a few hours ago. I click it open.

Lying in bed thinking abt you.

I read Trent's text a hundred times. He's in bed . . . thinking about me.

I remember fantasizing about him while I touched myself the night before I left. Is he doing *that* kind of thinking? Or the kind where he showered a thousand times before bed and wants to slit his wrists because he still can't get my stench off him?

I start to type in the question, but my heart squeezes into a knot, and I delete it. I used to be able to say anything to him, no matter how mortifying. Now I can't even ask a simple question.

I've ruined everything.

I've never felt guilt like this before, and it's compounded by the knowledge that, given the chance, I'd do the same thing again. And again. And probably again. But the truth is, although I won't deny that some of my dreams of Trent last night involved degrees of nudity, none of them were about sex. I dreamed of when we were younger, and he held me when I cried over my dead mother. I dreamed of times we sat blowing dandelion balls in the backyard and talking about things I don't even remember now, but were the center of our fifteen-year-old universe. I dreamed of our living-room wrestling matches, which I could only win by cheating and squeezing the ticklish spot below his kneecap—his Achilles' heel that only I knew about. I dreamed of our endless Warcraft quests. And I dreamed of the times we'd just sit together for hours while he played his guitar, and I sketched.

I've never had to try to impress Trent or pretend I'm something I'm not. He's always known all my warts. He knows that I only shave my legs when I absolutely have to, and how much I hate to lose, and that I bite all the skin off the insides of my cheeks when I'm nervous. He knows how insecure I am about anything to do with myself—my art, my looks, my body, my clothes. He knows that I'm the penultimate people pleaser, and he knows all of the really bad decisions I've made because of it. Peer pressure and I are old friends—which is why Rick and I did it without protection the night we lost our virginity. He said he'd be careful and pull out. He said it would be okay. He said he'd waited a year for me, and I couldn't take him that far and not follow through. So I followed through.

I'm sure there are lots of other things Trent knows about me that I don't even know about myself. I feel like, in a moment of weakness, I traded my only real friend for a few minutes of gratification.

But, *God*, were they gratifying.

Sleeping with Trent is probably the most selfish thing I've ever done. No one pressured me. No one pushed me. I wanted it just for me.

I lie back and run a hand down my body, remembering the feel of Trent's hands doing the same.

Shit.

I have to stop thinking about it. I have to shake the memory of sex with Trent from my head and remember the thing that really matters. I lucked into the most amazing family anyone could ever ask for. I'm not going to risk destroying it because I'm horny for my stepbrother. I have to let go of the lust and the guilt and move on. It sounds good in theory.

Now I just need a plan.

Chapter Five

THE CHURCH IS very old, with sculptures in every corner and crevice. The only light in the room filters through cut-glass windows that stretch to the high ceiling above. Carved beams held up by immense wooden pillars support the ceiling, and most of the walls are ancient, painted frescoes, some of which are starting to crumble. The art history major in me wants to study them for hours, but that's not why I'm here.

When I see the carved wooden confessionals at the back, I freeze. Do I really want to do this?

Oh, God.

I dip my shaking fingers into the holy water and cross myself as I move to the back pew. The act of contrition seems like a good place to start, so I kneel and fold my hands in front of me, bowing my head and closing my eyes.

"My God, I am sorry for my sins with all my heart.

In choosing to do wrong and failing to do good, I have sinned against you whom I should love above all things. I firmly intend, with your help, to do penance, to sin no more, and to avoid whatever leads me to sin. Our Savior Jesus Christ suffered and died for us. In His name, my God, have mercy. Amen."

I sit back in the pew, chewing the inside of my cheek, and look up at Jesus on the cross above the altar. Will he forgive me for having sex with my stepbrother? My face scrunches as the feeling of Trent on top of me flashes in my memory. But as much as it mortifies me, sitting here in a church and all, my body reacts without my permission, my pulse rising as an electric tingle races through my groin.

I'm going to hell.

I've just about convinced myself that no one's home, and it's okay to leave, when a door to one of the confessionals opens, and a white-haired woman steps out. She moves to a nearby pew and kneels, crossing herself.

I breathe deep and pull myself to my feet, walking slowly to the open confessional. I hesitate at the door, but then remind myself that this is Italy . . . where they speak Italian. I can confess my worst of sins, and the priest probably won't understand a word. I step in and close the door, then kneel in front of the thick red curtain separating the saint from the sinner.

"Nel nome del Padre, e del Figlio, e dello Spirito Santo. Amen," a deep sandpaper voice says from the other side of the curtain.

I cross myself as the priest prays the Sign of the Cross,

then bow my head and close my eyes. "Forgive me, Father, for I have sinned. It has been . . . well . . . a whole lot of days since my last confession. Probably a year or more. I accuse myself of the following sins. I . . . used the Lord's name in vain at least . . . oh, God—" *Shit!* My hands fly to my face. "Like that . . . I just don't think about it, and it comes out of my mouth. I've done it thousands of times. Maybe a million. Twice just since I walked into this church." I shake my head at myself. "I'm terrible. But that's not the worst. I've stolen from my friends. There was this scarf I got for Sam for her birthday that I decided to keep . . . so I guess it's not really stealing, but it felt like it, and there were the flip-flops that Katie loaned me that I never returned—I even brought them with me to Italy. And I swore at my stepmother when she wouldn't let me go out with my boyfriend until I cleaned the bathroom, but I knew he had this big romantic thing planned for our three-year anniversary and I was pretty sure we were going to have sex . . . which I guess I also need to con- fess . . . I had a lot of sex with my boyfriend before he turned into a douche—pardon my French . . . or English, I guess—but that was almost a year ago . . . when I still had a boyfriend. . . . and, what else . . . I sort of cheated on a history exam last semester because Drake Mulhollan left his book open where I could see it, and during finals I wished my roommate dead one day when she was having sex with her boyfriend all freakin' day so I couldn't get into my room to get my books—she didn't die, by the way . . . I mean, my wish didn't come true or anything like that . . . but I wished it, which I'm pretty sure is a sin. And then there was the time I lied to Dad about the dent in the car . . . and the baggie he found in my backpack wasn't really oregano . . . which, oh yeah, there was the pot thing too, but it was just a phase so . . ." I trail off, recognizing the fact that I'm babbling on to avoid the actual reason I'm here. I breathe deep and wipe my sweaty palms on my jeans. "And I stole my brother's T-shirt . . ." I swallow hard, "after we had sex," I blurt, then I'm running downhill again, words tumbling out of my mouth before I even think them, "and it was truly mind-blowing. It's all I can think about, and I want to do it again and, oh God—*shit*! See, I just can't stop myself from saying oh God. But my brother is so . . ." I growl in frustration and grab fistfuls of my hair. ". . . incredible. He's just fucking incredible— pardon my French. I've never felt the things he made me feel, you know . . . and God, I think I might . . ." I yank my hair as I shake my head hard. "I don't know. It was just sex, right? I mean . . . as much as he made me feel, it was just . . ." I bury my face in my hands. "He's my brother. Why can't I stop wanting him?"

"That is a question you will have to answer for yourself," the voice says from the other side of the curtain.

"*Oh God!*"

"That would now be a million and seven, by my count. I hope you brought your rosary to Italy as well as your friend's flip-flops."

"You speak English!"

"I do, child. Is there more you are in need of confessing?"

"Hell, no!"

"Hmm . . . Well, then. Let us pray. O God, whose only begotten Son, by His life, death, and resurrection, has purchased for us the rewards of eternal life, grant, we beseech Thee, that meditating upon these mysteries of the Most Holy Rosary of the Blessed Virgin Mary, we may imitate what they contain and obtain what they promise, through the same Christ Our Lord."

I hang my head and mumble along with the Final Prayer until he adds, "We are mere mortals created in your divine image, Lord. Please help your sheep to find the path to salvation and bless them with your mercy and grace for all the days of their lives. Amen.

"Do you come to the Lord with free mind and heart, ready to accept Jesus' guidance and absolutions of these sins?" he asks me.

"Um . . . yeah. I mean . . ." I add as my mind clears and I remember the drill, ". . . I am sorry for my sins and ask Jesus to forgive them as well as any I have forgotten to confess."

"Very well. You will be more mindful of your thoughts in regards to taking the Lord's name in vain?"

"Yes, Father."

"And you will respect your parents?"

"Yes, Father."

"And in the matter of your incestual relationship—"

"No!" My stomach lurches at the word "incestual." "Oh, God! He's not my *brother* brother!"

"Pardon?"

"He's my *step*brother."

He clears his throat. "Well . . . I'm assuming you're not bound in the sanctity of marriage?"

I throw up my hands. "Did you not hear a thing I said? He's my *brother*."

"I'm not sensing contrition."

I'd almost swear I hear amusement in his voice, and I pinch myself to be sure I'm not trapped in some warped self-flagellation dream triggered by my vast and immeasurable mind-blowing-sex-with-my-brother guilt.

I breathe deep and hang my head. "I just can't believe it happened."

"It sounds as though you need more than forgiveness for your sins of the flesh. You need to find a way to redirect your lustful energies."

"Yes, Father."

"I might have a suggestion. For your penance, you'll pray the Hail Mary fifteen times, then see the Reverend Moretti in the rectory across the street."

"What for?"

"He will have a project that will keep your mind occupied and your heart full."

"In other words, he'll keep me out of trouble."

"Idle hands are—"

"—the devil's workshop," I groan with a roll of my eyes at Dad's favorite saying. "I know."

"I absolve you of your sins in the name of the Father, the Son, and the Holy Spirit. Amen."

I cross myself as he says it.

"Go in peace."

"Thanks be to God," I respond automatically as I stand.

"Just knock on the door across the street," he says as I open the confessional door. "He'll be there."

I rocket out of the confessional, and because I'm looking back at the curtain and not watching where I'm going, I don't see the thing in front of me until I slam into it. All the air leaves my lungs in a whoosh, and it takes me a second to get my breath back. The thing is a person or a horse. I know this because it's warm, it moves, and it's bigger than me. That's all I know for sure until I turn around and see him.

"Oh! I'm sorry, Father," I say with a bow of my head when I see the person I've stumbled into is wearing a black button-down cleric's shirt and a white collar. He's taller than Trent, so something over six feet, and though he's slender, I can tell he's no stranger to the gym. He's cut and solid—which I know because he barely budged when I ran into him, and yet he left me breathless. He's got a hint of dark stubble on his cheeks and chin, where there's a dimple, and I'd guess he's older than me, but not by a lot. Maybe midtwenties. His wavy black hair is combed off his face, and, with his high cheekbones and straight, narrow nose, he looks like the half-naked guy in the Abercrombie jeans ads in my *Elle* magazines. Except he's not half-naked. He's in a priest's collar.

And I'm staring at him.

With his dark eyes and olive skin, I'm expecting Italian to pour out of his mouth when he opens it, so when his glance flicks to the open confessional door then back to me, and he lifts an eyebrow, and says, "Greater sins have been perpetrated, I'm quite sure," in a mild Italian accent, my knees go a little weak.

"Speaking of which"—I tip my head at the pews behind him—"I have a few Hail Marys, so . . ."

He steps aside, and one corner of his mouth curves up. "Then I'll let you get to work."

I brush past him and kneel in the pew, but my eyes have a will of their own. As I pull out my rosary and recite my first round of Hail Marys, they follow him to the altar, where he organizes things on the table for the upcoming Mass.

"Hail Mary, full of grace. The Lord is with thee. Blessed art thou amongst women, and blessed is the fruit of thy womb, Jesus. Holy Mary, Mother of God, Pray for us sinners, now and at the hour of our death. Amen." I close my eyes and mutter it out loud to bring my focus back to why I'm here.

When I've completed all fifteen Hail Marys and lift my head, the altar is empty, and I'm alone in the church. I stand, then genuflect at the end of the pew before scampering out through the vestibule into the bright, summer day. Across the street is a two-story beige stucco building that looks nothing like Father Green's rectory at home. There are no markings, so I'm not even sure it's the right place. I cross the street and hesitate for a second before knocking on the big wooden door, figuring I've got nothing to lose. If no one answers, I gave it the old college try, so I'm pretty sure that means I'm still absolved.

But when the door swings open a minute later, I'm

struck speechless. It's the priest who knocked the wind out of me—and just looking at him does it again.

"Can I help you?" he asks with the hint of a smile.

"Um . . . Father . . ." I don't even know his name. "The priest taking confession at the church sent me over here. He said to ask for the Reverend Moretti."

"You've found him."

"You?" I feel my eyes widen.

He steps aside and gestures that I should come in with a sweep of his slender hand. "This surprises you?"

I step past him into a small entryway. "It's just . . . aren't you a priest?"

"I'm not a priest . . . yet." He turns and leads me into a sitting room off the entry. It's small and dimly lit, with a gold, velvet-lined chair and a love seat surrounded by bookcases full of books that look ancient. He picks an open hardcover up off the love seat and sets it on a side table. "Sit."

I do. "But you dress like a priest."

He lowers himself smoothly into the chair across from me. "I'm a transitional deacon. There is a period of reflection between the time a priest finishes seminary and he can be ordained. I'll be ordained in eight months, at Easter observance. Then you can call me Father."

"So you could still change your mind?"

He shakes his head. "No. I've been called by the bishop and taken my vow of celibacy." He smiles, and something mischievous flashes in his eyes. "It's all over but the crying."

"Oh. So, Father . . . what's-his-name . . ." I say, waving

my hand toward the small window at the church across the street.

"Reynolds . . ." he finishes for me, leaning toward me with his elbows on his knees.

"Reynolds? That sounds American."

"It is. This parish is part of the Pontifical North American College. We're all American or Canadian."

Great. I managed to stumble into the only English-speaking church out of about a thousand within walking distance of my apartment. "But *you're* not American." I know this because he's got that delicious accent that, when he says certain words, sends a little shiver running over my skin. And he's dark, black hair and charcoal eyes set in flawless olive skin.

He raises his eyebrows. "I beg your pardon?"

"I mean, your accent. And you look . . . well . . . Italian," I say with a flip of my hand at the window, in case he forgot where we are.

"Never judge a book by its cover," he says, picking up the book that was open on the love seat. He flips it for me to see. On the cover is an artist's rendering of a black-haired boy in black-rimmed glasses with a giant mouse's head that he's wearing like a pointy hat. Curled up on the giant chessboard that the boy's folded arms rest on is another giant mouse, which still seems to have its head. There is an assortment of chess pieces on the board, and above it all is the title: *Harry Potter el la Pietra Filosofale.*

My face scrunches in confusion. "That's a really screwed-up cover."

He quirks a smile. "That it is."

"So, I'm getting that your takeaway here is, you're *not* Italian."

"My father is Italian by heritage, but I grew up in New York, for the most part."

"But . . . your accent . . ."

He winces for just a second, as if he's self-conscious about it. ". . . Is a jumble. A product of speaking Italian as a child and living with my non-English-speaking grandparents as a teen."

"They're Italian?"

"French, actually."

I just look at him.

"My mother's family is from Corsica." He clears his throat and crosses his legs, setting the book down and folding his hands over his knee. "But I'm quite certain Father Reynolds didn't send you here to discuss my heritage."

"He said I needed to talk to you about a project." I lift my hand and wiggle my fingers. "You know . . . idle hands and all."

He huffs a short laugh through his nose and leans back in his chair, studying me. It's super awkward for a minute until he breaks the silence. "How many Hail Marys did you say he had you pray?"

"I didn't." I narrow my eyes at him. "So, do you have a project for me or not?"

He nods slowly. "I'm sure I can find something. But first, I need to know a little about you."

"Such as?"

"Your name?"

I fold my arms across my chest. "Lexie Banks."

"You're American, yes?"

I roll my eyes. "Geez, what gave it away?" Maybe I shouldn't be so nasty, but I feel myself getting really defensive. This whole thing is just so embarrassing, and if he asks what I did to get sent here . . .

"Why are you here?" And there it is, the question I've been dreading.

Instantly, the wall goes up and I can almost feel myself get pricklier. "I don't really think that's any of your business. I already confessed everything to Father Reynolds."

An amused smile twitches his lips, but he fights it. "I meant in Rome?"

"Oh," I say with a cringe, feeling heat creep up my neck. But I also feel pissed. He seems to find my misery amusing—like a cat playing with the mouse before the kill. "I'm at John Cabot University on a year abroad."

"Studying . . . ?" he asks with a curious lift of his brow.

"Art history."

He looks at me strangely for a moment before tenting his fingers under his chin. "Ask, and it shall be given you; seek, and ye shall find; knock, and it shall be opened unto you."

"Excuse me?"

"Matthew 7:7."

I really wish he'd get to the point. "I know that's scripture. What I don't know is why you're suddenly spouting it at me. I already said my Hail Marys, so I think I'm covered with the prayer thing . . . for now."

He just looks at me for a moment longer, then untents

his fingers and uncrosses his legs, leaning toward me with his elbows on his knees. "Have you been through the Vatican Museums yet?"

"No. I just got here yesterday."

"We'll have to remedy that. Are you free tomorrow?"

I've been dying to see the Vatican Museums. It's on the top of my to-do list, but this feels more than a little weird. "I have orientation at John Cabot until four."

"Perfect."

"Listen. It's really nice of you, playing the welcome wagon and all, but this is supposed to be my penance, not social hour, so . . ."

He nods. "Fine. Meet me at six tomorrow evening at the obelisk in St. Peter's Square. We'll talk about the project then."

"The project is in St. Peter's?" I ask warily.

He stands and turns toward the entry, opening the front door in a not-so-subtle cue that we're done here. He levels me in his steady gaze as I stand. "Don't be late."

When I get back to my humble apartment with a bag of groceries, on which I just spent a small fortune, I unpack them into the kitchen. I grab my backpack and take it onto the patio, where I sit on the lounge and pull out my orientation stuff. There's a badge with my name and Notre Dame student ID picture on it that arrived with my key the week before I left, and an orientation schedule, a map of the lecture buildings, and a staff directory that I printed out from the e-mail they sent.

And my class schedule. Just thinking about my class schedule makes me tingle all over. I read through the list again:

AH 223 The Art and Architecture of Imperial Rome

*AH 243 Roman Funerary Art: Honoring
the Dead in Ancient Rome (On-site)*

*AH 296 Italian High Renaissance Art
(On-site; Mandatory trip to Florence)*

*AH 339 Venetian Art (On-site;
Mandatory trip to Venice)*

And the crowning jewel:

AH 376 Michelangelo

At the same instant that my phone vibrates, so does the floor beneath my feet as music starts cranking out of the bar downstairs. I wipe the drool off my chin before I pull my phone out of my pocket and check the text.

Sam.

Hey, gurl! Waiting for hot Italian boy pics. You be slacking.

I set my orientation stuff down and stand, wandering toward the ledge over the street at the edge of the roof. I lean on it and look down at the milling people outside the bar. *18 yo kid wanted to sleep with me last night.*

Ah! Fresh meat. Did u do it?

I roll my eyes, and just as I do, the same boy steps out of the bar. He grins when he looks up and sees me. "Ti amo," he calls up to me, holding out an arm.

Fucked his brains out. I text back, stepping away from the ledge.

U slut!

eye roll I text back.

So, you are my fave person.

?

You left your mother-of-pearl hair clip in Katie's car and she didn't find it till she was packing up to drive back to school yesterday.

So, that's where that went. I forgot I'd pulled it out when I was moping in Katie's backseat over Rick. But . . . *Why does that make me your fave person?*

Someone had to return it to your house.

?

And your smokin hot stepbrother answered the door.

My gut tightens the second I read it, and I feel sick. I can't answer. I can't even begin to form a thought that isn't, "Stay the hell away from him!"

Don't you want to know what happened? she asks after a minute.

No. No I don't. *What happened?*

Went to Lightly Toasted for a drink.

You'd think Lightly Toasted would be a breakfast joint where you'd get coffee, right? You'd be wrong. It refers to the phase of drunkenness between "I just showed up, so pour me a beer," and "I'm passed out on the floor, so don't step on me." The place is dimly lit and full of sofas and love seats covered with throw pillows in all the dark nooks and crannies. I've learned not to look too closely at what goes on in those nooks and crannies.

And? I type with a shaking hand.

What? You think I'd jump his bones right there in the bar?

Yes.

I'm playing this one low-key. Talking, flirting, and a little touching, but that's it. Luring him in with the demure act.

I lean my elbows on the ledge and hang my head, blowing out a laugh, but there's no humor in it. Mostly just relief. *You? Demure?* I type, but then I lift my head and see the boy is still down in the street . . . peeing into the alcove of my doorway. He shakes himself off and zips, then looks up. When he sees me watching, he smiles and blows me a kiss.

Great.

I look back at my phone. *Don't knock the hard-to-get act. It works.*

Good luck with that. Someone just peed in my doorway so gotta go. Keep me posted, I type. And I want her to. But I also don't.

I swipe to Trent's text from this morning. He went out with Sam, but then he was lying in bed thinking about me? I still don't know how to read that: between the lines or at face value. I haven't responded, and I'm feeling like I should. I shouldn't just ignore him. Or maybe that's exactly what I should do. Finally, I type in, *Went to church today. Confessed everything. Hoping not to burn in hell,* and hit SEND before I can change my mind.

Chapter Six

ORIENTATION STARTS AT nine, so I stumble around Rome—or at least my little corner of Rome—and find an adorable café for espresso and pastries beforehand. I point at the pastry case and direct the balding man behind the counter to something that looks like a chocolate chip croissant. He hands it and the espresso to me, and when I settle into a table in the corner and sip, I find out Italians like their espresso something akin to rocket fuel. The caffeine from this cup alone could power the next space mission. When I bite into the croissant, it's not chocolate, but it's sweet, and I moan a little as it melts in my mouth.

"I've died and gone to heaven," I say out loud once I've devoured the whole thing.

"If you really want to suck up, bring one of those for Professor Nance," a girl's voice behind me says, and I turn to see a petite girl sitting at the table there, staring full on at me with neon green eyes and sipping her espresso.

"Excuse me?"

She twists the pink tip of a strand of her short black hair around her index finger. "You're heading over to the orientation, right?"

Just when I'm starting to think this girl must be clairvoyant (maybe those are X-ray contacts that can see through a person's skull into their thoughts) she nudges my backpack with her foot. I look down and see the John Cabot badge that I clipped on the zipper tab this morning, so I wouldn't lose it.

"Do you go there?" I ask.

"Not yet. I'm a newbie too. But my sister came here last year and said Professor Nance plays favorites. His favorites are apparently the ones who bring him puddings."

I was trying to decide if the accent was British or Australian, and the "puddings" gives it away. "You're British?"

She bobs a quick nod. "From York. You?"

"America."

"That bit I knew from your accent," she says. "Where in America?"

"California. Not too far from San Francisco."

"I've been to San Francisco. Nice place."

I shrug. "It's okay, I guess."

Her iPhone starts to vibrate, jingling against her spoon, and she untwists her finger from her hair and picks it up. She reads something on the screen, barks out a laugh, then puts down her cup and starts typing with her thumbs. "She also just said to watch out for Claudio, Professor Nance's TA. Shagged half her class last semester and gave them all crabs." She grins up at me and wiggles her eyebrows. "Just in case you were thinking of sampling the local cuisine."

I've had plenty of "cuisine" lately. I'm not looking for any more. "Good to know."

She puts her phone down and sips her espresso. "What are you studying?"

"Art history."

"Ah, then you've come to the right place. But it means you'll miss out on the immense pleasure of Professor Nance and his crabby TA."

I'm sipping my espresso as she says it, and when I laugh, it geysers up my nose, burning the whole way. I cough so hard that I swear I dislodge a lung.

"Sorry for that." She hands me a napkin, which I take. "Have you been through the National Museum yet?" she asks, as I mop myself up.

"Not yet. I just got here a few days ago. But I'm going to the Vatican Museums tonight."

She grins. "Try not to cream your knickers right out loud."

My cheeks flame. "Um . . . yeah. So what are you studying?"

"Anthropology, which means I've come to the right place too. I've already creamed my knickers down in the catacombs and again at the Forum. Glad I packed a few extra pairs." She shifts her chair closer and holds out her hand. "I'm Abby."

"Lexie," I say, shaking it.

She picks up her phone and looks at the screen, then stands. "We should be shoving off."

I shoot the last of my espresso and scrape my chair back, hiking my backpack onto my shoulder. Despite what I told Dad, I didn't explore yesterday. I was too busy beating myself up for going to confession—which, I guess, I'll have to confess next time I go. "Do you know where we're going? Because I'm clueless."

"The main building is just around the corner," she says, leading the way to the door. She winds us through a narrow alley, and when we come out the other side, there's an archway over the road. "Here," she says, crossing the street to a pair of green double doors, which are propped open.

We follow a few other semilost-looking people through the door, one of whom is a tall, lanky, blond guy in jeans, a blue polo shirt, and a Red Sox baseball cap. So I'm guessing he's probably here for the orientation too. Abby grabs my elbow and tows me to a wide marble staircase directly in front of us, and we climb it to the second floor. There are a dozen or so other people waiting in the second-floor classroom that Abby leads me into, and Red Sox Cap Guy and another girl come through just behind us. A wiry man in a blazer, (despite the fact that it's got to be ninety outside and there's apparently no air-conditioning in here) with thick salt-and-pepper hair comes in a few minutes later and sits on the edge of the desk in the front of the room.

"Hello. My name is Professor Avery. Did everyone find us okay?"

We're here, I want to say, so pretty much, yeah. But reality is, I'd probably still be wandering the narrow Roman streets, twisting my ankles on the cobbles, if Abby hadn't saved my sorry butt.

After a few mumbled yeahs, he smiles, revealing stained teeth that could use an Invisalign intervention. "Well, we want to get you comfortable here before classes start next week. We'll be taking you on the tour, so hopefully you'll know where to go when the time comes. You also all have individual meetings with your curriculum advisors at either one or two, so check your orientation schedules."

"Um . . . ?" Baseball Cap Guy says. "What orientation schedule?"

"It was e-mailed on the tenth," Professor Avery says. "Did you not receive it, Mr. . . . ?"

"Higgins," the guy says. "Grant Higgins."

Professor Avery leans back and rifles through some papers on his desk, like it's magically going to turn up there. "We'll visit the computer lab and print you a copy," he says when he comes up empty. "Anyone else without a schedule?"

We all shake our heads, and Grant grimaces.

"Excellent. So you're all aware that John Cabot University is English-speaking. All your classes will be in English. We do, however, encourage you to interact with locals . . . explore the culture. Though learning is our primary objective, the greatest experiences you'll take home with you are the ones from outside the classroom. We offer a plethora of services and resources to make this the best experience possible for each one of you, so I encourage you to take advantage."

We spend the next few hours going over logistics, from the class schedules to the textbooks and fee schedules. We tour all the main buildings as well as the surrounding area. Abby elbows me as we're leaving the resource center and points at Grant Higgins, who looks relieved now that he has his orientation and class schedules. "Dibs," she says with a grin.

"I hate the Red Sox. He's all yours."

WHEN I SHOW up at St. Peter's Square that evening, the Reverend Moretti is already there, leaning against the concrete barrier at the base of the obelisk with his ankles crossed and his arms folded over his chest. His eyes tick to his watch as I stroll up.

"You're late."

"You said six." I glance at my phone. Six fifteen. "It's six . . . more or less." In all honesty, I know I'm late. I got distracted by the pretty pastries in the shop near my apartment. They had those same croissants, which I now know have currants in them. The way they melted in my mouth was so worth the wrath of the reverend.

He gives me the eye.

I give him the eye back. "It was a long walk. I had to stop for nourishment."

He turns on his heel without another word, and I

follow him across St. Peter's Square to the right side of the Basilica. Watching him weave through the milling crowd, it hits me how fluid his motions are. Even just walking looks graceful when he does it. He stops at the bottom of a ramp and makes an "after you" gesture with a wave of his arm and a small bow. I start up the ramp, and he follows. We push through a door at the top into a foyer with a wide staircase off to the right. The reverend flashes a badge at a guard there and says something in Italian. The guard looks me over and nods to the reverend, who holds an arm out toward the stairs. I start up them, and he follows.

"Where are we going?"

"I told you, to the museums."

He says it like he thinks I might be a little slow, and it pisses me off. I stop and look at him. "No. You said you had a project."

He tips his head up the stairs and arches an eyebrow at me. "Which is in the museums."

I plant my fists on my hips and stare him down. It's not that I don't want to see the museums. I do. More than anything. They're the reason I'm in Rome. But I don't like being left in the dark. "How do I know you're not just jerking me around?"

His causal aloofness slips a little, and he looks momentarily surprised. "Are you suggesting my motives are less than pure?"

Oh, God. I'm a moron. "No," I backpedal. "I just mean, why all the mystery?"

He starts climbing again, and I keep step with him.

"There's no mystery, really. The Church has several missions that target children. The purpose is twofold. We strive to educate them in their Italian culture in the hope that it will not only inspire them to better themselves in the eyes of God but also to protect their national heritage, of which the Church is a large part. With your interest in art history, you're the perfect missionary for this part of the program," he says with a wave of his arm at the double glass doors in front of us, just at the top of the stairs.

They swish open, and he presses his fingers into the small of my back and ushers me through into a long, wide hallway with enormous maps frescoed into the twelve-foot walls and the curve of the arched ceiling above. "Galleria delle Carte Geografiche," he says with a wave of his arm. "The gallery of maps. There are forty frescoes here that were painted between 1572 and 1585 by the renowned geographer, Ignazio Danti. They represent the Italian regions and the papal properties at the time of Pope Gregory XIII."

I move slowly up the hall, mesmerized by the details. It hits me fifteen minutes later, when I'm about halfway up the corridor, that this is the Vatican. There are more prized works of art here than anywhere else in the world. I feel suddenly dizzy with the overwhelming realization that I'm actually here.

I look back at the Reverend Moretti, and beyond him to the long stretch of empty hall. "Where is everyone? This is the Vatican Museum. It's supposed to be a madhouse."

"The museums close at six."

"But they let you just"—I wave my arms at the frescoes—"wander around in here?"

The hint of a smile curves his lips, and something flashes in his eyes. "They trust me."

"Perks of being an almost-priest, I guess," I mutter, turning back to the frescoes. I work my way slowly through to the end. "This is amazing," I say as the glass doors at the end of the corridor slide open.

One corner of his mouth curls, and he nods. "I thought you might like it."

I move through the door into the next gallery.

"Galleria degli Arazzi. The gallery of tapestries," he says.

I glance back at him as that kid-on-Christmas-morning zing of excitement ripples through me. "Brittany Simmons would so hate me right now." She's my class's resident haughty bitch. Every group has one—the person who thinks they rein supreme over everyone else. She was livid when I scored the year-abroad scholarship she thought she deserved.

"I feel obligated to remind you this is your penance for previous sins. It doesn't seem prudent to start racking up more so soon."

I spin and see him fighting a smile. "What am I supposed to call you, anyway?"

He raises an eyebrow. "Reverend Moretti will suffice . . . for now."

Something about this guy gets totally under my skin in that really annoying pebble-in-my-shoe way. I turn to the tapestry in front of me. "So, *Reverend Moretti*. This tapestry was fashioned from a Raphael original."

"Keen eye," he says, stepping up next to me and tucking his hands into his pockets, "but actually, these tapestries were all realized in the 1520s and '30s from drawings by Raphael's students. None of them are based on his original work, but some of his students picked up his tendencies, so there are similarities." He leads me halfway up the hall to a tapestry of Jesus and His disciples. "This one is especially interesting. It and many of the others are done in the Flemish tradition, which gives it a three-dimensional appearance. Walk past it slowly and watch Jesus' eyes."

I do, and not only do they follow me, but the long table at the end of which He's sitting points at me no matter where I stand. "So . . . wow."

He steps up next to me, his eyes following the lines of the artwork. "These hung in the Sistine Chapel for almost one hundred years." He glances at me. "Are you taking notes?"

I tap my forehead and smirk. "Right here."

He gives me the skeptic's eye for a long heartbeat, then turns and moves farther up the hall. We go through several more galleries in the next few hours and end in the Cortile del Belvedere, in front of the white marble sculpture of Laocoön and His Sons.

"This is where it all began," he says, admiring the sculpture of an immense and very naked Laocoön and his two mature, equally naked but significantly smaller sons, one on either side of him, struggling against a serpent that is wound around all three and biting Laocoön's hip. "Pope Julius II acquired this sculpture in 1506 when it was unearthed in a Roman vineyard near Santa Maria Maggiore. He sent a young Michelangelo and Giuliano—"

"—de Sangallo to check it out," I interrupt. "They told him it was the real deal and said he should snap it up and bring it back to Vatican City for preservation. It was the first piece in the Vatican collection." I fold my arms over my chest and stare him down. "Art History 101. What kind of amateur do you think I am?"

A smile ticks his mouth. "It's good to know you were paying attention." He turns back to Laocoön and smooths a hand over his perfect hair. "Tomorrow, we'll tackle the Sistine Chapel and St. Peter's Basilica."

I look at him for a long minute in the waning light. "You know everything that's in there. Why don't you just do this thing with the kids? Why do you need me?"

He makes a slow loop around the front of Laocoön, inspecting the piece from all angles. "Because I'm boring. No twelve-year-old wants to hear a deacon drone on about things that were created hundreds of years before they were born."

"So, why do you think they're going to want to hear *me* drone on about things that were created hundreds of years before they were born?"

He turns and looks at me, grasping his hands behind his back. "Because your task is to find a way to make it interesting—bring it to life for them, make them want to know more. Part of what we're hoping to instill in them is a hunger for knowledge that will carry through into adulthood."

I think about the tattoo over my heart, the kanji

symbol for knowledge—which makes me think about Trent's matching tattoo, rippling on his pec while I made love to him—which reminds me why I'm here. I shake off the shudder and look at the reverend. "But I don't speak Italian, so unless I'm expanding their cultural knowledge by ordering them a pizza, which is just about all I know how to say in Italian except, Va 'al diavolo, I don't get how this is going to work."

His eyes widen for a beat when I tell him to go to hell in Italian, but then he says, "I will be your mouth, when necessary." For some reason, when he says the word mouth, it draws my attention to his. And now I'm staring at it. When I don't say anything, he continues. "Children are extraordinarily perceptive. Only someone authentic, with a deep love of art, will radiate the enthusiasm needed to keep them engaged." He lifts a hand and rubs his chin. "I hoped that person might be you, but if you're not interested—"

"I didn't say that," I interrupt, because I am. How many people get to spend their free time hanging out at one of the most renowned museums in the world teaching kids to love art? This is an amazing opportunity. "How will this work with my schedule at school?"

"I'll need you one afternoon every other week, but we have a degree of flexibility in our scheduling. This is just one segment in a three-day series of presentations. I have a historian who will take them through the Forum and Colosseum, and an architectural student who will walk them through the Pantheon for the other two days. Once I have all your schedules, we'll coordinate them so your commitment with me will be consistent."

"How many Hail Marys did *they* have to say?" I mutter.

He tilts his head at me but doesn't answer.

I try to think of a downside, but I can't find one. "You've got yourself a tour guide."

A smile curves his lips. "Excellent."

It's not till I get home and look at my phone that I see that Trent responded to my text. I sit on the lounge on my patio, ignoring the bass vibration from the bar and the possibility that a boy might at this very minute be peeing in my doorway and open it.

Hope you said a Hail Mary for me. Heading back to school tomorrow. Same apartment, in case you feel like sending some Italian wine or anything.

So, that's it. It's over. We're good. Things are back to normal.

I've got my best friend back. What happened isn't going to ruin our family because it's over and done. We're archiving it into the dead files, where we'll never talk about it or think about it or dream about it again.

I breathe deep and am shocked that I finally can. It's like the elephant that's been sitting on my chest went looking for some other condemned soul to torture. All the tension in my muscles runs out, and suddenly I'm exhausted. I can barely keep my eyes open long enough to brush my teeth. God, I'm going to sleep well tonight.

I flop on the bed and call Julie before I'm totally out, and when I wake up in the morning, the phone is in my bed, and I don't remember most of the conversation or hanging up, which means I probably didn't.

All I remember for sure is I dreamed about Trent . . . in my bed.

I am so going to hell.

A LITTLE TOO FAR

I lapse in the bed and call into being. I recall my sins
and often finds them in the morning, the panic is in my
bed, and I don't remember most of the conversation of
anything when nearly I remember there.

All I remember for sure is promised about them

in my bed.

I lapse again it said.

Chapter Seven

"PORTA SACTA," THE Reverend Moretti tells me as we step through the entrance into the narthex of St. Peter's Basilica, stopping in front of a huge double door on the right front of the immense façade. Today, we're in the normal throng of visitors. No private tour, unfortunately. The reverend flashes his credentials and gets us past the long lines—more perks—but there's still a bottleneck at the main entrance. "The Holy Door," he continues. "It's also called the Door of the Great Pardon because its sixteen panels depict the sins of man and his redemption through God's mercy."

I study the panels of the bronze door.

"His Holiness opens it only on holy years for the pilgrimage."

"When is the next holy year?"

His gaze shifts from the door to me. "Not until 2025."

I scrunch my face. "So what happens on *unholy* years?"

He blows a puff of air through his nose that could almost be a laugh. "It stays bricked over on the inside." He leads me toward the main entrance, and we catch a slight lull in the crowd, so it only takes us a few minutes to get through the massive double doors into the central nave of the church.

"Holy crap," I say when I walk in and look up. I knew it was big, but . . . "Holy—" His hand on my arm and his stern gaze stop my next word. "Sorry," I whisper.

"Saint Peter's Basilica is the largest church in the world," he says, stepping deeper into the cavernous space. But he's already lost me because, in the corner to the right, behind Plexiglas, I see the Pietà—one of Michelangelo's greatest creations. One of the pinnacles of Renaissance sculpture.

I'm totally dumbstruck. I can't move. I can't even speak. I'm fairly certain I'm having my first truly religious experience, and it's probably a very bad thing that it's happening in a church, but it's over a sculpture. Mental note: Add idol worship to your list for confession.

It must take the Reverend Moretti a while to realize I'm not following him because it's a full minute later when his gentle hand grasps my elbow, directing me toward the crowd surrounding the sculpture. We wait while the masses snap their shots and move on, and several minutes later, we're standing at a black marble rail about eight feet from the Plexiglas. Five feet past that, on a high, oval pedestal, is the Pietà.

"I take it you recognize this?" he asks me, and I hear the smile in his voice.

I still can't speak. All I can do is stare. The detail is truly exquisite—the folds of Mary's robes; the way her fingers press into her crucified Son's flesh as she cradles Him in her lap. Jesus' ribs, the veins in His arms, His fingernails . . . every last detail is perfect.

"He was only twenty-three when he did this," I finally say, but it's a whisper, swept away in the noise of the crowd.

The reverend leans close to my ear. "I'm sure, then, that you're aware the process took less than two years and was completed 1499, and that this is the only piece that—"

"—Michelangelo ever signed," I interrupt without taking my eyes off the sculpture. "I also read that he regretted his moment of vanity later and swore never to sign another work by his hand."

"I've heard that anecdote as well."

"This is truly amazing," I say, still staring at the Pietà. "How could someone carve something this intricate with hammers and chisels. I mean, now, with modern tools, sure, but . . ." I lean on the rail, as close as I can get. "Think of the talent . . . the devotion and the passion that had to go into creating this."

He doesn't say anything for a long minute, and when I finally glance in his direction, he's leaning a hip on the marble rail, but he's not looking at the Pietà. He's looking at me. "Passion can sometimes bring out qualities in a person that they never knew they possessed."

"What is your name?" I blurt. I don't even know where

it came from, but suddenly I really want to know. "I mean your real name. Your first name."

"Alessandro," he answers after a beat.

"But I can't call you that."

It's not a question, but I still see him contemplating his answer. "It would probably be for the best if you didn't," he finally says, and his expression is hard to get a handle on—his full red lips pressed into a determined line but something in his deep charcoal eyes indecisive.

I look back at the Pietà. "I could stay here all day."

"I understand the sentiment, but," he says, pressing his fingers gently into the small of my back and shepherding me off to the side of the crowd, "there's lots more to see, including another great work of Michelangelo's."

"The Sistine Chapel," I breathe as tingles run up my spine.

And I realize Abby wasn't exaggerating about the creaming-the-knickers thing, because this is downright orgasmic.

I'VE HAD TWO weeks to come up with something that will keep kids interested in ancient art. Between that and the start of classes, my mind has been pretty occupied. Which is a good thing. Already, I've seen some amazing works on my "field trips" in my art history classes, and I've begun to feel comfortable enough that I've done some exploring between my apartment and campus on my own. Like, just yesterday I finally saw the famous thirteenth-century mosaics at Basilica di Santa Maria in

Trastevere. And I've stumbled on some places completely by accident. This whole city is the big black X on a treasure map.

But nothing can keep my mind totally off Trent.

We've been texting back and forth, but not for hours like we used to, and it's all been surface stuff. He tells me about his classes and his profs, and I tell him about some of the things I've seen around Rome. We're both avoiding anything deeper, and as much as it hurts that we can't talk like we used to, at least we're getting back to something resembling normal.

It's a start.

And I hear from Sam and Katie here and there. My last text conversation with Sam went something like this:

> Sam: *You getting any Italian ass?*
>
> Me: *I spend all my free time with a priest. What do you think?*
>
> Sam: *How old a priest?*
>
> Me: *Twenty-four.*
>
> Sam: *Hot?*
>
> Me: *Yes* (In hindsight, I should have lied.)
>
> Sam: *Don't know, Lex. Yrs of pent-up sexual frustration? Could be totally hot.*
>
> Me: O_O

Whether I have class or not, I set my alarm to call Dad and Julie every morning at eight so I catch them before bed, and every morning they grill me for details on everything I've seen and done. I text them pictures as I go, so they pretty much know where I've been, but Julie says it's more real when they hear it from my mouth.

Alessandro (which is what I call him in my head even though I can't to his face) and I have e-mailed back and forth several times while I've been working on the presentation, but I've only seen him once since the day in St. Peter's and the Sistine Chapel, and that was only for a minute, when I stopped by the rectory to pick up a book on the Vatican Museums he wanted me to read. When I've suggested meeting to go over my notes, he's begged off, saying we'll do a dry run when I have the whole thing hammered out. But, like it or not, the good reverend is going to have to see me today. I did some sketches I'm thinking of incorporating into the tour, and I need his input. I've e-mailed him every day this week asking to meet, and he hasn't answered.

I get the distinct feeling he's keeping his distance for some reason.

It's probably because I pissed him off when we walked into the Sistine Chapel, and I looked up at the ceiling, and hissed, "Holy shit!" at which point everyone around us gaped at me, and a grumpy Swiss Guard tried to throw me out. Alessandro had to intervene on my behalf, and he looked none too pleased about it.

It's not my fault I'm a Michelangelo groupie. Or maybe it is, but he's the one who said, and I quote the good reverend himself: "Only someone authentic, with a deep love of art, will radiate the enthusiasm needed to keep them engaged." He got what he wanted. He can't bitch about it now.

I *am* going to have to rein back my "enthusiasm" around the kids, though. The tours don't start for a few weeks, so I have some time to get over the orgasmicity of it all before then.

The Roman streets are always crowded, but Saturdays are the worst. I elbow my way through the pedestrians and street vendors clogging the sidewalks and spilling into the narrow roads, and finally make it to the rectory. I take a deep breath, square my shoulders, and knock.

No one answers.

I knock again.

Still nothing.

I spin and look across the street at the church. He could be there, but the truth is, after what happened in confession three weeks ago, I'm not really keen on running into Father Reynolds, so I've pretty much avoided the place.

Time to man up.

I march across the street and through the door, which is propped open. There are a few obvious tourists walking the walls and inspecting the frescoes, and there is a middle-aged woman kneeling in a pew, praying.

And there's an open confessional.

Damn.

I breathe deep and move in that direction. I breathe deep again as I step through and close the door behind me, and one more time as I kneel at the red curtain.

"Nel nome del Padre, e del Figlio, e dello Spirito Santo. Amen," the sandpaper voice that I now know is Father Reynolds's says, and I cross myself.

"Forgive me, Father, for I have sinned. It's been three weeks since my last confession . . . and I'm sure you remember that one, so we'll just skip to the new stuff, okay?"

"Ah. I do. And I also remember I sent you on mission with the Reverend Moretti. How is that going?"

"Well . . . that's really the reason I'm here. I'm looking for him, and he's not here or at the rectory."

"So, you have nothing to confess?"

I snort out a laugh. "I didn't say *that*."

"Well, then. First things first. The act of contrition."

I bow my head as we mutter the prayer together. When we're done, he says, "So, what have you to confess?"

"I'm trying to be more careful with my . . . okay, that's a lie. I just lied to you. I'm not trying to be more careful about anything. I still take the Lord's name in vain. All the time. Probably another hundred times since my last confession. And when I was at St. Peter's Basilica with the Reverend Moretti, I went all idol worship on the Pietà. And I cursed in the Sistine Chapel, and the Reverend Moretti had to sweet-talk the guard into not throwing me out."

"Sounds like the reverend is getting you in all sorts of trouble."

I point at him even though he can't see me through the curtain . . . I hope. "Right! That's what I said. It's all his fault, but . . . he hasn't answered my last few e-mails, and I need to see him, so . . ."

"One thing at a time, my child. Anything else you find yourself in need of confessing?"

"You know," I say. "Surprisingly, that's all I can think of at the moment."

"Very well. Do you come to the Lord with free mind and heart, ready to accept Jesus' guidance and absolutions of these sins?"

"I am sorry for my sins and ask Jesus to forgive them as well as any I have forgotten to confess."

"Very well. Once again, please be more mindful of your thoughts in regards to taking the Lord's name in vain."

"Yes, Father."

"And that includes times when you are inside churches with fine works of art."

"Yes, Father."

"I absolve you of your sins in the name of the Father, the Son, and the Holy Spirit. Amen."

I cross myself as he says it.

"It is Saturday. You will find the reverend at the youth center."

"Which is . . . where?"

"Take a right outside the door, then a left on Vicolo del Polverone. You'll see it one short block up on the left. Gray building with no windows and a blue door."

"Thank you, Father."

"Go in peace."

"Thanks be to God."

If I'd ever bothered to learn my left from my right, following directions would be so much easier. As it is, three lefts and four rights later, I finally stumble on Vicolo del Polverone. As luck would have it, right in front of me is a gray building with no windows and a blue door. Just to be sure there aren't two, I walk a block in either direction. When I'm fairly certain this is the place, I cross the street to the door, which is ajar. I push it open wider and peer into the gloom.

Around the edges of the room, there are weight benches with stacks of free weights, and punching bags hang from the ceiling. There are a few boys—teens as best as I can tell—working the bags. The middle of the room is dominated by a small boxing ring, complete with ropes. Two shirtless boys in protective headgear and gloves are sparing.

As my eyes adjust to the poor lighting, I scan the room for Alessandro, but he's nowhere. So maybe there really are two gray buildings with no windows and blue doors. As I'm turning to leave, I glance again at the fight in the ring.

The boy facing me sends a jab at the other boxer's face. The boxer ducks and shuffles to his left. The movement is so fluid, so graceful, that he makes it look effortless— more like a dance than a fight. The boy who threw the punch staggers a step, thrown off-balance by his miss, and the other boxer lays his gloves on the boy's shoulders to steady him and says something low in Italian. The sheen of sweat covering the boxer with his back to me shimmers, catching the little bit of light in the room, and I realize he's older than the boy he's sparring with. He's cut, his defined muscles rippling under smooth olive skin as he moves.

"Padre, c'è qualcuno qui," someone calls from the

punching bags. I turn and see all three boys there staring at me.

I look back at the ring in time to see Alessandro let go of the boy he's sparring with and turn. When he sees me standing in the door, his eyes widen for an instant. He pulls off the gloves and headgear and moves to the ropes, grabbing a towel that's hanging there and wiping his face and chest. He tugs a T-shirt over his head, and I feel a twinge of disappointment as that spectacular body disappears behind brushed gray cotton.

"Lexie," he says as he steps through the ropes. "What brings you here?"

"I . . ." I glance around and all four boys are still staring. "I had something I needed to show you . . . for the tour. You didn't answer my e-mail, so . . ."

An expression that could be either chagrin or regret passes over his face, but it's gone the next instant. "Yes . . . I apologize for my inaccessibility. I have several missions, and time is not always on my side."

"Could we maybe . . ." I look around, and everyone is still staring. ". . . go somewhere?"

He nods. "Just give me a few minutes to close up here and get cleaned up."

I wait outside on the sidewalk, and, a few minutes later, the four teens come straggling out. It's fifteen minutes later, and I'm just about to go back in after him, when Alessandro steps through the door in his crisp, black clerical shirt and slacks, collar snugly in place. His hair is damp, and he smells like soap. Fresh from the shower, obviously.

"Espresso?" he asks, turning to lock the door.

"Sure."

We walk up the sidewalk side by side. And, because the sidewalk is narrow, his arm brushes mine as we walk. Something buzzes in my chest as I picture him half-naked in the ring—the ripped muscles of his arms and back; the way sweat glistened off his pecs and abs when he turned. I shake the image out of my head and hope he doesn't notice my blush.

We find a seat in a nearby café and order. I can't resist getting a few of the currant croissants. I've already gained two pounds, and I've only been here three weeks. I can't imagine what I'm going to look like by the time the school year ends eight months from now.

I tear a corner off a croissant and pop it in my mouth. I close my eyes and give a little moan as it melts on my tongue.

When I open my eyes, Alessandro is staring at me, his expression totally unreadable.

"Did you always know you wanted to be a priest?" I ask, feeling suddenly self-conscious.

He sips his espresso and rests his cup on the table before answering. "No, not always."

"I couldn't do it," I say with a shake of my head.

His eyebrows rise. "No, you couldn't."

I glare at him as he takes another sip.

"You're a woman, Lexie. That's all I meant," he says, lowering his cup. "Women can't be ordained." He hesitates and quirks his head at me. "But there are other ways you could serve."

"Such as?"

He leans back in his chair and spins his cup slowly on the table, but his gaze stays fixed on mine. "The convent is always looking for faithful to serve God and the masses."

I snort a laugh. "That's just about the funniest thing I've ever heard."

He lifts his eyebrows at me again. "Then you don't get out much. Why would you find devoting your life to God funny?"

"It's just . . . me as a nun?" I scoff. "I mean"—my face scrunches like something smells bad—"how does anyone survive with the whole no-sex thing?"

He holds my gaze for a moment, then watches his hand swirl his espresso. "I'll grant you the calling isn't for everyone."

"Have you ever . . . you know?" The second it leaves my mouth I feel my cheeks start to flame. I can't believe I just asked that, but I really want to know.

He looks at me hard out from under long, dark lashes, and, for a minute, I think that's the only answer I'm going to get. But then he flashes a glance at the nearby tables— probably to decipher if anyone is listening in—and looks back at me. "Yes."

My heart pounds faster at his answer, and out of the blue the reason my body is reacting like this slams into me. Since the day I bumped into him at the church, I've thought he was a beautiful man, but seeing him in the gym, rivulets of sweat trickling over hard muscles . . . Yep. The tingle in my groin is unmistakable. I've got the hots for the good reverend.

I thought I was going to hell before, but this pretty much cements it.

But still, I want details: Who did he sleep with? How long ago? Was it good? Did he love her? Instead of asking what I really want to, I breathe out a shaky breath, and ask, "So how did it work? You just decided one day that sex was overrated, and you could live without it?"

He glances around us again, then leans toward me, his elbows resting on the table and his cup perched between his fingertips. "Believe it or not, Lexie, sex had nothing to do with my decision."

"So you never thought about what you were giving up . . . a wife? A family?"

"It was more about what I was gaining than what I was giving up. My path to the service of the Lord was long and convoluted."

I lean back into my seat, kick off my flip-flop, and tuck a leg under me. "I've got time. Hit me."

He breathes deep, then settles back into his chair, watching his finger trace circles on the glass tabletop. "My father was assistant chef at Windows on the World."

From the look on his face, I think that's supposed to mean something to me. It doesn't.

His haunted eyes lift to mine. "The restaurant on the top floor of the World Trade Center."

"Oh my God," I gasp as I finally understand the significance. I was seven when the attack happened. I remember watching on the TV in our kitchen that morning as one of the towers crumbled to dust. Tears streaked Dad's face as he poured milk on my cereal. I'll never forget it.

"His body was never recovered," Alessandro continues.

"I'm so sorry, Alessandro. That must have been horrible."

It's not until his gaze snaps to mine that I realize I used his first name. He smooths his white collar with a finger and thumb. "I was only eleven at the time and, at first, I didn't understand."

"It must have been hard to accept he was gone when you had no body to bury."

He shakes his head. "No . . . I understood that my father was dead, but I didn't understand why. I didn't understand that the Lord had a plan."

I just look at him.

He sighs and crosses an ankle over his other knee. His long, slender finger traces the inseam of his slacks mindlessly as he talks. "My mother . . . she wouldn't accept he was gone. At first, she poured all her time and energy into finding him, posting signs and scouring the city. Then, when she finally realized he wasn't coming home, she just curled up and stopped living. My older brother and I were left to our own devices much of the time. I was angry—at the world, at my mother. I lashed out. By the time I was thirteen, my brother and I were both in juvenile detention. That's where I learned to box."

I feel my eyes widen.

"While we were in the detention center, my mother tried to kill herself. My grandparents brought her back to her native Corsica, where they could care for her. They petitioned for custody of Lorenzo and me."

"So you came here when you got out of juvie?"

He shakes his head. "Not at first. Because our grand-parents were French citizens, there were visas and legal issues that needed to be cleared up before we could go. I'd just turned sixteen when my brother and I were released into a group home."

"In New York?"

He nods, and his wandering gaze locks on mine. "That was where I met Hilary."

I just look at him, but then I feel my eyes widen when I get what he's saying. Hilary. That's the who.

"She was with my brother for a short time, and when he was"—he winces a little—"done with her, she came to me."

"Oh." So . . . wow.

His whole face is pulled tight, and I wonder how painful it is for him to remember all this. "She was very young."

"But you were only sixteen, right? I mean . . . you were both young."

"That's no excuse." He breathes deep, and I watch his expression change from tortured to resolute as he puts it out of his mind and changes tack. "In any event, shortly after that, our visas came through, but my grandparents' caveat to taking us in was that we go to Catholic school when we got to Corsica. Until her breakdown, Mom had always made sure we were raised in the Church. Despite everything that I'd done, and that I didn't feel I deserved to be there, going back felt familiar—comfortable. Father Costa took us under his wing—became a father figure to us. He changed my life."

"How?"

He splays his hand on the table and presses back in his seat as if trying to ground himself. "I was drowning in guilt and anger that I'd internalized and turned back on myself. He gave me tasks. At first they were little things, like playing games with the younger kids at the church, but then he started sending me out to help families in the community—sometimes with light construction or repair projects, or checking in on the elderly and bringing them groceries. He even boxed with me because he knew that was my outlet. When I was a little older, he found me space in a building up the road from the church, where I could teach other kids." He smiles. "My first youth center." He leans forward onto his elbows and looks at me. "He helped me find healthier outlets for my self-destructive rage. Helping other people gave me purpose. He helped me to see I wasn't worthless—that my life could mean something."

"Long and convoluted," I say, running a fingertip around the edge of my espresso cup.

He nods slowly. "But the Lord showed me my path, and now I follow it."

"What about your brother?"

He breathes deep and taps a fingernail on his cup. "He didn't hear the calling."

From the look on his face, I have the distinct feeling things might not have turned out well for Lorenzo. He doesn't look like he plans on elaborating, and I don't push him on it.

"So, you had something you needed me to see?" he asks, his morose expression clearing.

"Yeah . . . sorry." I reach for my backpack and pull out my folder. "I did these by hand, and I don't have a scanner here, so I couldn't e-mail them." I lay the sketches of the ceiling of the Sistine Chapel on the table. I tore these sketches out and put them in a folder this morning because I didn't want Alessandro to see the one just before them in my sketchbook—the one I did of him looking at Laocoön on our first trip to the Vatican, his expression an interesting combination of clinical appraisal and unbridled awe. "Each sketch is one panel from the ceiling." I slip a page with a triangular panel sketched on it out of the stack. "I figured I'd cut them into the right shape and you said there'd be ten to fifteen kids in each group, so each kid would get two to three panels," I say, waving my hand at the pages in front of him. "You know, so they could put it together when they got back to school like a giant jigsaw puzzle. I could have them find the scenes from their pieces on the ceiling and tell me what they thought the scene was depicting. Then they could keep their pieces and color them in later if they wanted."

He fans the pages out on the table and looks them over. "You did these?"

I nod when he looks up at me. "They're really simplistic, but that's the point. That way, the kids can sort of make Michelangelo's work their own, you know . . . so it becomes more personal for them."

He slips the panel of Adam's creation out, inspecting it more closely. "These are exceptional. You're more the artist than I would have expected."

My face pulls into a scowl. "It's not like it was my idea or anything. Michelangelo's the genius. I just spent a few minutes on each one . . . because there are, like, thirty-three of them and I have classes and homework and—"

"They're perfect," he says, quieting me with a hand on mine. "This is a great idea. Exactly what I was hoping for."

"Thanks."

His hand is still on mine. He doesn't move it as he lays the creation of Adam down and picks up the panel depicting the temptation of Adam and Eve.

Why is he holding my hand? Is it just a priestly gesture? I always get nervous when people look at my work. He sensed that from my rambling, and he's trying to comfort me, that's all. Right?

So why is a rabbit thumping in my chest?

Finally, he lets go of my hand and slides the sketches back toward me. "Ask, and it shall be given you; seek, and ye shall find; knock, and it shall be opened unto you."

"You keep saying that. Why do you keep saying that?"

His eyes fix on mine. "I needed the perfect missionary for this job, and the Lord sent you."

"Actually, it was Father Reynolds who sent me, on account of the fact that there weren't enough Hail Marys I could possibly say to cover my sorry ass," I mutter.

He laughs. I mean actually laughs . . . right out loud. "You are truly something."

I cringe. "I guess that's better than the alternative."

He pushes his chair back and reaches for mine, sliding it back from the table. "I have Mass. Will you be joining us today?"

I stand and shake my head. "I don't think Father Reynolds can handle any more of me today."

Something mischievous flashes in his eyes as a corner of his mouth twitches. "Oh to be a fly on that wall."

Chapter Eight

"I'M FALLING IN love," I tell Abby as we sit at a sidewalk table at the café where we first met.

John Cabot is in Trastevere, a quaint Roman neighborhood just south of the Vatican. Its narrow, cobbled streets are full of cafés and bakeries and gelato stands, and the whole place turns into campus when school is in session. Everywhere I look, I see familiar faces: either students I have classes with or people I see in the university hallways. The streets are as familiar to me now as the walking paths crisscrossing Notre Dame. And what I realize as I sit back and start on my second currant croissant is that, after only five short weeks, Rome is starting to feel like home.

"I mean, look around you," I continue. "How could anyone not fall in love with this place? The food, the history, the art, the laid-back atmosphere, the—"

"—men," Abby interrupts, her gaze following a pair

of Carabinieri as they stroll past, the heels of their black boots thudding heavily on the cobbled road. They're in full uniform: black pants with a red stripe down the side, black jacket with silver buttons, black police cap with the Carabinieri crest on the front. It's finally cool enough now, at the beginning of October, that I don't feel so sorry for them anymore, but in the heat of the summer, that's gotta blow. "There is nothing quite as hot as a man in uniform," she says, following them down the street with her eyes. "Just looking at them makes me want to do something illegal."

I scowl at her. "I'm serious. I could see myself staying here . . . or coming back after graduation. I really love it."

"I'm serious too," Abby says, finally uncraning her neck and looking at me with eyes that are a very unlikely shade of hot pink. "I just want fifteen minutes in the backseat of a police car with that young one."

"Speaking of, what's happening with you and Grant?"

She rolls her eyes. "He's got a girlfriend back home. Serious, I guess. Can't be tempted, even by all this," she says, smoothing a hand down her curves. "So, in answer to your question: Nothing."

"Sorry."

"What about you? Any prospects?"

I'm shocked when the first face that flashes through my head isn't Trent. He's dark and beautiful, in a black shirt and a white collar.

"No," I say. "None. And I like it that way."

"A hot Italian comes up and whispers sweet Italian

nothings in your ear, and you're telling me you're not going to shag him on the spot?"

I think of Alessandro, leaning close to my ear at St. Peter's and telling me about the Pietà, which is just about the sexiest thing anyone could ever whisper in my ear. "He did. I didn't."

Her eyes spring wide, and I wish I could suck those words right back into my mouth. "You skolly! Who is it?"

I scowl at her. "Skolly?"

"I can see it all over your face. There is definitely someone here you'd drop those pretty little knickers for."

I snort out a laugh. "You are so far off base I can't even tell you. I don't have time for a social life."

She rolls her eyes. "That sodding church thing. I'm so glad I'm not Catholic." She smirks, and her gaze follows a bicycle messenger down the road. "I get to sin all I want."

"Speaking of which . . ." I finish my espresso and pop the last of my croissant in my mouth as I scrape my chair back. "I'm going to be late. See you later."

"Ring me later," she says, sipping her espresso. "I fancy a night out."

I smirk over my shoulder at her. "And you need a wing man?"

She smirks back. "No, but if you don't cock it up, I might get you lucky too."

I roll my eyes and step out into the sea of tourists on the sidewalk. As I weave through them toward St. Peter's Square, my phone vibrates. I make my way past a group of street musicians and tuck into the shade next to a boutique I'm passing, out of the line of fire, before fishing it out of my pocket. I fully expect it to be Alessandro hassling me because, let's face it, I'm always late, but when I look at the text, it's from Trent.

It's been over a week since I heard from him, and even then, it was little more than just, *Hi. How's it going?*

At this point, I can't kid myself anymore. It's glaringly apparent that Trent and I will never be able to get past the awkwardness. I mean, if we can't even have an unawkward text conversation, how's it going to go in real life.

I open his text. *Just checking in. Rome good?*

Yep, the obligatory "let's pretend that things aren't totally fucked up" text.

I'm good. Love Rome. You? I text back.

Good. Busy with wrestling and school.

Classes good?

Yep, You?

How can classes titled *Michelangelo* and *Italian High Renaissance Art* not be good? Then, before I can change my mind, I add, *Have you met anyone?*

Have you?

I type two letters. *No.*

Mom said you're doing some project with a guy?

A friend, I type back, not sure that really describes Alessandro.

I answered him, and I wait for him to answer me, but there's nothing. After a long minute of getting bumped by people passing me on the sidewalk, I type, *I'm late for a meeting. Gotta go.*

K. Bye.

And that's all I get. Does that mean he's seeing someone, and he doesn't want to tell me?

I've never lied or gone behind anyone's back. Ever.

I lean on the cool stone wall of the small boutique and rub a shaking hand down my face as his words from that night echo through my head.

Shit.

I hate this. I hate everything about it. I hate it so much that I would gladly trade back everything I felt that night with Trent for what we had before.

When I finally get my shit together and make it to the obelisk, Alessandro is waiting. He glances at his watch.

I hold up my hand and glare a warning at him. "Don't even."

He pushes away from the cement barrier at the base of the obelisk. "I take it today is not treating you well."

"Bingo."

"Well, let's see if we can remedy that." He turns, and I follow him through the crowd to the same ramp we went up the first time I visited the museums. The tour for the kids is only supposed to last ninety minutes, so it's a whirlwind, hitting only the highlights. The plan is to start at the Apollo Belvedere sculpture, then visit Laocoön and his sons on our way to the Michelangelo bust, which wasn't carved by him but by an unknown Greek sculptor centuries before Michelangelo was born. Then we speed through the map and tapestry galleries to the Sistine Chapel, and finish in St. Peter's Basilica at the Pietà.

I fish through my backpack for my notes as we weave

through the crowd to our starting point. When Alessandro stops at the Apollo, I'm still looking for them.

"I think I forgot my notes."

"You don't need your notes. You've got it all right here," he says, reaching up and tapping a fingertip on my temple.

"No," I say, rifling through my bag. "I mean the Italian. I printed out the phrases you sent me, and I tried to memorize them, but I'm sure I'm butchering the pronunciation and . . ." I stop digging and look up at him. "I think I'm going to need my notes."

"You don't need your notes," he repeats. "Just start here, with Apollo. We'll go through the whole thing in English today. Remember that these children are coming from the Catholic school. English and Latin education are mandatory there, so many of them have a basic mastery."

I'm stalling, and he knows it. I mean, I *did* forget my notes, I'm not making that up, but the truth is I just feel really stupid standing up here pretending to be some expert on all this stuff when I'm not. Sure, I cream my panties over a good Michelangelo, but who doesn't? Just because I might worship the man doesn't mean I can tell kids about him and make them love him as much as I do. They're going to see right through me. "Maybe I should work on those phrases some more. I mean, there's really no rush on the dry-run thing, right? We have another week before the first group."

He moves slowly toward me, like he thinks I might bolt. And he's probably right. He gently grasps my upper arms. "You'll be fine," he says very softly, obviously trying to talk me off the ledge. He reaches up, slides my backpack off my shoulders, and sets it at his feet. Then he leans closer: so close I can feel his breath in my hair when he whispers, "You'll be fine."

I breathe deep and back toward the Apollo, not sure if my heart is racing from stage fright or . . . something else. I clear my throat, and my eyes roll up, as if trying to peer into my brain. "Okay . . . so . . . the Apollo Belvedere"—throat clear—"was discovered near Rome in the 1400s and has been at the Vatican since 1511. It's a reproduction of a Greek sculpture, circa 580 B.C., most probably by Leochares." I lower my eyes out of my brain and cringe at Alessandro. "I feel so stupid."

"Well, you sound very smart. A little too smart. Remember, these are kids, Lexie. Think like a child. What would you find interesting about the Apollo if you were twelve."

I look up at his penis, then back at Alessandro. I put my hand over my mouth and fight to hold back the nervous giggle, but it erupts out of me anyway.

He breathes a short laugh and lowers his lashes, and I'd swear I see his face flush. "There must be something else that would intrigue a young Lexie Banks."

"Sorry to break it to you, but not really. I'm just that shallow."

He looks up at me and smiles. "Let's try it again."

"Okay . . . think like a twelve-year-old." I jiggle my arms to shake off the tension and breathe deep to pull it together. "This is the Apollo Belved—" But that's as far as I get before the giggles erupt out of me again. "Notice how . . . his penis . . . is chipped off . . ." I sputter through my laughter, but then I'm laughing so hard I can't stand up straight. People all around us stare at me as I cackle hysterically.

Alessandro grasps me by the waist before I topple over, which is imminent, and I'm surprised when I realize he's laughing too.

"Sorry . . ." I giggle. "I just . . . oh my God."

He scoops up my backpack and ushers me to a nearby bench, where the Asian-looking group of tourists who had laid claim to it spread like the Red Sea, making room for the crazy lady. I'm just starting to get myself together when Alessandro deposits me on the bench, giggles coming in short bursts instead of a continuous stream.

He lowers himself down next to me. "Well, that went well."

That's all it takes to set me off again. I bend at the waist and clutch myself as the giggles shake me from the inside out. Tears are streaming down my face, and I'm glad I didn't bother with too much makeup.

His hand rubs over my back as the hiccups start. "Maybe suggesting you think like a twelve-year-old wasn't the best advice."

The giggles slow as the hiccups become steadier. "I'm a mess," I say, wiping my eyes.

"That you are," he says, and I hear the smile in his voice.

THE ROMAN STREETS are alive at night in a whole different way. During the day, gawking tourists clog the sidewalks in a clumsy parade, their eyes and cameras trained on everything and nothing. At night, Rome pulses, and Piazza Navona is one of its hearts. There's electricity in the air that energizes everyone who makes their living on the streets, making them bolder. The street artists hawk their wares loudly in the center of the piazza, while couples stroll dreamily between the easels. The gelato vendors can't dish out their ice cream fast enough to keep up with the crowds, even in the chill of an October evening. And the Carabinieri in their crisp black uniforms with red stripes wander the piazza, openly checking out the girls in their scant clubwear.

Through her bright purple contacts, Abby watches each one of them stroll past as we sit at the outdoor café on the outskirts of Piazza Navona and eat. My eyes are still drawn to the art, as always. The more modern art on the street vendors' easels is eclipsed by the huge stone fountains in the center and on either end of the long piazza. The center fountain, surrounded by street vendors, is Bernini's Fountain of the Four Rivers, intricately depicting river gods from four different continents. I remember how chills ran down my spine the first time I saw it in Dan Brown's *Angels and Demons*. And now I'm here, in real life. Chills run down my spine again as I stare up at it.

"That one," Abby says, pulling my eyes away from Bernini's masterpiece. She nods toward a pair of Carabinieri who are walking within feet of our table. "He is totally edible."

"Speaking of edible, this is really good," I say through a bite of my dinner. I'm not sure what I ordered, but it's delicious. There are fresh vegetables and a chicken breast with paper-thin slices of lemon in some kind of tangy sauce. That's all I know. I was surprised when I got here to find that most Italian food isn't pizza and pasta. I mean, there *is* that, but that's not what's front and center on most restaurants' menus.

She raises her eyebrows at me, then adjusts her very-low-cut black lace halter top for maximum cleavage exposure before slowly pushing her chair back. The scrape of her chair legs on the sidewalk catches the Carabinieri's attention, and they slow to look at her.

"Scusami," she says, and slinks the few feet toward them. "My friend and I were wondering if there's a good club nearby."

"What kind of club you want?" the younger of the two says in stilted English. He's on the short side, but muscular, with cropped blond hair under his police cap. "Dance club? Piano?"

"Definitely a dance club," Abby says, twisting a finger into the pink tips of her straight black hair. She grins. "We're looking to large it up tonight."

I roll my eyes and sip my water as he fills her in on the local club scene. I glance over a minute later, and see that his partner has moved away, and Abby and the young Carabinieri are standing very close. She slips something into his hand, and he grins and leans in, saying something I can't hear into her ear. She brushes her fingers down his arm and turns back to me.

"I've got a date," she says, sliding back into her chair with a self-satisfied grin on her face.

I roll my eyes again.

She smirks. "Don't worry. We'll find you a special someone too."

We pay the check, and when we find the club, just a few blocks away, it's already crowded. The techno-dance music is so loud I feel it shake the floor, vibrating up my legs and making me feel seasick.

Abby slithers her way between people to the bar in the back and orders us two beers. "I'm going to get pissed tonight," she yells in my ear when she turns and hands me a mug. "Have a pint on me!" She pounds her entire beer in thirty seconds flat, then turns and orders another.

"What if your date shows up?" I ask.

"He damn well better. I've got plans for him."

"You think that's a good idea?" I ask, just now realizing she's serious about this.

"Best sodding idea I've ever had," she says, then pours half her new beer down her throat.

And then I get it. I lean closer so I don't have to yell so loud. "Is this because of Grant?"

"Grant bloody who?" she scowls.

"Listen, Abby. Sleeping with this guy isn't going to make Grant want you."

She finishes the rest her second beer in one swallow. "I'm just sampling the local cuisine," she says with a suggestive smile. "It's got nothing to do with that wanker."

She grabs my hand and drags me toward the mosh of undulating bodies near the DJ. We dance, and I'm a sweaty mess over an hour later when I see Abby's Carabinieri moving through the crowd toward us. He's traded his uniform for a white linen shirt that's open at the collar and a pair of dark jeans. I'm only on my second beer, but Abby's well on her way to getting "pissed," so even when she sees him and stumbles into his arms, I don't let her out of my sight. I back to the edge of the dance floor as they dance, their bodies grinding together, swaying slowly, even though it's a fast song.

A tall, not-so-bad-looking guy comes up to me and starts shouting over the music in rapid Italian. By the way his eyes flicker between me and the mass of people on the dance floor, I think he's trying to ask me to dance.

I squint apologetically at him. "I don't speak Italian. Sorry."

"Ah. You are American?" he asks with a thick accent.

I nod and when I look back at the dance floor, I see Mr. Carabinieri making a less-than-flattering face and holding Abby at arm's length.

"Excuse me," I say, pushing onto the dance floor. I realize Abby looks a little green as I get closer. "Are you okay?" I shout as I reach her.

"She is not well," Carabinieri Boy says.

I wrap my arm around her waist and pull her to my side. "I should take her home."

"No," Abby slurs. She flops her head in the Carabinieri's direction. "Marco."

"Abby, just let me take you home," I say, shooting a glare at Carabinieri Marco.

But just then, Abby lurches forward with a hand over her mouth. Marco drops her like a hot potato. I pull her to my side, and we just make it out the door when all six pints of beer and most of her dinner makes its reappearance.

I stand with her, one arm around her waist to hold her up and the other pulling back her hair, while she heaves onto the sidewalk.

"Where are my shoes?" she asks when her convulsions slow.

I look down as she backs away and see her bare feet are splattered with vomit. "I'll buy you a new pair."

She's still staring at her feet. "Bloody shame. Those were my favorites."

"Come on. I'll take you home."

She stands unsteadily, and we start in the direction of my apartment. Even though she puked up volumes of beer, she's still pretty drunk. After a block, I'm mostly dragging her so I decide to take my life into my hands and hail a taxi. It's not that far back to my apartment, but I'm not going to make it if I have to carry her. When we get there, I shove her ahead of me up the stairs and dump her on the love seat, then go to boil water for tea. I bring a wad of damp paper towels back with me while the water's boiling and work on cleaning up her feet.

She kicks my hand away. "Where's your loo?"

"Over there," I say, pointing to the door in the corner.

She hauls herself up. "I'm going to shower." That's obviously the easiest answer to the puke-on-the-legs situation, so I don't argue as she staggers across the room toward the bathroom, undressing as she goes. First, the short skirt hits the floor, then the halter, which leaves her in just her sheer lace thong. I try not to look until she closes the door, then I pick up the trail of clothes and fold them onto the arm of the love seat.

The water starts, and, after a minute, I hear Abby singing loudly and very off-key. The teapot whistles, and I head back to the kitchen and make us both a cup of tea. When Abby emerges from the bathroom fifteen minutes later, wrapped in my towel, she looks a thousand times better. And her eyes are a very natural pale gray.

"I'm knackered," she says, combing her damp, black hair back with her fingers. "Where's your bed?"

"Don't you want some tea?" I ask.

She presses a hand to her stomach, and her face twists. "Things are still a bit touchy in that department."

I nod and sip the last of mine, then put the cup next to hers on the end table. "It's in here," I say, moving past my dining-room table to the door up front. She follows me in, drops the towel to the floor, and crawls under my sheets, heaving an epic sigh.

I usually sleep naked, but I'm thinking with another naked girl in my bed, maybe not so much. I grab Trent's T-shirt from the armoire and pull it over my head, inhaling deeply. His smell is almost gone from it.

I think Abby's asleep when I come back from the

bathroom and click off the light, but as I settle in next to her, I hear the rustle of sheets as she turns to face me. "Men are complete prats, the whole bloody lot of them."

"I don't know," I muse, bringing Trent's shirt to my nose again. "There might be one or two who redeem the whole bloody lot."

Chapter Nine

IT'S D-DAY. I'M so nervous that I don't really sleep that well and wake way before my alarm. I have class this morning, but I'm supposed to meet Alessandro at the Vatican at noon for our first tour. He thinks I know what I'm doing. I know he's wrong.

I put on my smartest outfit: a blue blouse with a straight black skirt and low black pumps, then inspect myself in the mirror. Even though I look like someone's grandmother, I decide it will have to do. I pack my things for school and my drawings and notes for the tour because I won't have time to come home in between, and head to my favorite bakery for a currant croissant even though I'm not really hungry. I spill onto the sidewalk and hurry to class, but just as I'm walking into the building, my phone vibrates.

I press CALL and lift it to my ear, realizing in my panic this morning, I forgot to call Dad and Julie. "I'm sorry! I just—"

"Lex," Trent slurs into the phone, stopping my words in my throat. "It's me."

"Hey," I say, surprised. I do the math quickly in my head and realize it's almost midnight there. "What's up?"

"I just . . . shit Lexie . . ." He trails off, and there's a lot of background noise—pounding music and people laughing and talking too loud.

"Where are you?" I ask.

"Just a stupid par—" His voice breaks off, and there's a loud thudding sound.

"Who are you talking to?" a slightly whiny girl's voice asks in the background.

"Get off me and give me back the goddamn phone," Trent slurs, his agitated voice coming from somewhere off in the distance.

"Who is this?" the girl asks into the phone.

"Trent's sister," I answer sharply. "Give him back the phone."

"Whatever," she says, then Trent's voice is back.

"Lex? You still there?"

"Yeah, I'm here." I lean on the wall of the building and rub my temple, which is starting to pound. I want to climb through the airwaves between us and see him. "Are you okay?"

There's a long pause, where all I can hear is the party noise. "I just needed to hear your voice," he finally says. "I miss you."

"I miss you too," I tell him, leaning harder into the building.

"I just . . . I want you so fucking much right now. Shit, Lexie. I can't even . . ." He trails off again.

I close my eyes and focus on breathing. "You're drunk, Trent. Where are you?"

"Just some friends of George's apartment," he slurs.

George is Trent's wrestling partner, and despite the fact that he's a scholarship athlete, he's a serious tweaker.

"Are you okay to get home?" I ask. "Is there someone there who can help you get home?"

I hear another thud in my ear.

"Seriously, Becca. Get off me," Trent says, his voice away from the phone. There's some rustling and a muffled female voice, then the line goes dead.

I want to call him back, but what would I say? "I want you too?" Could I say it?

I will. If he calls back, I'll tell him.

My heart pounds, and my hand starts to shake as I stare at my phone, willing it to ring. It doesn't.

"He was just drunk," I tell myself. "Drunk and horny. That's all."

Right? He just wants me because he's drunk.

I start my feet moving into the building, and I'm late for my Renaissance class. For the rest of the morning, my head spins with what to do. I put my phone on my thigh and stare at it some more. I'm sure Trent is asleep now—probably passed out somewhere. I hope he's not with that girl, Becca. Either way, I can't call him back.

After class, I march across Trastevere to the Vatican and am actually early for a change. "I am so unprepared," I whisper to Alessandro as we lead the first group of kids across the courtyard to Apollo.

He doesn't answer but rests his hand on my back, and I instantly feel stronger. I force myself to stop chewing my cheek and try to tap into his serenity. He's always so calm, and if there's one thing I need right now, it's to stay calm. I can't dissolve into a writhing heap of giggles in front of fourteen twelve-year-olds and their nun teacher. I've spent the week since my meltdown working more on my composure than the material, which, as Alessandro pointed out, I already have in my head.

"I still think you should do this," I tell him.

We reach the Apollo, and he grasps my hand. "You'll be fine," he whispers.

I breathe deep and turn to the group, who are gathering around the statue. "Hi, everyone. I'm Lexie, and this is the Reverend Moretti," I say with a nod toward Alessandro. "Can everyone understand me?"

Most of the group nod.

"Their English is quite good," their teacher, Sister Clarice says. She's in the full nun getup, and it's a little unnerving.

"Good," I say with a nod. I look up at Apollo. "So does anyone know who this is?"

They all just stare at me blankly. So, I take that as a no.

"Who knows something about the Greek gods?" I ask.

A smallish boy in the back raises his hand.

"What's your name?" I ask him.

"Antonio," he says, very quietly.

He's shy. I can tell by the way he sort of sinks into himself when there's any attention on him, just like I used to do when I was his age.

I smile at him. "Have you ever heard of Apollo?"

Several other kids raise their hands, but I keep my eyes on Antonio. He nods.

"Do you know what he was the god of?"

He glances at his teacher, who nods her encouragement. He points up. "Sun."

"Excellent, Antonio." I give him a smile. "Apollo is the Greek god of sun and light, and a lot of other things as well. This statue of him has been here at the Vatican for over five hundred years, but it's actually a copy of a much older statue, one that was made well over two thousand years ago." I step aside to give the kids a look without me in the way. "Does anyone have any questions?"

No one does, so we start across the courtyard to Laocoön. I glance up at Alessandro, and he looks relieved. Probably because I made it through the whole Apollo spiel without melting down or mentioning genitalia.

By the time we get through the galleries to the Sistine Chapel, the kids have all started to warm up, asking questions and telling me the tidbits they know about the art. As they get more comfortable, they also get more curious, and it starts to feel a little like herding cats. I need both Alessandro and Sister Clarice to keep track of everyone.

The line for the chapel is long, as usual. As we move slowly down stairs that lead to the entrance, I tell them,

"Inside the chapel, we're not allowed to talk above a whisper, so I'll give you these now." I pull the copies of my sketches from my bag and hand them out. "On the ceiling, you'll see a famous painting by Michelangelo. Your sketch matches a scene from the ceiling. I want you to find the scene, and when you do, show me what you have."

We step through the door into the crowded chapel, and the same grumpy Swiss Guard who tried to throw me out a month ago is here. I swear he recognizes me because he follows me around, waiting for me to make a fatal mistake so he can boot my ass.

I try to lose him in the crowd, then I see Alessandro. He's leaning a shoulder against the partition near the exit, one ankle crossed over the other and his hands tucked loosely into his slacks pockets. I make a beeline for him, and the Swiss Guard follows.

"Make him stop following me," I hiss between my teeth when I reach Alessandro. I turn and smile sweetly at the guard as he approaches. When Alessandro doesn't say anything, I give him a "go on, tell him," glance. He tips his head at the guard as if to say, "keep an eye on her." I turn and glare at him, and when he lifts an eyebrow at me, I want to rip it off his face. I spin and move through the horde toward Sister Clarice.

One by one, the kids come up to me with their sketches and point to the ceiling panel it matches. I whisper to each to look carefully at the scene and tell me what they think is happening in it. Some know their scripture, because they tell me about the Creation, Noah, and Adam and Eve, while others make up elaborate stories to go with their pictures. When they've all found their scene, I move them toward Alessandro at the exit.

He nods when we reach him.

I nod back.

We snake our little parade through the throng into St. Peter's Basilica, and I lead them up all five hundred feet of central nave to the Papal Altar with the dome of St. Peter towering above it.

Once everyone is gathered, I turn to them. "What did you think of the ceiling in the chapel? Pretty amazing, huh?"

They all nod, and one girl holds up her sketch. "I want to paint this like Michelangelo."

I smile. "You can take those home and paint them or color them or whatever you want. But did you know that Michelangelo didn't really want to paint that ceiling?"

Many of them shake their heads.

"The ceiling of the Sistine Chapel was done by Michelangelo on orders from Pope Julius II. He tried to tell the Pope to get somebody else because he wasn't a painter, but the Pope forced him to do it." I glance at Alessandro to see if he's pissed I just dissed a pope, but there's an expression on his face that I can't read at all.

I look back at the kids and scrunch my face. "Have your parents ever made you clean up your room?"

They all make faces and grumble.

"To Michelangelo," I continue, "painting the Sistine Chapel was like having to do his chores. He considered himself a sculptor and an architect, not a painter. But . . ." I say, holding up a finger and smiling, "there is something he considered one of his greatest achievements, and it's right here in this basilica. Does anyone know what it is?"

Several of them point behind us to the Pietà (which, admittedly, still makes me cream my knickers a little), but Antonio, the little shy boy who knew about Apollo, points straight up, and his eyes brighten.

I take a few steps toward him. "Tell us what you're pointing to, Antonio."

"The dome," he says with an almost smile.

"You are absolutely right. St. Peter's Basilica is so big that it took 120 years to build it. No person can live that long, right?"

A group nod.

"So, they went through a lot of architects before the basilica was finished. Michelangelo was one of them, and he's the one who figured out how to stack a bunch of really huge rocks into the shape of an enormous dome and not have them fall down—because if the dome fell on the Pope, that would really suck, right?"

Another group nod, and a few stifled giggles.

I can't believe these kids are so interested. And I can't believe how much fun I'm having. I'm so full of nervous giddiness, I have to force myself to slow down my speech so these poor kids can keep up. "The dome of St. Peter's was one of Michelangelo's last masterpieces, and he didn't even live to see it completed. He designed it in 1547, and he died in 1564. Stories say he was making changes to the design on his deathbed. The dome wasn't completed until 1590."

"Can we climb?" a boy shouts, pointing to some

people walking along the viewing platform on the first ring of the cupola, 250 feet above our heads.

"We will climb on another day," Sister Clarice says, and a few of the kids grumble while a few others squeal.

"There is one other great work of Michelangelo's in St. Peter's, and many of you pointed to it earlier," I say, turning and leading them toward the Pietà. As we get close, I tell them, "Michelangelo carved this sculpture, the Pietà, depicting Mary and Jesus after the crucifixion, when he was only twenty-three. How old are you guys?"

"Twelve!" someone shouts.

"Really? I thought you were at least twenty," I say, looking out over them. "So . . . maybe not quite yet, but in a few years, do you want to try to carving something like this?"

"Too hard," a boy right up front says. He's leaning over the rail to get a closer look.

"This was Michelangelo's passion, though, so to him, it wasn't hard work. Name one thing you love to do."

"Football!" the boy up front says. A few others yell some things in Italian, and I swear I hear Warcraft from someone.

"Would some people consider what you love to do hard work?"

The boy pushes off the railing and faces me. "Yes, if they weren't a good footballer."

"Is it hard for *you*?" I ask, tipping my head toward him and smiling.

"Not really," he says, puffing out his chest.

"So, when you're doing something you love, sometimes it doesn't *feel* hard, even if it is. That's how Michelangelo felt about sculpture."

Some of them are beaming at the Pietà, as if they're dying to give it a try. I hope some of them do. (Not that I'm suggesting it's a good idea for a bunch of twelve-year-olds to go home and take sharp things to a block of marble. But maybe with clay.) Others are looking around the cavernous space in awe. And the little boy, Antonio, is looking at me. He makes his way slowly through the group and stops in front of me. "I want to build churches," he whispers. He looks toward the center of the church, up at the monstrous dome. "I want to build domes like Michelangelo."

I lean into the marble rail next to him. "Then I think you should. If you love something, and you're willing to work for it, your dreams can come true."

He smiles.

I smile.

When I look up at Alessandro, he's leaning against the far wall with his hands in his pockets, one ankle crossed over the other. I'm not even sure he's paying attention.

Everyone says their good-byes, and I wave as the kids file out of the basilica behind Sister Clarice.

Alessandro makes his way through the crowd to where I am. "Come with me," he says, then turns and walks briskly toward the exit.

I don't follow. Instead, I ball my hands on my hips, and shout, "That's it? No 'Wow, Lexie, that was really great.' Or, 'Gee, Lexie, you pulled that off despite yourself.'"

He turns and levels me in his gaze. "Gee, Lexie, you pulled that off despite yourself."

I'm not going to let his accent throw me, so I ignore the tingle in my stomach. "I swear to Go—" I catch myself, but not before Alessandro lifts an eyebrow at me. I storm over to him and get in his face. "Listen, Reverend, if I didn't think this was my only chance not to burn in hell for what I did, I'd be so out of here." That's a total lie. I'm here for the art. But admitting that doesn't buy me any leverage.

He looks at me curiously for a second, and he's so close I can see the thin black rims around his charcoal irises. "Alessandro."

"What?"

"I want you to call me Alessandro." His hard shell cracks a little, and his face softens. But then he glances at the milling crowd and backs off a step, lowering his lashes. "You were truly spectacular with those children . . . and I have something I'd like to share with you." His eyes lift to mine. "Can I show you?"

God, why can't I breathe?

Because he's an attractive man. A *very* attractive man. It's normal to feel attracted to an attractive man, white collar or not, right? . . . Even though half the time I want to wring that collar right off his neck.

Which is something else I'm sure I need to add to my list for confession—both the wanting to wring his white-collared-neck part, and the lusting-after-his-bones part.

I am so burning in hell.

"Fine. Let's go."

Chapter Ten

THE LIFT DUMPS us onto an open expanse of flat roof, where there's a gift shop (even the Church exploits tourists) and a few picnic benches. We're on the roof of the basilica, and as Alessandro strides off toward the dome, he says, "There are 320 stairs."

Panic kicks in my chest. "We're going up?"

He glances at me and smiles. "It's one of my favorite spots in all of Rome."

I'm already more than a little wired from the tour, and I feel another shot of adrenaline hit my veins. My feet stall, and it takes Alessandro a few seconds to realize I'm not beside him. He turns and looks back at me. "Is there a problem?"

"Um . . . I'm sort of," I cringe, knowing just how stupid this sounds. "I'm scared of heights."

He takes the few steps back to where I am and stops in

front of me. "The observation platforms are all enclosed. There is no possible way you could fall."

My heart is thumping in my chest just thinking about all the possible ways. "Unless the platform gives way, or the rail comes detached from the wall, or there's an earthquake or a—"

His palm cups my elbow, shutting me up. "So you will deprive yourself of the most breathtaking view in all the city because of a phobia?"

I look up at the dome and feel my legs turn to Jell-O as cold sweat breaks over my body. "Somebody must have taken pictures up there, right? I'll just Google it."

"Like most everything else, pictures don't do it justice." His hand squeezes my elbow, and we start moving again. I let him guide me to the base of the stairs.

Breathe.

Breathe.

Breathe.

I can do this. I *want* to do this.

I try not to think as we climb the flight of stairs to the cupola. Alessandro's hand is on my back, urging me forward, and I ignore the pounding of my heart and focus on moving my feet.

It's just a flight of stairs, I coach myself. But I don't let myself look up or down.

When we get to the top of the stairs, Alessandro smiles at me. "You're doing great."

"Yeah, but . . ." I trail off as my eyes flick to the dome. I'm going to try really hard not to puke in front of him . . . or *on* him.

He ushers me along the walkway, and when we get to the base of the cupola, and I look up, I see a gradual ramp enclosed inside a yellow-tiled tunnel. We start up it, and my chest loosens a little. With no windows to the outside world, I can almost convince myself we're not actually 200 feet above terra firma.

"This isn't so bad," I say. "Is it all enclosed like this?"

He nods. "With the exception of the observation platforms inside the basilica and at the top."

The top. That's all I have to hear before my knees are quaking again.

We spiral up the ramp, which, after a few minutes, dead-ends at a door. I stop short when I realize it leads inside the basilica onto the viewing platform at the first ring of the cupola . . . 250 feet above the basilica floor. "Is there a way to just . . . skip it?" I ask, looking for another opening or doorway.

"No," he answers, grasping my elbow, "and trust me, you don't want to."

He guides me onto the platform and, for a second, my head swims, and I'm sure I'm going to pass out. Sweat trickles between my shoulder blades as I press my back against the wall inside the dome, as far from the edge of the platform as I can get. But as my fingertips dig at the wall for purchase, I feel sharp edges and roughness, and when I turn, I'm face-to-face with the mosaics of St. Peter's. There are beautiful examples throughout the basilica—reproductions of great works of art by Raphael and others—but none are as expansive as the mosaics that were laid inside the dome, covering the entire undersurface. They're obviously more modern than the mosaic at Santa Maria in Trastevere, laid in the late 1500s, and in a completely different style, but no less stunning. I step back for the bigger picture and bump into the rail behind me.

When I realize where I am, I cry out in surprise and my arms flail, trying to claw me back to safety. But then there are strong hands on my upper arms, pulling me into a firm body.

Alessandro.

"You're fine, Lexie," he says in his most soothing voice, which would make me weak in the knees if I weren't already weak in the knees.

But he's a liar. I'm *not* fine. I'm hyperventilating.

He guides me away from the rail to the wall, and I bend over and fight for breath. The wisps of hair that I curled around my face this morning when I pulled my ponytail back are plastered to my forehead with sweat.

"I need to . . . go back . . . down," I manage as I gulp for air. I climb my hands up my thighs until I'm upright.

He loops his arm around my waist, steadying me as I wobble on my feet. "I'm sorry. I shouldn't have forced you into this."

We turn toward the door we came through, and that's when I catch sight of Bernini's bronze baldacchino: the canopy of the Papal Altar. It's so close, I can almost reach out and touch it.

I look at Alessandro and grasp his hand where it rests on my waist to be sure he has me, then we inch toward the rail. I stare down at it, memorizing every detail from this angle. "This is incredible," quakes out of my chest with my shaking.

He grasps my arm and draws me close, supporting my shaking body. "That it is."

When I look at him, he's gazing out over the baldacchino. I mop my face with my sleeve. "I want to go all the way up."

His gaze turns to me, and there's a question in it.

I grasp his arm. "I think I can do it."

He nods, and a smile creeps over his face. "If you're sure." He guides me around the cupola to a door farther along the platform. "Are you ready?"

I nod, and we step into the stairwell. Like the ramp, it's totally enclosed in yellow tile except for the occasional slits in the wall where a person could look out . . . if that person weren't me.

I focus on breathing as Alessandro guides me up the stairs, but it becomes harder as the stairwell narrows. I'm not normally claustrophobic, but there's something about knowing I'm 400 feet above the ground in a cramped stairway that leads to a platform where I'll surely fall to my death.

When the walls of the stairway start to slant with the curve of the top of the dome, I have to stop. "How much farther?" I pant.

"Almost there," Alessandro assures me, but it's not at all reassuring. "This last bit is a tight spiral staircase."

I look in front of me and see exactly what he just described. There are deep stairs in a tight spiral with a thick rope dangling down the center. I know my eyes are about to bulge right out of my head. "Are you *serious*?"

He turns and rests his hands on my waist. "We can go back if this is too much."

"No," I say, setting my resolve. I've come this far. It would be beyond stupid not to go the last few feet.

He slides a hand around to my back and urges me toward the stairs. "I'll be right behind you."

We twist up the spiral, and when we get to the top, there's a breeze coming through the door. This is it. Alessandro steps up behind me and rests his hands on my hips. "Are you all right?"

"What do you think?" I grasp his hands and hold on, just to make sure he's got me, then step out the door. I look out over Rome, and all the blood drains out of my head. When stars flash in my eyes, and my knees buckle, I'm sure I'm going down, but Alessandro pulls me into the curve of his body and holds me tight. I turn in his arms and bury my face in his shirt, holding on to him with a death grip.

Breathe.

Breathe.

Breathe.

His hand strokes my hair, slow and smooth, and I try to synch my breathing with the motion. Slowly, my senses return, and I realize I'm plastered to the front of an almost-priest. I back out of his embrace. "I'm okay," I scrape my sweat-soaked hair off my forehead. "You know ... provided I don't look anywhere but at your chest." ... Which is spectacular, by the way.

"The rail is as high as your shoulders, Lexie. You could jump, but there's no way you could fall."

With the word "jump," my insides flip, and I feel woozy again. "Thank you for that visual," I tell him. As I stare into his chest, afraid to even look at his face because it's too small to totally block the view of what's behind it, I feel a cool breeze in my face, drying my sweat. "You're sure you have me?" I ask.

He grasps my hips firmly. "I am."

I press my hands against my eyes and slowly turn. When my back is against his front, I lower my hands and open my eyes.

He was right, it's breathtaking. Just the sight of Rome, 400 feet below, leaves me gasping for breath. But I refuse to cower into his shirt again. I start inching my feet sideways, around the platform. "Is that the Pantheon?" I ask, realizing that if I focus on picking out landmarks, I'm not thinking about how high I am.

"It is." He starts to lift an arm to point but I grab it before he can take it off me. "And, to the left and a little closer," he says, laying his hand on my hip again, "is Piazza Navona."

We keep moving, and, slowly, the fist around my lungs loosens a little. By the time we make it around to St. Peter's Square at least fifteen minutes later, I can actually breathe.

"I've got to take a picture," I say, fishing in my pocket for my phone with a shaking hand. "My family will never believe I did this unless I send proof." I snap a shot and text it to Dad and Julie. I hesitate, then add Trent to the text. My phone rings almost instantly, and I glance at the screen. "Hi, Julie," I say when I answer.

"You are *not* on top of St. Peter's!"

"Actually, I am."

"She's really there!" I hear her call to Dad. "Oh, Lexie! I'm so glad you got up the nerve. Isn't the view spectacular?"

"I never would have come up here on my own. I had a little help."

"Oh? Are you with a friend?"

I glance behind me at Alessandro and feel his hands on me, holding me tight. "Yeah. The Reverend Moretti talked me into coming up after our first tour. It went really well, Julie. I didn't choke or anything."

I feel Alessandro's fingers squeeze tighter as Julie says, "Congratulations, honey. I knew you would be wonderful."

"Thanks, Julie. Give Dad a kiss for me."

"Have you talked to Trent recently?"

She knows we've always talked constantly in the past, so if I say no, she'll know something's wrong. But if I say I just talked to him this morning, she might ask what he said. "I've been so busy with school and the tour and all, I just—"

"Well, you should call him. He just made first team, so your dad's in heaven."

"First team? Really?" Trent has never put in the training hours to earn one of the top spots on his wrestling team. "Is it because he's a senior?"

"Your father says no. He says Trent's wrestling like a man possessed."

"Oh. Well . . . okay. I probably should go, but I'll call you tomorrow."

"We love you, honey, and we're so glad you're doing well."

"Love you too, Julie. Bye."

When I disconnect, I look over my shoulder at Alessandro. "I told you they'd never believe it."

He smiles. "You're going to go home an entirely new person."

If only.

I'm actually starting relax a little. My breathing is coming easier, and I don't feel like I'm going to pass out or throw up. I inch closer to the rail. "This really is amazing. Thanks for making me do this."

"It's your reward for a job well-done."

"I thought absolution of my sins was my reward," I mutter.

He bobs a nod. "That too." He looks out over the river and bites the corner of his lower lip. "I am not supposed to ask this, and you don't have to answer, but"— his eyes flick back to mine—"what is all this penance for?"

He opened up to me and told me about his dark past. Could I open up to him?

No. It's too mortifying. The only person I could ever tell about something this mortifying is Trent.

And I can't tell Trent about this because this *is* Trent. *I want you so fucking much right now.* He said it, but I feel it. I want him. I can't deny it. Which means there's something really wrong with me.

But as I look up at Alessandro, his gaze is so warm,

urging me to trust him, and I realize I *want* to tell him.

He leans on the rail but keeps one arm firmly around me. "I shouldn't pry. I'm sorry."

"Have you ever done something so . . . unforgivable that you couldn't even look at yourself in the mirror?"

His lips purse, and the skin around his eyes pulls tight, but despite his obvious discomfort at the topic, he holds my gaze. "There are many things I've had to beg forgiveness from the Lord for."

"But I mean something that you can never fix. Something that ruined everything."

He leans forward, his elbow on the rail and looks at me intently. "I shot a man, Lexie."

The jolt is physical.

"That's why my brother and I were in juvenile detention," he continues. "I was with Lorenzo when he got the notion to rob a street vendor. He threw the old man to the ground and kicked him a few times, then handed me the gun when he went to grab the money. But the old guy got up and jumped Lorenzo, so I shot him."

"Did he . . . die?"

He shakes his head. "The Lord spared both of us that day." He rubs a hand down his face. "But I've dealt drugs to children. I beat a boy within an inch of his life. These are all things I'm still paying penance for and will continue to for the rest of my life. There is very little the Lord won't forgive if you look into your heart and truly repent."

I feel so stupid now, my problem so insignificant. But the thing is, I'm not sure if I "truly repent." I've already confessed the sex to Father Reynolds. I've tried not to think about it—to move on like Trent is. But I can't stop remembering. I can't stop thinking about him.

"Talk to me, Lexie," he says softly, his arm around me squeezing.

I blow out a slow breath. "I slept with my stepbrother, and . . . I think I may be in love with him."

The whole story spills out of me, and as I get deeper and deeper into it, I almost forget I'm 400 feet in the air. I tell him about our first kiss in Trent's beanbag chair six years ago. I tell him how excited that made me feel and how, ever since then, I think I've always wanted more. I tell him how when Trent first left for college, I slept in his bed for a week, until his scent wore off the sheets, and sometimes touched myself and dreamed he was there with me. I tell him how ashamed I am for not stopping when Trent asked what we were doing that night. I tell him how my selfishness ruined everything Trent and I had, and would ruin my whole family if our parents ever found out. I tell him how the guilt is eating me alive and how I've tried to focus on other things like school and the Vatican tours to keep my mind off it, but I can't stop thinking about him and dreaming about him.

Alessandro listens, but he never interrupts the flow of the words pouring from the deepest part of my soul. When I'm finally done talking, everything goes quiet. The world below feels like it's in a different universe. It's not until I shiver that I notice that the sun is setting. The air is noticeably cooler, and when I lean into Alessandro for his warmth, I realize it's just him and me, alone at the top of the world. Everyone else is gone. I'm scared to look at him, but when I do, there's no judgment in his eyes. Only compassion.

A strand of hair blows across my eyes, and he loops it behind my ear. "If you ask the Lord for guidance and open your heart to His answer, you will know the right course, Lexie. But you have to trust: both Him and yourself."

I feel like a fool for ever lusting after Alessandro. I press my shoulder into his and smile a shaky smile. "You're going to make an amazing priest."

He lets go of me and backs toward the exit, holding his hand out to me. "It's getting cold. Let's get you down from here."

I turn and take one last look over the city. I don't go weak or shaky. I don't feel sick. I don't break into a cold sweat. I don't even grab for the rail. "This is beautiful. Thanks for bringing me up here."

"My pleasure." He smiles. "Do you ever eat anything but currant croissants?"

I clasp his outstretched hand, and I feel so much lighter as we move to the stairs, like I've finally left the weight of the world behind. "I eat all kinds of things."

"Perfect. I'm cooking."

I look at him, eyes wide. "You cook?"

Alessandro's hand is cool and firm in mine as we start down the stairs. "My grandmother taught both me and Lorenzo. We'll stop at the market on the way to your place."

"My place?" My voice squeaks a little around the nerves that rise in my throat at the thought of Alessandro in my apartment. With me. Alone.

He looks back at me when my arm yanks his as I stop moving, and he cocks his head. "Unless that's a problem. I can't have guests at the rectory."

"No." I start moving again. "No problem." Right? I mean, it's not like anything's going to happen. I take mental inventory of the state of my apartment—cereal bowl in the sink . . . unmade bed . . . clothes on the bedroom floor. Nothing too embarrassing.

But still, as we wind our way back down the stairwell to terra firma, I feel much less claustrophobic than I did on the way up—mostly because I'm distracted by what might happen when we get to the bottom.

Chapter Eleven

THE BAR NEXT door is in full swing when Alessandro and I get back to my apartment with two grocery bags full of fresh vegetables (some of which are totally foreign to me), fresh figs, some chicken breasts, and a bottle of red wine (for the sauce, he tells me). We have to shoo some people away from my doorway to get in. We climb the stairs, and I lead him to the kitchen, which is nowhere near big enough for two people.

"Do you need any help?" I ask.

He steps in and sets the bags on the small counter between the ancient refrigerator and the stovetop. "I'll need a pot and some utensils," he says, looking around and pulling my cutting board down from where it's tucked against the wall near the sink.

"Well, you can see there are not too many places to put things, so you should be able to find what you need either in those two drawers," I say, pointing past him at the only drawers in the room, "or in the cupboard next to the oven."

He slides the top drawer open and pulls out a knife. "This is perfect."

"So, if you're good, I'm going to get cleaned up." I feel gritty from sweating so much on our climb, and I've got to get out of these clothes. Plus, I can only imagine what my makeup looks like. I'd be better off without it.

His eyes catch on mine for a second, then he nods. "I've got dinner covered. Go ahead."

I strip in the bathroom and flip on the water. Once it's warm, I climb into my microscopic shower. I shampoo, and while the conditioner is in, I soap up and shave my legs for the first time in days—all the way up and then some.

The water's starting to run cold by the time I'm done, and I climb out. It's only as I towel off that I realize I forgot to grab my bathrobe from the bedroom. I'm so used to being able to run around naked that I didn't even think of it. I tuck my towel around me and click open the door, peeking out toward the kitchen. Once I determine the coast is clear, I scamper across the living room toward my bedroom, but I haven't even made the dining-room table when Alessandro calls, "I forgot to ask if you have any olive oil." His head pokes out of the kitchen, and when he sees me standing here in nothing but a towel, his eyes widen for just an instant before he ducks back into the kitchen. "It's okay. I can make do with butter."

"No," I say. "I've got olive oil. It should be in there somewhere."

"Too late," he calls back, and I hear something sizzle in a pan.

"I'll be right out," I tell him as I back toward my room, but just before I slip through my door, I see him peek out of the kitchen again.

I drop my towel on the bed and smooth on some lotion and my deodorant. On my way to the armoire, I tug the duvet back into place, fluff the pillows, and scoop the dirty clothes off my floor, tossing them into the hamper.

I pull open the armoire and peer in. I shouldn't care what I put on, right? It's not like I'm trying to impress him—which also explains why I just spent twenty minutes in the shower shaving all the way up to my hoo-hoo.

This is stupid. He's an almost-priest. And a friend, I think, even though there are times I'd pay to see him thrown into the Colosseum with a tiger or a bear or whatever. I grab my favorite pair of well-worn jeans and a black cotton tank off the top of my clean laundry and tug them on. I rake my damp hair back with my fingers and clip it onto the back of my head, then inspect my face. No major zits at the moment, so I decide to smudge a little blush on my cheeks, brush on some mascara, and call it done.

When I open the door, the first thing I see is that Alessandro has set the dining-room table. But then the smell of his culinary creation literally makes my mouth water, and I follow my nose to the kitchen.

"That smells amazing," I say as I come around the corner and lean on the doorframe between my toy kitchen and the sitting room.

He's stirring the pot, and he looks up at me. "I hope you like it," he says, shifting his attention back to the pot. He stirs its contents with one hand as he gives the sauté-ing garlic and onions in the pan next to it a few flicks of his wrist. He lifts the pan and dumps the contents into the pot, in which there are chunks of chicken and sliced vegetables stewing in a cream-colored sauce.

"Do you need any help? I could stir . . . or something."

He picks up my peppermill and grinds some into the pot. "I think I have things under control."

"What is that?"

"It's my grandmother's chicken stew with a twist," he says, lifting the wine bottle. "Do you have an opener?"

"Oh." Do I? "Did you look in here?" I ask, squeezing past him in the tiny space and pulling open the lowest drawer. I crouch and rifle through it. In the back, I find an old-fashioned corkscrew. "Voilà!" I say, standing and handing it to him. I push the drawer closed with my knee as he takes it from me.

He runs the pointed tip of the opener around the foil at the top of the bottle and peels it back like an old pro. As he twists the corkscrew into the cork, I can imagine those biceps, the ones I saw at the gym, rippling under his shirt with every turn.

"So, how long until it's ready?" I ask as he pulls the cork.

He pours about a third of the bottle into the pot and stirs again as the sauce turns a rich, burgundy color. "The flavors need to marry, so about half an hour."

I lean toward the pot and inhale. "You're going to have me drooling before the half hour's up."

He smiles and reaches into my cupboard for two tumblers. "Do we need a bib?"

"Maybe," I say, smelling the pot again.

He pours a few inches of the remaining wine into each of the tumblers and hands one to me. I take it and raise my eyebrows as he sips from his. He lowers his glass and looks at me.

"You're allowed to drink? I mean . . . outside the sacrament?"

One side of his mouth curves up, and his eyebrows arch. "We're allowed to enjoy life, Lexie. The priesthood isn't meant to be purgatory."

"I didn't mean it that way, it's just that . . . I'm pretty sure I've never seen a priest drink before except in church, though I haven't really spent too much time with one . . . socially, I mean."

He takes another sip and swirls the wine in his glass, inspecting it. "I chose well."

I sip mine, and it *is* good. I'm not much of a wine drinker, but this is smooth.

He turns for my sitting room, and, in three strides of his long legs, is at my love seat. He lowers himself into it.

I follow and sit next to him, taking another sip of wine. I dribble a little—so maybe I really do need a bib—and catch the drop that escapes over my lips with the tip of my tongue.

His eyes brush over my face and stall at my mouth. "You look lovely, by the way."

"Thanks."

"So," he clears his throat and settles deeper into the

love seat, examining his wineglass. "I didn't think today could have possibly gone any better. How did you feel about it?"

"Great. I felt great. I mean . . . I guess I was a little nervous at the beginning, but once the kids started to warm up, it was just so . . . fun. It was fun to see them get so excited about Michelangelo and the art."

He nods and excitement sparks in his eyes. "It *was* fun."

"I mean, I've never really been a kid person, you know? But it's like it made the whole thing new for me as well. I felt myself getting so excited, like a kid at Christmas, and when they started asking questions and telling me about their Sistine Chapel scenes"—I look at him, and I can feel myself beaming—"it was just the best feeling."

"You were wonderful with the kids. You're a natural." The ghost of a smile flits over his face as he sips his wine. "Have you thought about children of your own?"

I'm sipping my wine, and I almost choke. "Um . . . well. Not really. I guess someday, if I get married, then . . . maybe."

His expression softens as he looks at me. "You'd make an excellent mother."

I tip my glass to my mouth, feeling totally self-conscious, and out of the corner of my eye catch his gaze drifting down the V of my tank top, where it lingers.

A shiver runs over my skin as I take another sip. There's something about those intense charcoal eyes on me that makes me feel . . . dangerous. It must be the forbidden thing, I think. And, *shit*. There's that tingle in my groin again. I *can't* have the hots for an almost-priest, no matter how good-looking he is. It's just wrong in so many ways. I clear my throat. "So, do you know anything about wine, or was this just a lucky guess?"

His gaze lifts back to my eyes. "I know a thing or two."

"Such as?"

He shifts in his seat, just a little closer, and his knee presses into mine. "Such as, there are a few family-owned wineries in the Lakes Region that produce very small quantities of very good wines. This," he says with a swirl of his glass, "being one of them."

I take a bigger sip. "I could use your help picking some wines out for my family. I promised them some."

"It would be my pleasure."

I shift in the small love seat, and now our arms are touching at the elbow. "I really want to thank you for everything today."

"I did it for selfish reasons. I love to share my favorite places with my favorite people."

There's a whoosh in my stomach at his referring to me as one of his favorite people. "I don't just mean for the dome . . . though that was huge. I wasn't even scared by the time we came down. But I really mean for listening. There's no one I could ever talk to like that back home. Well . . . except Trent. He was the one I went to whenever I needed advice. He's the only person I've ever been able to be so open with, so . . . I just really appreciate that you were willing to listen—and that you didn't, I don't know, tell me I was too repulsive to live or whatever."

He puts his glass on the side table and takes my hand

in both of his. "You are not repulsive"—his eyes flick over me again—"in any way. I want you to feel like you can confide in me, Lexie. I'll do anything I can to help."

I don't even know how long we sit here, staring into each other's eyes, my hand sandwiched between the two of his, but suddenly, Alessandro lets go of my hand and stands. "I think the stew may be burning."

As he vanishes into the kitchen, I let out the breath I was holding.

He stirs and seasons for the next few minutes, and when he's determined through several taste tests that it's ready, he scoops the stew into bowls. He pours more wine as I carry the bowls to the dining room, where I light the candles on the table. "What? I don't have company very often," I say when he comes in with the wine and looks at me funny. "Actually, you're my only company. So far."

We eat and talk, mostly about his grandmother's favorite recipes. He promises to share some of them and tells me where the best produce and meat markets in the city are.

When we're done, I carry the dishes to the sink. He rolls up his sleeves, but I push him out of the kitchen. "Oh, no. You cooked, so I clean."

He smiles. "I won't argue with you. Cleaning up is the only part of cooking I dislike."

Despite his "dislike," he ends up grabbing my dish towel and drying the dishes, then wiping down my counters. "I should have thought of dessert," he says, hanging the dish towel on the magnetic hook on the side of the refrigerator.

"I've got dessert covered," I say, gesturing for him to sit down on the love seat. "Wait there." I pull down the bag of Skittles I've been misering, pouring some into a bowl. I bring it to the love seat and set it down between us. "Dessert is served."

"Skittles," he says, grabbing a few in his fingertips and popping them in his mouth. "Lord, I miss these."

I crack a smile. "Careful, Reverend."

He smiles back. "I haven't had these in eight years, since I left New York."

"I haven't see them in any of the local grocery stores."

He shakes his head a little mournfully. "You won't find anything like this in the small grocers in Trastevere. You have to get outside the old city, where there are more modern supermarkets."

"Do you like it here?" I ask.

He nods, popping more Skittles into his mouth. "I do."

"Will you stay here after you're ordained?"

His hand in the Skittle bowl hesitates for just a second. "That is not up to me. I'll be sent wherever the bishop believes I can best serve the parish."

"Do you *want* to stay here?"

He looks at me a long minute, then nods again. "I'm hoping to return to Corsica, but if that's not in the cards, I would very much like to stay here."

"I can see myself living here. I hope I get the internship and can stay through the summer at least."

"What internship?"

"John Cabot offers internships at some of the local museums. I'm really hoping to score the one at Galleria Nazionale d'Arte Antica."

"You would stay?" he asks. "If you got the internship?"

"I would. Through August, anyway. Otherwise, my visa is up in May."

"Would a reference be helpful?"

"You'd do that?" I ask, surprised.

He smiles, and something in it stalls my heart. "It would be my pleasure."

"Thanks."

He dips his hand back into the Skittle bowl, then gains his feet. "I really should be getting back to the rectory. I've already missed the evening vigil."

"Oh. Sorry."

He shakes his head as he moves the few feet to the door. "No need to be sorry. I wasn't expected to be there, but I usually am anyway." At the door, he pulls me into a hug. I press my face into his chest and breathe him in, warm and musky. "Today was lovely, Lexie. Thank you for sharing it with me."

"You're welcome, but I should be thanking you," I say as he pulls away. "You gave me this wonderful opportunity, and took me to the top of the world, and let me horrify you with all the details of my sordid love life. I meant what I said before. You're going to make an amazing priest."

His eyes cloud for just a second, but then he smiles. "I was not horrified, and I'm very glad to have your stamp of approval." He squeezes my hand. "Good night, Lexie. I'll see you in a few short weeks for our next tour."

"Good night," I say. But as I close the door behind him I think to myself, nothing about a few weeks sounds short.

It's midnight, and I'm just climbing in bed after finishing my homework when the phone vibrates on my nightstand. I pick it up and look at the text.

Trent.

My heart speeds up as I open it. It's in response to the text I sent from the top of St. Peter's.

You seriously went up there?

Yeah, I text back. *It was amazing.*

Looks like it.

I wait for more, something about his call, but there's nothing.

Did you get home okay last night? I finally ask.

There's a long pause. *Yeah.*

Again, I wait in vain for more.

I was worried about you, I coax.

Sorry.

Sorry? That's it?

Did you mean it when you said you wanted me? My shaking finger hovers over the SEND button.

My shaking finger still hovers over the SEND button.

My shaking finger hovers longer over the SEND button.

Then I delete the text.

Glad you're okay. Night, I text instead.

Night, he texts back.

Chapter Twelve

THE ITALIANS DON'T celebrate Thanksgiving. Go figure. But it's all good because I spent the last three days in heaven (aka: Venice) on a class trip. I'm just starting to come down from my Venetian high as I sit in my funerary art class, not even caring that it's Thanksgiving today, when my phone vibrates. I flip it out of my pocket and read Sam's text.

Just got home from a totally hot date.

In class. Talk later, I text back.

My phone vibrates again as I'm stuffing it back in my pocket. *You're not even going to ask who?*

Fine. Who? I text back.

Your super hot stepbrother.

I'm going to throw up. *Talk later.*

I shove my phone in my pocket and try to pretend I'm not hyperventilating as I do the math on my fingers. It's almost noon here, so nine hours behind us . . . that means it's six, five, four . . . three. It's three in the morning there. She just got back from a date with Trent at three in the morning?

I'm definitely going to throw up.

I mean, it's not like I've been sitting around pining for Trent. My classes and school trips and the tours with Alessandro and the kids have kept my mind occupied. Since my meltdown on the dome with Alessandro five weeks ago, I've felt better about the whole thing. I'm really trying to get over him. I include him in the group texts I send to Dad and Julie with pictures of the places I've been, but I rarely hear more back from him than the occasional, *cool*.

Alessandro and I see each other every other Friday for our tours with the kids, but since that first tour, he's e-mailed me at least once a week, and usually more, saying he has something to show me. He's taken me to see frescoes and mosaics and sculptures tucked away in obscure churches around the city that I never would have found on my own, and we always end up at a café for espresso or gelato.

We talk about everything over espresso, including his past and mine. He makes me laugh, and he makes me feel smart—like I basically have my shit together, which we both know I don't. But it's nice that he lets me pretend. Just last week, he asked if my feelings for my stepbrother were waning. I said they were, and, at the time, I didn't think I was lying.

But then I get this text, and my heart squeezes into a hard knot.

Damn.

I take out my phone and read through Sam's texts again. She's wanted to get her hooks into Trent since we were juniors in high school. Now she finally has. The irony is that, up until a few months ago, I would have been happy for her.

I look up, and everyone's packing up and leaving, so Professor Bertolli must have dismissed us. I look at the blank page in my notebook and hope I didn't miss anything important while I was obsessing. I scoop everything into my backpack and head out the door. I have two more classes today, and one is Venetian Art, where I know we're going to talk about our trip. Under normal circumstances, I'd never consider ditching, but my brain is scrambled and my guts are in knots and I'd be useless anyway, so I start up the street toward home.

I glance into the pastry case as I pass the café where Abby and I met, and even the currant croissants don't look good to me. But then through the window I see Abby. She's sitting at a table in the back corner with Grant. My feet slow without my permission when I realize Abby's crying. She rubs a forearm under her nose as Grant stands. He shrugs a backpack onto his shoulder and stuffs his hands in his pockets, then leans down and kisses the top of Abby's head before moving in my direction.

I lower my head and start walking again until I'm sure he's passed, then loop back to the door.

Abby's still at the table, a napkin pressed to her face.

"Abby," I say softly as I approach.

She stops sniffling but doesn't lift her face from the napkin. "What?"

"I'm sorry. I shouldn't have butted in," I say, backing away a step.

She lifts her head and looks at me. Her eyes are red-rimmed, one of her neon blue contacts a little askew, and she's got raccoon eyes from where her mascara has smudged. She pushes the chair Grant was just in toward me with her foot. "Sit."

I slide into the seat and lower my backpack to the floor next to me. "What happened?"

She rolls her eyes, and the contact fixes itself. "I turned daft, that's what."

I'm not really sure what that means, but I can guess. "You and Grant . . . ?"

She nods. "The lot of us from our anthropology class went out clubbing a few weeks ago after our exam. We got pissed, and I brought him home and shagged him." She looks up at me. "I only ever wanted his body, you know."

I nod.

"But he's crashed at my flat every night for the last two weeks and"— she grimaces and rubs a finger under her eyes, which only makes the mascara smudge worse—"I want more than just his body now. I told him I was in love with him."

Well, that explains why I haven't heard from her in a few weeks. I haven't even seen her at school, which makes me wonder if they even got out of bed long enough to go to class. Now doesn't seem like the time to ask, though. "But he's still with his girlfriend?"

Her face pulls into a pained squint. "He says he won't break up with her."

"What did you think was going to happen when you both go home? I mean, you'll be on different continents in a few months, right?"

"Do you think my heart gives a shit about that?" she spits.

"Sorry, I just mean . . . it's hard to keep things going long-distance." All my experience tells me it bites balls. Either you think everything's great when it's not, like with Rick, or you know everything sucks, and you do nothing but agonize over it, like with Trent. I scoot my chair closer and loop an arm around her back. "Shit, Abby. This really blows."

She leans her head on my shoulder. "I've shagged dozens of guys, but I've never been in love before."

There's no easy answer. There's nothing reassuring I can say to her that's not a lie. So the server brings us espresso, and we just sit in silence. At some point we change from espresso to wine, which seems to do more to improve Abby's mood.

"You should spend the weekend at my flat," she says, sipping her second glass. "We can buy junk food and watch Italian porn."

"As appealing as that sounds," I say, "I'm going to Santa Maria Maggiore with Alessandro Saturday."

She rolls her eyes. "If the man weren't wearing a white collar, I'd swear there was something going on between you two."

"Well, he is, and there's not."

"So, Sunday?" she asks. "We can find porn with nuns and a priest and have a Mass of our own."

"I'll come over Sunday, but no porn. I'll bring a couple movies and junk food." My apartment doesn't have a TV, and I don't really miss it, but a movie sounds like fun. "So . . . are you going to be okay?"

She breathes deep. "I'd be better if Grant contracted a painful, flesh-eating disease."

I grimace. "Sorry, can't help you there."

She drains the last of her wine. "Yeah. I'm good."

I sip my wine and push back from the table. "Okay . . . well . . . I should head home, but I'll see you Sunday."

"Don't forget the porn!" she calls after me, as I move toward the exit. A group of guys I recognize from school sitting near the door look up at me and grin.

I shrug at them and step onto the sidewalk. It's dusk, and the air is getting cooler by the second. The sky is hung with low, gray clouds, but, thankfully, it's not raining yet. I walk fast to keep from freezing, and also to beat the rain, and my mind wanders back to my own problems.

When I wasn't consoling Abby, or watching her drown her sorrows, I was thinking about Trent and Sam. I sat through my classes with my muscles bunched and my stomach in knots. And now, now, with nothing to distract my thoughts, all the tension comes back.

By the time I get to my apartment, I'm in physical pain. I want to call Sam. I *need* to call Sam. But it's only six here, which means it's nine in the morning there. If I call now and wake her, she'll know something's up.

Instead, I go to the kitchen and look for something

to pull together for dinner. Nothing looks good, and I finally end up making a cup of tea and getting ready for bed. I finish in the bathroom and grab Alessandro's Vatican Museum book and my sketchpad on the way to my bedroom because I had another idea I want to try out for the kids. I strip and climb into bed, propping the pillows behind me on the headboard, then flip to the sculpture section of the book and look over some of the pieces.

I start sketching the Colonna Venus, but as my hand works, so does my mind.

If Trent and Sam are together now, how am I going to handle going home for winter break? I'm on an airplane in three weeks. Is that long enough for the whole thing to sink in, so I don't flip when I see them together?

I can do this.

I can.

I have to.

I breathe deep and set down my sketchpad.

It's been three months since I've seen him. This should be getting easier, but it's not. I have to decide if what I feel for Trent is love or just lust. Because if it's just lust, I can't risk destroying our family over sex.

But if it's love . . .

If I'm in love with Trent, could I tell him? If I did, then what? If by some remote chance he loves me too, which is doubtful considering his current behavior, we'd still never be able to follow through. What would people think? I can just imagine the rumor mill on this one. It would go something like: They've been having sex since their parents got married when they were five. Remember back in sixth grade when she gained all that weight and went away to summer camp? She was pregnant with Trent's two-headed love child and she had it in the woods and they chained it up in a cave so no one would ever find out. Now it's Gollum.

We could never tell. Dad and Julie would be mortified because, let's face it, they'd probably assume it had been going on for a while too. Their friends would gossip, they'd be ostracized from their social groups. Everywhere they went, people would talk about their incestuous kids behind their backs.

I'm just on the edge of a panic attack . . . at that place I can still stop it if I just calm down. Air. That will help. I stand and push my window open, leaning out and gulping the cold air.

The catcall from below catches my attention and I look down into the street. The boy, the one who wanted to sleep with me, then peed in my door, is looking up at me. And that's when I remember I'm naked. I reach for the curtain and pull it around me.

"Facciamo ballare il tuo letto stanotte, gnocca!" he calls up to me. My eyes widen as he unzips his pants and pulls out his junk. And when I look up, the wrinkled old woman is on her balcony, wrapped in a crocheted throw, staring at me. Her eyes narrow, and she tsks me. Three shakes of her finger and three clucks from her mouth that echo off the walls. One, two, three.

"Oh, shut up, Grandma Moses. I'm having a bad day," I growl.

Despite Grandma Moses and Horny Boy, I don't leave

the window. The fresh, cold air helps to calm my nerves. I stand here until I can breathe. When I reach for the window to pull it closed, I look down and find Horny Boy peeing in my doorway again.

Just shoot me.

I climb back into bed and look at my clock. Seven thirty. So that means it's . . . twelve, eleven, ten. It's ten thirty in the morning there. Not too early to call and not be suspicious. I pick up my phone and dial Sam.

"What?" she says when she picks up. Yep, I woke her.

"So, tell me about this hot date." I almost pull off casual.

"Sleeping. Call later," she grumbles.

"I can't call later. I'm going to bed. It's late here," I lie, knowing she's not going to expend the energy to do the math.

I hear her heave a sigh, then the rustling of sheets. "Okay. Fine. Trent is a fucking god, and I'm totally in love with him. 'Night."

"No!" I yell, afraid she's going to disconnect, but then I rein myself back. "I mean . . . you always expect details from me, so . . ."

"You don't think it would be a little weird to know details of your stepbrother's sex life?"

At the word "sex," my stomach loops, and I feel sick. "Trent and I talk about everything." . . . And I'm already intimately acquainted with certain aspects of his sex life.

"I don't know, Lex. I'm not sure he'd tell you *this*." She's starting to wake up. I can tell by the lascivious lilt to her voice.

That panic attack is threatening again, and I move back to the window, careful this time to stay behind the curtain. "What happened to 'hard to get'?"

"We are so far past that. We've moved into the can't-get-enough phase of our relationship."

I lean out the window, afraid I'm going to throw up, and Grandma Moses and Horny Boy are gone, thank God. "So you guys are . . . ?"

"We haven't done the deed, if that's what you're asking, but it's only a matter of time."

My relieved breath blusters in my ear through the phone, and I pull it away from my mouth. They haven't slept together . . . yet. Small prayer answered.

"So, when do you come home for Christmas?" she asks.

"Um . . . my flight's on the eighteenth."

"I'll be home on the twenty-first, and the first place I'm heading is your house."

"Great," I say, feeling anything but. "Can't wait to see you."

"Well, maybe if your uber-hot stepbrother lets me up for air, you will." And there's the tone again.

"All right . . . well . . . I'm going to bed, so talk soon."

"'Night, bitch."

"'Morning, bitch."

I disconnect and close my window, then crawl into bed and flick off the lights. There's still time to tell him I love him. I could do it.

I could.

But I won't.

Chapter Thirteen

"WHAT WOULD YOU do if you thought you might be in love with someone who may or may not be in love with someone else?"

Abby pulls the DVD out of the case and shoots me a glare.

I wince under the heat of it. "Sorry. I forgot."

For the last three weeks, I've watched Abby and Grant pretend like they don't know each other. When they pass each other at school, or on the street, they either keep talking to whoever they're with (me most often in the case of Abby) or lower their eyes and ignore the other's existence. And it makes me think of Trent. We're basically doing the same thing, just long-distance.

I've spent every day between Thanksgiving and finals trying to get up the nerve to call him. I've had his number queued up on my phone at least a dozen times, my shaking thumb hovering over the green CALL button, but I've never pushed it. No matter how many times I rehearse what I want to say in my head, I can't make it come out of my mouth.

"Appreciate the concern, Lexie. I really bloody do." She turns back and slips the DVD into the player. It's our third Sunday movie marathon in a row. Last week I let her pick the movies and we ended up with *Cinque Ragazzi e Una Ragazza*, which roughly translates into "Five Guys and a Girl," and *Grande Disossata*, which means "Big-Boned." And, Jesus, was he ever. I'm pretty sure there was no actual plot to either movie, so I don't think we missed much by not understanding the dialogue. Most of the characters' mouths were full for the entire movie anyway, so they weren't saying much. After that, I told her she was in charge of food, and I'd bring the movies. Today, we have *When Harry Met Sally* and *Magic Mike*, the latter of which I chose not only because Channing Tatum is yummy (and looks a lot like Trent), but also to keep Abby from giving me too much shit about the former. But I had to get *When Harry Met Sally* when I saw it on the English rack at the rental place.

One afternoon back in high school, after a five-hour Warcraft marathon, Trent had turned off the game, and it just happened that the TV was on AMC. *When Harry Met Sally* was starting, and we got sucked into it and curled up on my bed and watched the whole thing. Movies never make me cry, but for some reason that one did. I was sniffling back tears during Harry's "I came here tonight because when you realize you want to spend the rest of your life with somebody, you want the rest of your life to start as soon as possible," speech to Sally at the New Year's Eve party near the end. Trent had put his arm around me and pulled me into his lap. He kissed my forehead and stroked my hair, and I'd totally let loose and sobbed into his shirt. I remember how I felt right then—so desperate and out of control that it made me dizzy and sick. I had no clue what it was about or where it had come from at the time, but looking back, I realize my heart knew I was desperately in love with Trent even then. That breakdown was my heart fighting with my mind, which just couldn't accept it yet.

Abby puts in the DVD and settles onto the couch next to me, picking up the bowl of popcorn and setting it in her lap. "Who's the bloke?"

"Just someone from back home," I say as Harry Connick, Jr. starts crooning "It Had to Be You," and the opening credits of *When Harry Met Sally* start to flash on-screen.

"Is he hot?" she asks.

I roll my eyes but answer truthfully. "Yes, but that's not why I love him."

She huffs a derisive laugh. "Yeah, and I'm the Virgin Mary."

And that makes me think about Alessandro. I'm leaving tomorrow, and I'm surprised at the pang when I realize I'm not going to see him before I go. I struggled with whether to get him something for Christmas and finally decided against it for three reasons: 1) I don't want him to think I think there's anything "personal" going on between us; 2) I don't even know if almost-priests do the whole gift-giving thing; and 3) even if they do, what the hell do you get an almost-priest?

I stare mindlessly at the movie as Harry and Sally meet. "I love him," I finally say, "but I shouldn't. We could never do anything about it even if he's not in love with someone else."

"Bugger!" she shouts, and it scares the snot out of me. When my eyes fly to her, her tennis-ball yellow contacts are about to pop off her eyeballs. "It's the bloody priest, isn't it?"

I roll my eyes again. "I said it was someone from *back home.*"

"Yes, you did," she says with a skeptical squint, "but you're a sodding liar. I've seen the way you get when you're talking about the places he took you."

"Because I like art." I jam my thumb into my chest. "Art history major, *remember*?"

She sinks deeper into the couch, dejected. "So then, who?"

"No one. Forget it," I say, turning back to the TV. I sip on my tea and lose myself in Harry and Sally's cross-country conversation.

"What are you going to do?" Abby asks a long time later, so softly I hardly hear her. When I look at her, it's obvious she's really asking for advice.

"Damned if I know."

THE BASS FROM the bar downstairs vibrates my bed as I fold only the clothes I'll need for three weeks at home into my bag. I bawled my eyes out at the end of *When Harry Met Sally* again, and I would have given anything for Trent to have been there to hold me this time. Abby asked if I wanted to stay the night, but I hadn't even packed, and my flight is in the morning, so I headed home. I also really needed to get my thoughts together. If I'm going to say something to Trent, I need time to figure out exactly what it's going to be.

"I've thought a lot about what happened between us before I left, and I realize it happened because I've always wanted it to. I love you, Trent."

See. Not so hard. But as I play it back in my head, I realize how stupid it sounds. I've told him I love him a hundred times, but I've never meant it like this. What if he doesn't understand? What if he doesn't feel the same?

The only thing that's kept me from going totally insane is that Trent and Sam go to different schools. Sam's at UC Santa Cruz, and Trent's in LA—five hours apart by car. They haven't seen each other since Thanksgiving, which, according to Sam, guarantees that Trent will be crazy for her by winter break. They've already gotten the foreplay out of the way, she says, because they've been sexting all semester, so as soon as they get home, they're sealing the deal.

Which gives me exactly one day before it will be too late.

I'll beat them both home by two days. Trent will be home on the twentieth, and Sam is coming home on the twenty-first. I need to be ready, or I'll miss my window.

"I've really missed you, and I've been thinking a lot

about us. I realized that I've been in love with you for a long time and—*ugh*!" I throw up my hands. "I so totally suck at this!"

I drop onto the bed next to my bag and rest my head in my hands. "Think." What can I say so he understands that I'm serious?

I try to picture his face, how he'd react if I said it. Because there's the very real possibility that he's totally repulsed by what we did and just wants to forget it.

"Shit." *Shitshitshit*.

It seems counterintuitive to pray about what to say to the brother I had sex with to make him understand I'm in love with him, but I do it anyway. I rest my head in my hands and breathe deep. "Please, God. I know I've screwed up a lot of things . . . well, mostly everything, I guess, and I don't live how You want me to, but I need to know what the right thing is here. Should I tell Trent I love him? Because I do. I really do, and I think maybe I always have. I know it's probably a sin, but I can't help it. If we'd just met, like, at school or the mall or been living *anywhere* other than under the same roof, then there'd be nothing wrong with our being together . . . but shit—pardon my French—what if he's trying to forget the whole thing? What if he's already in love with Sam? What if he says no, that he doesn't want me? Telling him will just make everything worse. And what about our parents?" I weave my fingers into my hair and yank. "What am I supposed to do? Just send me some kind of sign. I'll take anything."

I jump as the buzzer for the door rips through my

silent apartment. Nobody ever rings that bell. Probably just drunk kids from the bar.

I stand and move to the window, throwing it open and looking down at my door . . . and see Alessandro. He smiles up and waves.

"I'll be right down!" I call. I pull open my apartment door and skip down the stairs before I realize I'm wearing nothing but a thong and Trent's Loyola Wrestling T-shirt. I run up the stairs and grab the pair of jeans off my living-room floor, tugging them on, then head back down. It's misting outside, and Alessandro's hair and black wool jacket are covered with tiny sparkling droplets of water. As if he weren't already too tempting, he looks like someone sprinkled sugar on him to make him just that much more tasty.

"I'm sorry not to call, but I was on my way back to the rectory from the youth center when I realized I still had your Christmas gift." He pulls a small, black felt pouch from his jacket pocket.

His eyes slip for just an instant to my chest, and I realize the cold air has hardened my nipples, which is impossible to miss through the thin cotton of Trent's T-shirt. I grab his hand and pull him through the door. "Come out of the rain."

We tread up the stairs to my apartment, and I pull him inside. "Tea?" I ask as he peels off his jacket and hangs it on the back of a dining-room chair.

He settles into the love seat as I move to the kitchen. "Something hot would be perfect. It's chilly out there."

I fan myself a little as he runs a hand over his dark

waves, and the water beads up and rolls onto his collar. *Nope, nothing hot and perfect around here,* I think to myself as I put the teakettle on to boil. "Isn't it late to be at the youth center?"

"I've been working with a kid, Franco, quite a bit," he answers as I come in and sit next to him. "He's got potential."

"So you're putting in overtime?" I ask with a smile.

He smiles back. "No rest for the weary."

I remember the way his muscles rippled under his skin in the gym that day and resist the urge to fan myself again. "You never seem weary to me."

"The Lord sustains me," he says, matter-of-factly, as the teakettle starts to whistle.

I pull myself off the love seat and pour our tea. When I come back with our cups, he's standing at the window to the patio, looking out at the rain. "When do you leave?" he asks, turning back toward me.

"Tomorrow morning."

His lips press into a line, and he gives a small nod. "I thought so."

"I'm back on the sixteenth of January. When is our next tour?"

"The nineteenth."

"Oh! My birthday. Perfect."

He moves toward me, lifting his cup out of my hand. He produces the black felt pouch from his pants pocket and hands it to me. "I wanted you to have this before you left."

I cringe. "I didn't get you anything."

A smile ticks his mouth. "I didn't expect anything."

"But . . ." I say, holding up the pouch.

"I'm afraid it's not much."

I set my tea down on the side table and flip open the flap of the pouch. When I turn it into my hand, a small coin drops into my palm. I flip it over and examine the front. "St. Christopher."

He nods. "The patron saint of travelers. I want you to be safe."

"Thank you." I pull him into a hug, and it's only when he stiffens that I remember I'm naked under my T-shirt, and I'm pressing my boobs right into him. I let him go quickly and sit. He lowers himself down next to me and sips his tea.

"I've decided to tell Trent I love him," I blurt.

His eyes lift to me, and his lips press into a line. "If that is the direction the Lord has sent you, then you should."

Is it? When I asked for a sign, I got Alessandro. Is there some other message there? "The more I think about it, the more I realize I've loved Trent for a long time. Even when I was with Rick, there was always something between Trent and me. It's like I just wouldn't let myself feel it, you know? But making love with him brought it all to the surface, and now I can't pretend it's not there. I love him."

He bites the corner of his lower lip between his teeth as he nods. "Then it sounds like you know what to do."

"I do. I will." I will. I sip my tea and set my resolve. It feels more doable now that I've said it out loud. I prayed for a sign and got Alessandro. I needed to talk it out, and now I know this is the right thing to do. I lean my head into his shoulder. "Thanks for listening."

He loops his arm over my shoulders and pulls me close to his side. "The strength for all righteous tasks can be found in the Lord." It sounds more like he's talking to himself than me, but I draw strength from it—from him.

I can do this.

"I'll miss you," I say after a long while.

"I'll miss you too." He kisses the top of my head and lets me go. "But I'm afraid I've got to go."

We stand, and I open the hand that's still clutching the St. Christopher metal. "Thank you for this."

He shrugs on his jacket. "Just be safe and call when you get back." His hand slips around my neck and he kisses me again, this time on the cheek, then reaches for the door handle. He hesitates for just a second, and it looks like he wants to say something else, but finally, he pulls the door open and disappears down the stairs.

I watch for a second after he leaves, then go to my bedroom window and watch him walk down the street. And when I look up, Grandma Moses is standing in the drizzle, tsking me again. This time, I don't even know what my offense is.

I'M NERVOUS WHEN I get off the plane in San Jose. I've still got two days before Trent comes home Wednesday, but seeing him is all I can think about. I've gone over and over what I'm going to say, and I think I have something that works, but whether I'll actually be able to get it out of my mouth when the time comes is still questionable.

I grab my bags and clear customs, then head for the exit. I spot Dad and Julie in the sea of people waiting outside security before they see me. Julie nudges Dad and points when she finally sees me on the escalator. She's bouncing on her toes by the time I clear the secured area.

"Oh, honey!" she says, wrapping me in her slender arms. "Oh, you look so beautiful! Oh my word, I can't tell you how much we've missed you!"

Dad takes my backpack and my roller bag from me as I peel myself out of Julie's embrace. He gives me a one-armed hug and a kiss on the cheek. "How was your trip, kiddo?"

"I had to change terminals in Heathrow, which was a pain in the ass because I had to go back through security, but otherwise, no problems."

"We expect a full report on your first semester abroad on the trip home!" Julie says, bouncing on her toes again.

Dad starts toward the elevators, and Julie and I follow. "You already know most everything," I tell her.

She grasps my hand as we walk. "We know you've seen a lot of sights and you like your classes, but we haven't heard much about the people you've met or friends you've made."

I shrug. "There really aren't many. I mean, the people are great, but I've only really gotten to know a few."

"Like your deacon?" she asks with a squeeze of my hand as we step into the elevator to the parking garage. "It seems he's been a godsend." She lets out a little giggle. "Literally."

"He's been great," I say. "The school tours we're doing have given me the opportunity to get up close and personal with Vatican artwork. It's been incredible." I've never told them how the whole thing came about—as my penance for sleeping with Trent—and I hope they never think to ask.

"I want to hear all about everything you've done together." She presses her shoulder into mine as the elevator opens, and we follow Dad into the garage. "I still can't believe he got you to climb the St. Peter's dome."

There's a tingle in my stomach with the memory. "Me either, but it was amazing."

When we find the car, Dad loads my luggage in. Julie is grilling me for information before we've even left the garage—everything I learned in my classes, what foods are my favorites, have I learned any Italian—and I answer her questions as best I can. She asks again about friends, and I tell her about Abby, leaving out the parts about drunken clubbing and Italian porn. I'm relieved when she finally runs out of questions and starts telling me about things at home—until she gets to Trent. She clasps her hands in front of her face excitedly. "He'll be home on Wednesday and we'll all be together again." She looks at me over her shoulder. "I know he's dying to see you."

"What?" It's out of my mouth before I can rein it back.

"He can't wait to see you," she says, like I just didn't hear her.

I heard her. I'm just having a hard time believing it. He hasn't texted me in weeks. "Me too," I say.

Chapter Fourteen

I SPEND TUESDAY trying to pretend everything's how it's always been. I sleep late, trying to get adjusted to the time change, and because none of my friends are home yet, I spend the rest of my time going through pictures with my parents. But I can't stop thinking about how this is going to go. I have the words, but I don't know how Trent is going to react to them.

When I hear his motorcycle pull into the driveway Wednesday afternoon, my insides are wound so tight that I'm sure I'm going to throw up.

"Lexie!" Julie calls up the stairs, "Come on down! Trent is here!"

I focus on breathing and move to the window. Trent cuts the engine and pulls off his helmet. His chocolate curls are shorter than I've seen them in a while, and as he lifts his leg over the bike and pulls his duffel off the back, it hits me that he's bigger. As in, bulging biceps and pecs stretching the cotton of his Army green T-shirt. My heart thrums just watching him.

"Lexie!" Julie calls again.

"Coming!" I pull myself away from the window as Trent strides up the front walk to the door, and before I'm even on the stairs, I hear Julie calling out the door to him. I tread slowly down the stairs, and when I spill into the foyer, Julie has Trent wrapped in a bear hug. He lifts his eyes, and, as they connect with mine, an electric jolt hits me, just like when I stuck Dad's keys in the light socket when I was a kid I smooth my hair down, sure it must be standing on end.

"Hey, Mom," he says, his eyes still on me. His forehead crinkles in a question, but I don't know what question he's asking. "I'm not the long-lost offspring. That would be Lexie."

"I just worry about you so much on that death trap," she says, shooting a glare out the door at his bike. "I wish you'd get a car."

"I'm fine, it's not a death trap, and I don't want a car," he answers as he pries himself out of her grasp and pushes the door closed.

Dad gives him a quick man hug, two pats on the shoulder, then break. "Good to have you home, son. Need help with your things?"

"Thanks, Randy, but all I have is this," Trent says, holding up his duffel.

"Lexie!" Julie says. "Come give Trent a hug."

I move slowly from where I'm frozen at the bottom of the stairs to where he stands, near the door, staring at me with a look that seems to say either, "Do I really have to do this?" or, "Does she really want to do this?"

I wish I knew which.

"Hey," he says, pulling me tight into his arms. "Missed you."

"Me too," I say, but it's automatic, because all I can think about is the warm, spicy smell of him and the feel of his body—his actual body, not just some fantasy—pressed against mine. I can't stop my fingers from sweeping over his biceps, memorizing the contours of his muscles, and I feel his goose bumps. "You look . . . great."

"Trent's decided to get serious about his training," Dad says, giving him a pat on the back.

"Oh?" I look at Trent, and his eyes drop to the floor.

"He's moved up a weight class with the extra bulk, and he's still undefeated this season."

Trent shrugs. "It's no big deal."

"It's a *huge* deal." Dad beams. "His coach thinks he may be looking at a top four finish at the NCAA Championships in March."

"Wow."

Trent's jaw is tight, and his neck and ears turn pink. "It's really not a big deal." He steps past me toward the stairs, rubbing a hand over the back of his neck. "I'm going to shower and unpack."

"Okay," Julie says. "Dinner's in an hour. I made your favorite. Beef stew," she tells his back, as he climbs the stairs.

He doesn't answer, and, a few seconds later, his door clicks closed.

I climb the stairs behind him and hesitate at my door, trying to figure out what just happened. The way he looked at me, I thought maybe . . . But then his mood shifted, and now I'm not sure what to do.

I find myself at his door. I lift my hand to knock, but instead, lay my palm flat and listen, my heart rate approaching the speed of sound. I start to knock again, but back away from the door.

Not yet. Now's not the right time.

I slip through my door and flop onto my bed, staring at the ceiling. When I hear Trent head to the bathroom and turn on the shower a minute later, I listen and go back over what I want to say. I finally have it perfect, but what if he doesn't want to hear it?

When Julie calls up the stairs that dinner's ready, I'm still lying on my bed. Trent has been rustling around his room, and I've been following his movements as he unpacks, hoping for what feels like a good time to go in. I never got up the nerve.

He startles me when we both open our doors at the same time.

"After you," he says with a nod at the stairs.

"Yeah, okay . . . sorry." *Just shoot me.*

I feel him behind me as we move silently down the stairs, and I'd swear his gaze has weight. It presses heavy into my back. We settle into our spots as Julie shuttles bowls of stew from the stove to the table.

"Smells great, Mom," Trent says.

Julie lowers herself into her seat, and I realize from the quiver of her lower lip that she's near tears. "It's just so wonderful to have everyone home. I wish this wasn't such a rushed trip. The holidays are meant for family." She scowls. "Why would they schedule a tournament between Christmas and New Year?"

Trent shrugs. "It's the same every year."

"Well, it's not right."

Dad gestures to the living room, where the sounds of a football game waft from the TV. "There are bowl games from the middle of December to the first week in January. None of those athletes get to go home for the holidays."

Julie turns her scowl on him. "That doesn't make it right."

"So, Lexie," Dad says, obviously trying to change the subject, "tell Trent about all your Roman escapades."

"Oh, well . . . I'm doing tours for kids at the Vatican Museums . . ." I look at Trent, whose eyes are on me, "but you knew that already."

"I think it's wonderful that this priest—"

"Deacon, Julie," I interrupt. "Alessandro is a transitional deacon. He won't become a priest until April."

"Oh, of course. Anyway, I think it's wonderful he's taken Lexie under his wing," she continues. She looks at me. "He's shown you a good deal of the city, hasn't he?"

I nod. "Yeah. He's been really great."

"You'll have to show Trent all your pictures later," Dad says through a bite of stew.

I glance at Trent, who's looking at me out from under

his long, dark lashes with slightly narrowed eyes, as if he's angry . . . or maybe in pain. "Yeah . . . I will."

"How did the brackets work out for the tournament?" Dad asks Trent, his curiosity obviously overriding his fear of Julie's wrath.

Trent's jaw tightens, and his gaze shifts to a potato that he's pushing through his stew with the back of his spoon. "We're in the top half with Eastern Michigan, Penn, and Oregon, so it's going to be tough." His gaze flicks to mine, and there's something a little desperate in it. He obviously doesn't want to talk about wrestling. In another world, he would have told me what was wrong without my even having to ask, but in this new, awkward world, I'm not asking, and he's not telling.

Dad starts in on different wrestlers and their stats, and Trent focuses all his attention on smashing the carrots and potatoes in his bowl into mush.

After dinner, I help Dad clean up the kitchen, and when I go back upstairs, Trent's door is closed. I almost go back into my room, but a shot of courage carries me to his door. I knock.

No answer.

He's probably listening to his iPod. Or maybe he heard me. Maybe he just doesn't want to talk to me.

What if he just doesn't want to talk to me?

I breathe deep and lift my hand, hesitating for just a second before knocking harder.

"Yeah," he calls.

I crack open the door and poke my head through. Trent's guitar leans on the stand in the corner, which surprises me. He usually takes it to school, but it definitely wasn't on his bike when he got home a little while ago. He's propped against his pillows, texting someone.

Sam? Are they sexting? My pounding heart stalls for a second before regaining its erratic rhythm.

"Warcraft?" I ask when he looks up at me.

He pulls his earbuds out, draping the cord over his neck, and I hear some pounding rhythm wafting out of them—something sharp and angry. He hesitates for a long heartbeat, as if this is something he has to think about it. "Yeah, Warcraft would be good," he finally says with a nod.

I slip through the door and close it behind me. If I'm going to say what I want to, I definitely don't want Dad or Julie overhearing. I chew my cheek as I pick up a remote and settle onto the foot of his bed.

He queues up the game, and when he joins me on the bed, he spares me a glance. "How were your flights?"

"Good. Everything was good."

"Good," he says stiffly, navigating Jethro over the lip of the cave entrance to the forbidden grotto, engaging the orcs guarding it, who explode in a shower of purple guts.

I bring Galidrod online, and he joins Jethro. We shoot orcs for a while in silence. I take the chance to study Trent's face, hoping for a better feel for what's going on with him, but he's giving nothing away. He's never been a mystery to me before. I've never had trouble reading him, but everything changed that night. Somehow, getting closer than humanly possible drove us father apart than we've ever been.

His eyes flick to me as Jethro finishes off the last orc. "You're chewing your cheek. What's up?"

Damn. He knows me too well. "I was really hoping we'd get a chance to talk before you leave." Shit. My voice is shaking.

He looks at me and gives a small nod, his gaze so intense that it unnerves me. "What do you want to talk about?"

Just say it. I'm in love with you. "What's the deal with wrestling?" This is so not the direction I wanted to go, but it's the only thing I can force out of my mouth.

He pauses the game, puts down his remote, and rubs his palms on his jeans. "What about it?"

"You wanted to quit, and now all of a sudden you're, what? The Rock or something? What's with that?"

His gaze burns all the way through my retinas as his fingers curl into fists on his knees. "I am trying to forget what we did, Lexie," he says through a tight jaw. "Wrestling gives me . . ." He trails off and shakes his head, his face pinching. Is that expression regret? Chagrin? Disgust? What? "It gives me a way to do that," he finally finishes.

"Oh." Now it's more than just my voice shaking. It feels like the temperature in here just dropped ten degrees, and I'm shaking all over.

He's trying to forget. He wants to forget.

The doorbell rings downstairs, and I hear Julie yell, "Coming!" as Trent finally drops his intense gaze. "Listen, Lexie. I know this is what you—"

But that's as far as he gets before Julie is calling up the stairs, "Lexie! Sam's here!"

My stomach lurches. Sam? She wasn't supposed to be home until tomorrow.

"What were you going to say?" I ask, needing him to finish. I need to know exactly where I stand with him.

"Oh! But I'm sure you want to say hi to Lexie too," I hear Julie say in the weighty silence between my question and Trent's answer. Sam mutters some response, and Julie sounds annoyed as she calls up the stairs. "Trent! Come on down!"

His gaze flicks to the door, and he stands, tugging his earbud cord from around his neck and tossing his iPod to the bed. "Nothing. It doesn't matter."

But it does matter. *God*, it matters.

I follow him down the stairs, and just as I reach the bottom, Sam throws herself into Trent's arms and gives him a wet smack on the lips. "I missed you, gorgeous." She's totally beaming. I've never seen her like this before.

"Hey," he says.

"Hi, Lexie!" Sam squeals when she lets Trent go, but she won't take her hands off him to move to where I am. "You look amazing, gurl! Please tell me that glow is because you're in love with some fabulous Italian!"

I shrug. "Sorry, no. No fabulous Italians," I say, and Trent's gaze lifts from the floor to me for just a second. "I thought you were coming home tomorrow."

"We had a paper due for my communications final, which was all I had today, so I handed it in early and came home to surprise a certain someone," she says, grinning like a love-struck fool and squeezing the arm that's around Trent's waist tighter. "Right now, I have plans for your stepbrother, but we'll have to catch up soon. Maybe after Trent leaves for the tournament?"

"Yeah, okay. That sounds good." I hear my voice say it, but it's like my body's just going through the motions on autopilot because all I can think is, *Please don't sleep with her!* My mind screams it over and over. But I can't say it.

" 'Kay. I'll give you a call." She lets go of Trent just long enough to give my shoulders a quick squeeze. "Don't wait up for us," she whispers in my ear, and my throat tightens.

"All right. Bye."

Sam grabs his hand, and they slip out the door. Trent's eyes lift to mine just as she pulls him through, and there's a question there that I just can't read.

Then they're gone, the door thudding shut behind them.

And that's it. There goes any chance I had to say what I wanted to say. All I can do is stand here, staring at the closed door as all my insides explode in a shower of purple guts.

Chapter Fifteen

SAM PULLS UP to the curb in her mother's green Volvo a little after 3:00 A.M. I know this because I'm wide-awake, sitting on the edge of my bed with my arms crossed on the windowsill and my chin propped on my forearms. I was hoping they'd be back early, like by midnight. But, three? Three is a full hour after the bars close. They had to fill that hour doing something. My insides twist at the picture that forms in my mind—Trent, naked; Sam naked. I squeeze my eyes shut and force the image out of my head.

I told myself at eleven that if Trent wasn't home by midnight, I'd go to bed and forget about the whole plan. Then I told myself at midnight that I'd give him another hour. My stomach started to knot around one fifteen, and it's been getting progressively worse to the point where I'm fairly certain anything left in it after the dinner I picked through will projectile onto the glass in front of me if I try to move. So I don't.

I wipe the cloud of breathy fog off the window with the side of my hand as Trent swings the car door open. In the yellow glow of the dome light, I see Sam lean toward him expectantly. She looks a little rumpled, and, at the realization, my stomach lurches again. I swallow back the acid rising in my throat and look away as Trent leans in to kiss her. When I chance a glance back outside a second later, he's already halfway up the walk.

I stand and turn when I hear him shuffle through the front door. Sam pulls away as Trent climbs the stairs. A moment later, I'm standing with my palm pressed against my door without knowing how I got here as Trent moves past it. I reach for the door handle—and freeze.

What am I going to say? *Hey Trent, how was your date? Yeah, my neck's a little stiff because I'm been sitting at my window watching the street all night waiting for you to come home because, guess what? I love you. Yep, you heard me right. I. Love. You. So, what do you have to say to that?*

I lower my hand and back toward my bed, sitting hard when the edge takes my knees out from under me. I sit and listen to Trent brush his teeth and move up the hall to his room. I listen as he strips off his clothes and climbs into bed. I listen as everything goes silent except for my ragged breathing and pounding heart.

This is so not how things were supposed to go.

Between still adjusting to the nine-hour time change and my up-all-night stalkery, it's noon before my eyes finally open. I rub them hard and sit on the edge of the bed, hanging my head under the weight of a new day. I'm wearing Trent's T-shirt . . . but not the gray Loyola Wrestling one I took to Rome. I threw that in his dirty clothes last night while he was gone and grabbed the one he was wearing before he showered—the Army green one. I lift it to my face, breathing in his spicy scent, and feel my insides liquefy at the memory of my face buried in his neck, breathing in that same scent as he loved me. Every muscle in my belly contracts hard as I relive the sensation of him on top of me, inside me, and my heart implodes.

I flop back onto the bed with an elbow over my eyes and groan. I remember watching an old movie that went something like this. I think it was called *Fatal Attraction*.

I hear Trent in his room, knocking around near his closet on the other side of my wall, and the knot in my stomach is instantly back . . . if it ever actually went away. He's only here for four days, I remind myself. He has the Midlands Championship next weekend, and the team is flying out the day after Christmas to prepare. So I only have to make it four days without letting on that I pretty much want to die.

I pull off his shirt and grab my bathrobe, clicking my door open and peeking out before taking the plunge into the hall. The hall is empty, but as I tiptoe quickly past Trent's room toward the bathroom, I hear his voice drift through his door.

". . . just painfully awkward, you know?"

My feet stall on the carpet, and I nearly fall on my face.

"No," Trent says after a short pause. "We had the conversation back in August, and she knows this isn't going anywhere, but it's obvious even though she hasn't come out and said it that she's looking for more than I can give her."

Another pause.

"She knows I'm into someone else, I don't return her texts, I'm not even that nice to her . . . I just don't know how much more obvious I can be."

I start up the hall again, my stomach in my throat, and escape into the bathroom, but not before I hear Trent say, "I just thank God I'm only home for a few days. Everything about being here totally blows."

I spend the rest of the day in bed, which I only get away with by telling Julie I threw up in the shower. It's not a lie. She thinks I must have caught a flu bug on the plane from Rome, and I don't dispute that. The flu ruse buys me a full day where I'm not allowed to have contact with anyone, especially Trent, who has a chance to win his weight class at the tournament in a few days. But by Christmas Eve, Julie starts threatening to take me to Urgent Care if I'm not better by that night. So, guess what? I get better!

I'm still weak, of course, so she doesn't make me come down early on Christmas morning, but I am expected to make an appearance when Aunt Liz, Uncle Terry, and the triplets arrive at two, which I do. We take turns opening presents, showing off what we got, and thanking everyone, then we move to the table for Christmas dinner.

The triplets are Mike, Marcus, and Mindy, and they're fertility babies. Aunt Liz is older than Julie, but it took years of trying à-la-natural and a few rounds of fertility treatments before she and Uncle Terry conceived, so the triplets are five years younger than me. Thankfully, Julie decides, 1) that the boys should sit together and puts Trent between Mike and Marcus, and 2) that I should be between her and Dad in case I'm still contagious, so I get out of having to socialize, or even look at Trent, who's busy fielding questions about college and wrestling from the boys. After dinner, I help Julie and Aunt Liz with the dishes to avoid the living room, where Trent and the boys are watching football while Dad and Uncle Terry talk politics. When we're done, I beg off pumpkin pie by telling Julie I'm wiped out. She gives me her blessing to go back to bed.

As I climb the stairs, I look over my shoulder in time to see Marcus launch himself at Trent. "Wrestle me!" he yells, and they both thud to the floor as Marcus knocks Trent off his chair. I watch for a minute as they roll around on the floor, laughing, and Trent lets Marcus get the upper hand. I can't help smiling as I start toward my room again. I click my door closed and flop back onto my bed.

This is it, the last time I'll see him for months. If there's anything I need to say, I need to say it now. I lie here waging my internal war, rehashing all the reasons why Trent and I can never be together. It's better if I just let him go, right?

Right?

Damn.

A light mist has started by eight, when Aunt Liz and the fam pull out of our driveway in their white Caravan. I wait to hear Trent on the stairs, determined that I'm not going to chicken out this time. I'm going to tell him. But the longer I wait, the more nervous I get.

Where the hell is he?

My question is answered when I hear his bike roar to life outside. I lurch for the window in time to see him rocket out of the driveway like he's been shot out of a cannon. He fishtails a little on the wet pavement as he guns the engine and disappears from sight, still accelerating.

"Merry Christmas," I whisper into the silence he leaves behind.

Around ten, when Julie knocks on my door to check on me and say they're going to bed, I'm on Facebook. It's rude not to respond to everyone's Merry Christmas posts, is what I told myself when I logged on an hour ago, but what I've really been doing is stalking Sam's and Trent's feeds for details about their relationship. I can't believe I didn't think of this before.

Trent's wall is mostly other people tagging him in photos from school or wrestling. He hasn't added anything other than a comment on said pictures for months. But Sam's is a different story.

She is "in a relationship with Trent Sorenson," and according to her post from 3:30 A.M. the night she and Trent were out, she *Just got back from an amazing date with the hottest man on the planet. I iz in luv!*

There are a couple dozen comments on the post. Most of them are along the lines of, *ooh, la, la!* or, *Hope it ended with your panties in a bunch*, and they all make me want to throw up.

I scan for more and find love poems dedicated to "the hottest man on the planet" and YouTube links for love songs dedicated to "the hottest man on the planet" and when I scroll all the way back to Thanksgiving, I find a picture of them together on a love seat in a dark corner of Lightly Toasted. She's giving him a tonsil exam with her tongue. The post that goes with the picture says . . . wait for it: "The hottest man on the planet!"

He's with Sam. I have to accept that. He knows what we did is wrong, just like I do. If he knew I'm in love with him, how much worse would this be? How much more awkward? But still, I find myself opening my door and walking to his room. I move to the alcove near his closet and pick up his guitar, just to feel the weight of it and remember that, once upon a time, he loved me. Once upon a time, I was the most important person in his life, and he wrote me a song to prove it.

Even if we can't get that back, it doesn't change that it was real.

He's leaving in the morning, and I won't see him again until at least May. Maybe August, if I score the internship. Do I just leave it like this?

I think I have to.

I lie on my side in his bed, my arms hugging his guitar to my chest, and remember. I remember all our talks, and our wrestling matches. I remember our Warcraft marathons. I remember curling into Trent's arms when I was sad and how he took it all away. How he made everything better. I close my eyes and turn my face into the pillow when the tears start.

I open my eyes, and it's dark, so I close them again. But then I realize my arm is asleep. I move it, and it thumps against something hard.

Something with strings.

My eyes fly wide and I look around. I'm still in Trent's room, hugging his guitar. And there's a warm body spooned behind me and a heavy arm draped around my waist.

I unwrap my arms from the guitar, shifting it off the bed and leaning it gingerly against the nightstand, then lift the arm off my waist very slowly. Once I'm extricated, I sit up carefully, trying not to jiggle the bed or make any noise.

I have no clue what time it is or how long I've been in here, but when I turn and look behind me, I see Trent, curled around the spot where I just was.

I get up as slowly as I can, considering both my heart and mind are racing, and lay the guitar back in the stand, then tiptoe past his bed to the door. Just as I'm passing, he groans and rolls on his back. I freeze until he goes still again. But I don't start moving when he settles. I just stand here, staring at him.

God, he's beautiful.

Before I can stop myself, I'm moving back toward

the bed. I bend slowly and brush my lips over his rough cheek. He stirs and moans a little, but doesn't wake.

What did he think when he found me here? He didn't wake me. He just curled up next to me, like he would have before everything went sideways. Could we still get what we had back?

I want that so desperately.

I tiptoe to the door and slip through, and before I'm even in my own bed, I know what has to happen.

The sound of Trent in the shower wakes me. I wait for the water to turn off and listen for the sounds of his returning to his room, then slip out of bed and pull on a pair of jeans under his T-shirt. At my door, I breathe deep, then pull it open. I breathe deep again as I lift my hand to knock on his door.

"Just a sec!" he calls, and, a few seconds later, his door swings open. He's standing in front of me in a pair of well-worn jeans that sit low on his hips and nothing else. And, *damn*. "Hey," he says when he sees it's me.

Despite my visceral reaction to the sight of his cut body, it's his eyes that draw me in. They're warm and soft, and I know I've made the right decision. "Can we talk?"

"Yeah, sure." He steps aside to let me pass.

I move past him into his room and close the door. "I bet your wondering what I was doing in your bed last night"—I pluck at his shirt—"wearing your T-shirt."

His eyebrows go up, but he doesn't say anything.

"I really miss us, Trent." I swallow. "I miss how I could

tell you everything and how I knew you'd never judge me. I miss how safe I used to feel when you held me. I miss that you knew me better than I knew myself. I miss my best friend *so* much," I add, as a tear rolls over my lashes. "What we did stole him from me. I want him back."

He bites his lips between his teeth for a second. "I miss you too," he finally says, pulling me into his arms.

We stand here forever, my face buried in his chest, and as much as I want to kiss him and feel his touch on my body again, I squelch all those feelings and just live in this, the comfort of my best friend.

Finally, I pull away. "So, it's done? We're good?"

He smiles that lazy smile and gives the ends of my hair a tug. "We're good."

I walk over and lift his guitar out of the stand. "Will you sing it to me?"

He takes the guitar and sits on the edge of the bed. "I'm a little rusty." He gives the strings a strum, then tunes it by ear.

"Why didn't you take your guitar to school? You always have before."

He sighs and looks at me, his eyes sad. "You are my inspiration, Lexie. You always have been."

I scrunch my face at him. "But . . . what does that have to do with leaving your guitar home?"

"You of all people should know art is inspiration. I was angry and confused. I didn't know what was going to happen with us. Anything I wrote would have been shit."

He was feeling it too. I should have known, but I was so wrapped up in how I was feeling that I didn't think about it. "I'm sorry," I say, sitting next to him and hugging him. He stops picking at the strings and hugs me back. "I never want to lose you, Trent."

He kisses the top of my head and sends shivers through me. "You won't."

I let go, and he strums the strings again.

"You ready?" he asks, smiling at me.

"Always."

As he starts on the first verse of "Someone, Somehow," I feel tears sting the corners of my eyes. I've always loved his singing voice: smooth and deep with just a hint of gravel when he kicks the emotion up a notch. By the time he gets to the chorus, I can't keep them from spilling over.

> You fill the hollow places life as left behind.
> And now your soul is tangled into mine.
> When I needed an angel you were there,
> you, to all my secrets I bare.
> I needed you then,
> and I need you now.
> Someone, somehow.

I lean into his side as he finishes, and he wraps his arm around my shoulders and squeezes.

Warm and comfortable and *mmm*. This is the feeling of my best friend. I never want it to stop. "Thanks."

He tips his face into my hair. "For you, there's nothing I wouldn't do."

I turn to face him and lift my hand to his face, trailing

my fingers down the line of his strong jaw. Very slowly, I close the distance between us and press a gentle kiss to his lips. He closes his eyes and holds his breath, and when I pull away, his eyes are still closed.

I stand and move to the door. "Don't you dare leave without saying good-bye."

He opens his eyes and nods. "You got it."

An hour later, when I come down the stairs and see Trent standing in Julie's embrace with his duffel bag in his hand, two things happen. 1) I have a minor panic attack at the thought of not seeing him for the next several months, but 2) when he smiles his lazy smile—the one that always makes me feel warm inside, the panic evaporates. And then I see the guitar case at his feet, and everything lightens.

He holds his arms out to me, and I step into them, and when he wraps them around me, I know I have my best friend back.

"Love you," he says low in my ear.

"Love you too," I whisper back.

He kisses my forehead, then lets me go, and Dad gives him a clap on the back. "Go get 'em, son."

Trent smiles and nods. "See you in a few weeks."

He picks up his guitar and turns for the door. We all spill onto the walk, watching him strap his things onto his bike and climb on. He turns and gives me his lazy smile, then tugs his helmet over his head and flicks the bike to life. As much as my heart aches as he speeds off down the street, it's so much lighter that I'd swear I'm floating.

I HAVE MY strategy, and so far it's working, but I don't want to tempt fate, so when Sam twirls her straw through her smoothie as we sit at the Juice It Up in the mall, and says, "So, how much do you really want to know about Trent's sexual prowess," I say, "Nothing. I changed my mind. That's between you two."

She pouts a little, like she really wanted to share. "If you say so." But then her eyes light up. "Hey, I bought something for your birthday, but since you'll be gone by then, you have to open it now." She pulls a small, brown paper bag with a blue bow on top out of her purse. "These are for use on your trip, and you're not allowed to come home before they're gone."

I scrunch my face at her as I take the package, afraid of what it might be. She watches as I pull it open and peer inside. I roll my eyes and hand her back the condoms. "You should keep these."

She huffs out a laugh. "What? You think I didn't buy myself a box too? Have you *seen* your stepbrother?"

I feel myself wince.

"You *will* find a hot Italian, and you will wish you had those," she says, nodding at the bag.

"Doubtful," I say. I've already met a hot Italian, and there's no way I'm going to need a condom.

"You can't tell me in a city full of beautiful Italian men, there's not a single one who wants to sleep with you."

"Gee. I didn't know that was the only criteria. 'Hey, you want to sleep with me? Yeah? Okay, let's go!'" I roll my eyes.

"I'm just saying, you never know when love is going to strike."

I shove the package in my shopping bag and sip my smoothie. "We should go. I told Julie I'd be home for dinner."

My birthday isn't until January 19, but since I'm flying back to Rome tomorrow, Julie insists on celebrating tonight. She makes my favorite: lobster saffron risotto, and after dinner comes out with a cake, twenty-one candles blazing like an inferno on top of it.

"Make a wish!" she says as Dad warbles out the ". . . and many moooore," at the end of "Happy Birthday."

I blow out the candles and hold the wish that Trent and I can be how we used to be. No awkwardness, no holding back, just best friends.

And I toss Trent's T-shirt into Julie's dirty clothes as I'm packing that night. I'm done obsessing.

Chapter Sixteen

MAYBE IT'S BEING thousands of miles from anyone I feel accountable to, but it's liberating to be back in Rome. Or maybe it's Abby. She's crazy, I know, but she's growing on me.

I got home late last night and fell into bed. When I woke late, there were three texts from Abby that she was coming over. I was going to answer them after I dragged myself through the shower, but I wasn't even dressed yet when my doorbell started buzzing.

I'm unpacking all my freshly home-laundered clothing back into my armoire, and she's lying on my bed, texting someone and giggling.

"You realize you sound twelve?" I say, looking up at her when she giggles again.

She lifts her head and glares at me. "Bugger off."

"So, who is this person that has the power to reduce you to a giggling twelve-year-old?"

She lifts her head again, and this time she's grinning like a dork. "It's Grant. We're sexting."

I feel my eyes widen. "What happened to the girlfriend?"

She pushes herself to a sitting position against my headboard, a smug smile on her face. "He went home for holiday and realized she just couldn't compare to this," she says, running a hand over her curves.

Warning bells are going off in my head. "So, they broke up?"

She shrugs. "They will."

I tuck the last of my T-shirts into my drawer. "Just be careful, Abby."

Her thumbs are flying over the keyboard on her phone, and she's grinning again. "Always am. I'm a great fan of the Trojans."

"I mean with your heart."

She looks up at me with an expression so sincere that it looks totally foreign on her face. "We have chemistry, Lexie. You can't fight chemistry."

Who am I to argue that? I spent all last semester alternately swimming in and drowning in Trent's and my chemistry, and I think I've finally made shore, but it has definitely taken its toll.

She looks back at her phone and giggles again.

"Are we still doing my birthday movie marathon?" We'd talked about it before break, and she'd actually suggested a night of clubbing. After last time, though, I know I can't count on her to have my back if I get trashed, so I talked her into something a little more chill. She only caved when I'd capitulated to hot Italian porn and agreed to bring wine.

Her eyes lift from her phone. "Oh, shit! When is that?"

"Day after tomorrow."

For the first time ever in the history of our friendship, she looks contrite. "Grant and I are going to Florence for the weekend. I will find a hot Italian to take your mind off the fact that I'm a bloody horrible friend?"

I smile and shake my head. "Spare me the hot Italian. We'll do it some other time."

My phone starts vibrating off the nightstand, and I move across the room and pick it up. Speaking of hot Italians . . .

"Hi, Alessandro," I say when I connect.

"I hope you had a pleasant flight."

I can almost hear his smile, and I smile in response. " 'Pleasant flight' is an oxymoron."

He laughs. "Well, I am happy you're back. I just wanted to remind you about our next tour this Friday."

"Like I've ever forgotten," I say with a roll of my eyes.

"I'll concede that you don't forget, but punctuality isn't your strong suit."

"I'll be there, *Dad*." Now I sound twelve, but I feel suddenly giddy talking to Alessandro. I really missed him though I'll never admit it to his face.

"I'll be waiting with bated breath." Something in his voice stalls my heart, and I take a deep breath to massage it back into rhythm.

"See you then."

When I look up at Abby, she's got that grin plastered to her face. The one that says sex all over it.

"What?"

"You and the priest?" she asks with a lift of her brows.

I roll my eyes.

She tucks her legs under her and leans toward me, onto her hands. "Is he a virgin?"

"No!" I snap before I think better of it.

Her eyes widen. "Did you pick his cherry, Lexie?" she sings.

I throw up my hands. "Oh my God! Will you stop?"

She leans back and scrutinizes my face, and that lascivious smirk is back. I fight not to press my hands to my flaming cheeks. "Bloody hell," she finally says. "This is better than the movies."

WHEN I RUSH up to the obelisk right on the minute, Alessandro steps forward and grasps my shoulders, kissing me on one cheek, then the other. It's only the traditional Italian greeting—nothing special—but he's never been this physical before, and it surprises me a little. When I pull away, he studies my face.

"How was your holiday?"

"Fine. It was good."

His eyes narrow a little, as if he's trying to read between the lines, and I know he's wondering about how things went with Trent, but then he gently grasps my elbow and moves us off toward the back entrance to the museums. "Selfishly, I'm happy to have you back."

What does he mean by that? Did he miss me?

Before I can respond, if I could actually think of something to say, he sweeps a hand toward the doors, and adds, "Your public awaits."

As I start walking toward the ramp, I feel my cheeks flush. It was stupid to think he missed me. He's happy I'm back for the kids, of course. Otherwise, he'd have to do the tour himself.

"So, if I remember right, today's your birthday," he says as we walk.

"You remember right." I smile internally that he remembered.

"Have you made plans?"

"I was supposed to go to my friend Abby's, but she's having chemistry, so I don't think that's happening."

He looks at me curiously for a second before saying, "It's against Italian law to spend your birthday alone."

"What?" I say, squinting at him. He's got to be joking, right?

He cracks a smile. "I'm cooking."

My stomach flutters. "Oh. Okay, I guess."

We reach the door, and he holds it open for me. "I'll be by around seven?"

"I'll be waiting with bated breath," I say, parroting back his words.

We stroll to our meeting spot, and, as the kids gather around the Apollo, I smile at Alessandro, remembering how nervous I was the first time we did this. Now I feel comfortable here, like these museums are my second home. Now that all my angst over Trent is resolved, I realize I'm not just here as an escape. I'm here because I love it.

And, more and more every day, I want to stay.

The apartment is a thousand degrees when I get home. I try to adjust the thermostat on the wall of my bedroom, but the wheel is stuck, and the old metal radiator is going full steam. I grab my phone and call the landlord, but he doesn't answer. It wouldn't matter if he did. He doesn't speak English, and I don't know how to say "thermostat" or "radiator" or "burning alive" in Italian.

Just as I'm stuffing the phone back in my pocket, it vibrates.

I smile at the caller ID. "Hey, you," I say when I connect.

"Hey. Happy birthday."

It's so good to hear Trent's voice. "Thanks. How was the tournament?"

He blows a sigh into my ear. "I won."

"Oh my God! That's amazing! Dad must be in heaven."

There's a long pause. "Not so much."

"Why?" I say, feeling my brows pinch.

"Because I quit the next day."

I can't even speak for a second, my mind reeling. "Wow."

"Yeah." He gives me a second to absorb, then says, "So tell me what's going on there? Any big birthday plans?"

I want to push him, to make him tell me everything that's going on with him, but we're still healing. Maybe we're not ready to tackle *everything* quite yet. "Um . . . well, you know Alessandro?"

"Alessandro?"

"The almost-priest I've been doing all that work at the museum with?"

"Oh, yeah."

"He's cooking for me tonight. He should be here in about an hour."

"A cooking priest, huh?"

I hear the smile in his voice. "First, he's not a priest yet, and second, he's pretty damn amazing in the kitchen."

"Yeah, well, just make sure he's not expecting you for dessert."

"Jesus, Trent! He's a priest!"

"Not yet," he says, laughing.

I roll my eyes right out loud.

"Seriously, though. It sounds like you guys are pretty close."

"We are." I think of all the things I've told him—things I never would have dreamed I could tell anyone other than Trent. "He's a really good listener."

There's a long pause, and I can almost hear Trent wondering if I've talked to Alessandro about him. "Good," he finally says. "I'm really glad you've had someone to talk to."

"Yeah. He's amazing. I really feel like I've gotten to know Rome because of him."

"That's great, Lex," he says, and there's something resigned in his voice.

In the silence of the pause, I can hear him breathing. I close my eyes and imagine the warmth of his breath in my hair.

"Well," he says after a minute, "I just wanted to wish you a happy birthday and tell you I miss you, so . . ."

"Thanks."

"I love you," he says in a voice that makes something deep in my chest twists a little.

I close my eyes again and breathe. "Talk soon."

"Talk soon," he repeats, then the line goes dead.

I hold the phone to my ear a minute longer, hearing those words over and over. "I love you too," I whisper before lowering it.

I fan myself, then move around the apartment, opening all the windows. The cool air from outside makes it feel less sauna in here, but it's still warm.

I head to the shower and decide to shave again, but the whole time I'm getting ready for my "date" with Alessandro, I can't stop thinking about Trent. When I come out of the bathroom, I look through my armoire and slip the black silk tank Sam picked out for me off the hanger. It's my birthday, and I feel like dressing up. Alessandro always looks so put together. No reason for me to always be a slob.

I strap on my black lace bra and the matching thong, and slide the tank over my head. Sam's right, the beads do draw attention to my boobs, and I think for a second about changing. I rifle through the hangers for the black skirt we bought to go with the top and shimmy it up my silky legs. Midthigh, so not indecent, but will he think

I'm sending him signals? Am I sending him signals?

I look at myself in the mirror, and my cheeks are flushed. *Jesus* it's hot in here. I fan my face as I move to my bedroom window to open it wider, and there's Horny Boy, on the street in front of my apartment. He must live on this street or something.

He looks up and sees me and his hand moves to the zipper of his jeans. "Vieni a letto con me, dolcezza."

"No!" I say, holding up my hand.

A grin spreads across his face as he inches the zipper down.

I run to my nightstand and pull out Sam's box of condoms, then sprint to the bathroom. I rip one open and fill it with water, then tie the end and run back to my window.

He's got his junk out, and he's just starting to aim for my doorway.

"No!" I say again, and throw my water balloon.

He jumps back and laughs as it explodes at his feet.

"Conosco un modo migliore per usarlo," he says, grinning up at me.

I run to the bathroom and fill two more, bringing them back with me. I throw them, and they explode on the pavement nowhere near him. I've got horrible aim.

He gives himself a stroke and smiles up at me. "Vuoi assaggiare?"

But then a man steps between us. He puts his hand on the boy's shoulder and says something to him low enough I can't hear it. The boy puts his junk away and scurries back into the bar. When the man turns and smiles up at me, I'm relieved to see Alessandro's face. He arches an eyebrow. "Pest problems?"

"Yeah, thanks! I'll be right down!"

When I throw open the door at the bottom of the stairs, Alessandro is standing there with two grocery bags. He smiles, and it strikes me that there's something different about him. I can't put my finger on it, exactly, except to say there's a little bit of swagger to him that I've never noticed before. "Your personal chef has arrived." His eyes drift over me. "You look lovely."

I'm barefoot, in a short skirt and a tank top in the middle of winter. "Thanks, but not quite season appropriate," I say with a shiver. "The heat won't turn off in my apartment, so it's hot up there. The landlord isn't picking up."

Horny Boy staggers out of the bar door just a few feet away. It seems to take his eyes a second to focus, but when they zero in on Alessandro, he grins. "Perdonami Padre, perchè ho peccato." He cackles and staggers back into the bar.

Alessandro clears his throat and looks back at me. "Can I come in? Maybe I could take a look."

"Yeah," I say, standing aside. "Sorry about that."

We move up the stairs into my apartment, and he heads directly to the kitchen and sets his bags down. "It *is* warm in here. Where is your thermostat?"

"In my bedroom," I say, pointing back past the front door and the dining-room table.

He hesitates for just an instant, but then peels off his jacket and hangs it on the back of a dining-room chair on his way to my room. I follow him through the door.

"Here," I say, pointing to the wall next to my bed. I watch his eyes briefly scan the room, catching on the bed for just an instant, before landing on the box of condoms on the nightstand.

Shit.

I feel my cheeks flame as I sweep them into the drawer and shut it, and I can't look at him. "The, um . . ." throat clear, ". . . the stupid wheel is stuck. I can't turn it down."

He moves to the wall and pulls the cover off. "This is old," he says, looking it over. "Sometimes the mechanism just gives out." He fiddles with the wheel, but can't get it to move. "Hmm . . ." he says, looking around the room again. Finally, he lifts a foot and bends to slide off his shoe.

"What are you doing?" I ask, something in my stomach kicking at the thought that he's undressing.

"When all else fails . . ." he says, then bangs the heel of his shoe into the thermostat twice.

I step back, and my eyes widen. "*I* could have done *that.*"

He smirks a little as he spins the wheel, and the old radiators hiss off in unison. "But you didn't."

"Thanks . . . I guess."

He puts his shoe back on and makes his way to the kitchen. I prop myself in the kitchen door. "Can I help?"

"No. This is my gift to you." He washes his hands, then pulls a bottle of wine out of one of the bags and digs in my drawer for the corkscrew. "Your only job is to relax and enjoy," he says, coming out with it. He opens the bottle, pulls down two tumblers, and pours the wine.

"Is this another one of your favorites?" I ask, taking the glass from his hand and sniffing at the top.

"It is."

"You still haven't taken me wine shopping."

He looks up from where he's pulling a pan from my cupboard. "That's right. I forgot. We'll have to do that soon."

"So, how was your Christmas?"

He glances my way as he peels a clove of garlic. "It's our busy season, so . . ." I widen my eyes at him, and he cracks a smile. "It was lovely. Yours?"

I take a long sip of wine before answering. "Stressful. Trent was home."

He stops peeling and turns toward me. "Did you . . . were you together?" His face is a shade pinker than it was a minute ago and a little pinched around the eyes.

"No, we didn't sleep together if that's what you're asking. Well . . . actually we did." I add when I remember Trent's last night home. "I fell asleep in his room one night while he was out, and when I woke up, he was curled around me in bed. That's when I realized how much I needed my best friend back."

Alessandro nods. "So you talked?"

"We did. I think we worked everything out. I mean . . . my romantic feelings aren't totally gone, but I have to ignore them. We agreed that we were going to try to get back what we had."

He pulls my cutting board and a knife down and starts chopping garlic. "And you feel good about your decision?"

I nod. "The second we talked, I felt lighter. It had been weighing so heavily on my conscience, you know? I struggled with it every day, and it was wearing me out. But now, I have my brother and my best friend back. We're moving past what happened. So, yeah. I feel really good about the decision."

He smiles at me. "I'm glad you were able to work things out with him. Love of family is the one of the most important things."

I watch him move around my kitchen for the next half hour, no less graceful here than in anything he does, and when he finally has everything simmering in the pot on my stove, we sit together on the love seat.

"Do you ever see your family?" I ask, swirling my second glass of wine.

He nods slowly. "My grandfather isn't well, so I go back to Corsica whenever I get the chance."

"Did you see them at all over Christmas?"

"No, I'm afraid not." He quirks the hint of a smile. "As I mentioned, it's our busy season."

I smile back.

"But I have a trip planned for my holiday next month."

"How long will you go?"

"Three days. That's all the time I have. But it's enough to check up on them and be sure Mémé has everything she needs to care for Mom and Pépé."

"Your mother is still living with them?" I sip my wine and watch his face.

He settles deeper into the cushions. "She's never been right after her breakdown. She needs someone to care for her."

"What will happen if she outlives your grandparents? I mean, you couldn't . . . you know, go back and take care of her, could you?"

He sips his wine. "I've requested my home parish, and Father Costa has also put in the request, but the bishop holds sway over my placement. He'll send me where he believes I can best serve the needs of the parish."

"So, if you can't go home, what will happen to your mother?"

"Father Costa will see that she's cared for."

"What about your brother? Could he take care of her?"

He lifts his gaze to mine. "Lorenzo's been dead for almost two years."

I feel myself flinch. "I'm so sorry, Alessandro. I didn't know."

"It was the path he chose. Sooner or later, his sins were bound to catch up with him." He sounds so reasonable about it, but there's a shake in his hand that wasn't there a minute ago.

I reach for it and fold it into mine. "Things haven't been easy for you."

"The Lord tests us all in different ways." His fingers curl into mine, and he sips his wine again.

"I'm just sorry that all that has happened to you." I settle into his side, and his thumb rubs circles on the back of my hand.

"It's all led me to right here." We sit and listen to the lid of the pot clank as the contents gently boil. "Would you like to come?" he asks suddenly.

I lift my head off his shoulder. "Where?"

He looks down into my eyes. "To Corsica. Would you come with me?"

"I . . ." Would I? I shift in my seat so I'm facing him and tuck a leg under me. "Your grandparents wouldn't mind?"

"I'm sure they'd be thrilled to meet you."

I roll it over in my mind, trying to find the downside. "You said it's for three days?"

He nods. "You'll miss some school."

"I'm sure I could get notes," I say to myself, then to him, "I'd love to go."

A smile blooms on his face, and he squeezes my hand before standing. "Dinner will be on soon."

Once dinner is on the table, we sit and eat and talk about everything under the sun. He tells me about Corsica, obviously excited for our trip, and we talk about how to keep the tours going after we're both gone.

"When will they assign you?" I ask as I drain my fourth glass of wine.

"As soon as I'm ordained. I'll most likely leave the week after Easter."

"That's soon," I say, surprised to feel a sudden pang at the thought of being here in Rome without him.

"Easter is April 5 this year, so two and a half months."

I lift the bottle. Alessandro holds up a hand when I try to pour the last of it into his glass, so I pour it in mine instead.

"You might want to slow down," he warns.

I smile. "I'm legal everywhere now. I'm celebrating." But as soon as we're done eating, and I stand up to clear the dishes, I realize five glasses of wine was probably three too many. I stagger into the wall next to the door when I lose my balance, and the silverware clatters off the plate in my hand onto the tile floor. "Shit," I say, then burst out giggling and look at Alessandro. "Pardon my French."

"I assure you, that is *not* French." He takes the plate from my hand and loops an arm around my waist, guiding me to the love seat. "Sit. It's your birthday, so I'm cleaning."

I sink into the cushions and roll my head back. "I'm drunk."

"Yes you are," he says from the kitchen, and I hear the smile in his voice.

"It's your fault, nursing one glass of wine all night. Someone had to drink the rest."

He laughs. I close my eyes. The room spins, then fades, and my mind goes totally blank.

All I know is my bladder is about to burst. I flop an elbow over my eyes, but it doesn't stop the rock hammer pounding into my left temple. I roll and bury my face in the pillow, and everything goes dark. That helps a little.

Wait—the *pillow*?

My eyes fly open and I sit up, but that causes the rock hammer to turn into an ice pick. "Shit!" I say, grabbing my head in both hands to keep it from exploding. "Shit," I say again, softer when I see where I am. "How did I get into bed?" I ask out loud, but the sound of my voice hurts my head, so I stop talking.

The last thing I remember, I was on the love seat after dinner, and Alessandro was cleaning the kitchen. What happened after that?

I rack my brain, but that hurts too, so I lie back and bury my face in the pillow again. I'm in the same tank top and skirt I was wearing last night.

Did Alessandro put me to bed?

Forget it. I'm not going to worry about it now. Sleep. I just need to sleep for another day or two, and I'll be fine.

My thoughts swirl into random images, and I'm not really paying attention until one of those random images turns into Alessandro, leaning over me. His hand sweeps my hair off my face and he leans closer. His lips brush against mine. "Good night, Lexie. Sleep well."

"Oh, God," I mumble into the pillow. Alessandro *did* put me to bed. "Oh, God," I mutter again. Please tell me I didn't throw myself at him or anything stupid. Last time I was on the rebound, I slept with my stepbrother, so anything's possible.

I want so much just to go back to sleep and forget the whole thing ever happened, but my bladder has other plans and drives me out of bed. I hold the furniture for balance as I weave my way to the bathroom. As I sit here peeing, I think about showering because, let's face it, I stink, but I don't have the energy, and I definitely don't plan on going anywhere today, so instead, I splash some water on my face, gag myself with the toothbrush, and stagger back to bed. But as I pass the dining-room table, I see the note. I snatch it up and read Alessandro's surprisingly messy scrawl.

I hope you slept well. Call me when you're up.

When I get back to my room, I check my phone, and there's a text from Trent.

Happy day after your birthday. Hope your dinner was great. Love you.

Thanks. I text back. *Hungover. Going back to bed. Love you too.*

I settle into the pillows, and the change of position makes my head throb. After a minute it stops, and I dial Alessandro. When he picks up, there's a lot of noise in the background. "Hello, Lexie," he says. "I trust you survived the night."

"Barely," I mutter into the phone. "Where are you? I can hardly hear you."

"In the ring at the youth center," he answers. "It's Saturday afternoon."

"Afternoon? Really?"

He laughs, then says, "Rapida, Franco!"

"What?" I ask before it registers he's not talking to me.

"Sorry for the distraction. How are you feeling?"

"Like shit."

"Ah. Next time I'll have to ration you."

I pull the pillow over my head. "You're a bad influence on me."

The background noise lessens, and a moment later, he says, "Am I?"

"Yes. I've never been that drunk before in my life."

"If memory serves me right, I tried to warn you."

"Well, my memory doesn't serve me at all . . . except . . ." The image of his leaning down and kissing me flits through my head.

"What do you remember?" he coaxes.

"Did you . . . ?" I shake my head and pain shoots through my skull as my brain sloshes. "No, forget it."

Even if he did, it doesn't mean anything, right?

"I have something else I'd like to show you," he tells me after a second. "Since there's no tour next Friday, I was hoping I could steal you away for a few hours."

"Ooh! Mystery."

"It's not all that mysterious, I'm afraid, but I thought you might find it intriguing."

"What is it?"

"There is a traveling exhibit of Pompeian artwork housed at the National Museum this month."

"Oh my God! Are you *serious*? Why didn't they tell us about that at school?"

"I can't speak to your professor's motivations, but I can speak to mine. I've been wanting to see it but thought I'd wait for you to get back."

"So, Friday?" I confirm. "It will still be there?"

"Through the end of January."

"I am so in."

"Excellent. I'll see you then. And happy birthday again."

When he disconnects, I roll my face back into the pillow. My plan is to sleep until class on Monday, and if my head hasn't stopped throbbing, maybe Tuesday.

Chapter Seventeen

WE'VE BEEN TO the National Museum before, of course. It was one of the first places Alessandro took me. They have three rooms in the back that, when we were here in September, had a traveling display of second- and third-century pottery. We make a beeline for those rooms.

"I really want to go to Pompeii before I leave," I tell Alessandro as we walk into the exhibit. "I've seen Florence and Venice on my class trips, and I get to see Corsica next month"—I smile at him—"so thank you, but I've never been south."

"It's only three hours by train to Pompeii," he says. "We could go."

It's everything I can do not to jump up and down and clap like a five-year-old. "That would be unbelievable."

We spill into the first room and take our time perusing the artwork. Mt. Vesuvius buried Pompeii under volcanic ash in A.D. 79, so all this art is from the first century or earlier. And it's incredible. There is statuary and painted pottery and a few frescoes that were removed from crumbing walls and preserved. Each piece has a plaque with a bit about its history and where in Pompeii it was found, complete with pictures. We spend the next two hours working through the first two rooms.

"This is just beyond cool," I say over my shoulder to Alessandro as we round the corner into the third and smallest room. He grasps my arm just as I run into a sign propped on a stand.

He grins as I gasp. "Best to contain your enthusiasm long enough to watch your step. I sincerely doubt your credit-card limit would cover damage to anything in this room."

"Sorry," I say, righting the sign, then turn to the room.

Directly in front of me is a statue. It's mostly just a pair of torsos with legs, because the heads and arms have fallen off, but there's no mistaking what they're doing. The naked man's torso is seated on a stump, and his huge erection, which has definitely *not* fallen off, is pressing into the half-dressed female torso from behind.

Something stirs between my legs, and I can't look at Alessandro.

"Well, that's something, isn't it?" he says, and when I finally get up the nerve to glance at him, he's lifting his eyebrows at me, half a smile on his lips.

"Um . . . yeah. Something."

I turn my flaming face to the wall, and on it is a fresco

of a man and woman going at it doggie style. "Oh my God!" I say, and turn away. "What the hell did that sign say, anyway?"

I walk back and look at it. In both Italian and English is a warning that the exhibit in this room contains erotic art. "No kidding," I mutter. "Let's go," I say to Alessandro, but he's moved deeper into the room. "Lexie, this is art. I'm interested to see it."

"Really?" I say, stepping back into the room.

He turns to me and lifts an eyebrow. "People have sex. Does that embarrass you?"

If I were here on my own, I'd want to see this for sure. He's right. These are authentic ancient pieces that I couldn't see anywhere else. But I'm not here alone. I'm here with a very sexy man in a white collar who may or may not have put my drunken ass to bed on my birthday last week and kissed me.

"It's just . . . I—"

He grasps my hand and pulls me to his side. "This is fascinating, Lexie. Read this," he says, pointing to the plaque next to a picture.

The picture was taken in Pompeii, so apparently this fresco is still there, in the House of Vetti. It's an image of Priapus, the Greek god of fertility. Jutting out from under his tunic is an erection that would hang to his knees if it weren't resting on a scale in front of him, where he's apparently weighing it.

"It says frescoes and statues of Priapus were common in the doorways of ancient Roman households," Alessandro says, running his finger over the words on the plaque. "It was considered good luck to stroke the penis upon entry."

Oh. My. God. How is it that I'm standing here with an almost-priest listening to him talking about "stroking the penis upon entry"?

"Yeah . . . wow," I say, turning away and pressing my hands to my flaming cheeks. "That's . . . um . . . fascinating."

He moves to the next piece: a mosaic from the baths, so the plaque says, of a woman on her back giving the very horny man (judging by the size of his erection) kneeling over her a hand job.

My face is just about to burst into actual flames.

I move ahead of Alessandro and scan each piece, pausing just long enough so he'll think I'm really looking at them. I'm waiting in the second room when he finally comes out several minutes later.

"I think that paints an interesting portrait of human nature, don't you?" he asks.

"Yeah. Definitely."

"It hasn't changed much in two thousand years." I look at him to see if he's messing with me, but he's looking over a mosaic on the wall, his expression serious. "Have you seen enough?" he finally asks, turning his attention to me.

I've seen *more* than enough. "Let's go."

WHEN SAM CALLS while I'm making dinner, I'm surprised. She texts me occasionally, and I work pretty hard to steer the conversation away from Trent, but she's never called me here.

"I scored tickets to take Trent to see Ed Sheeran on Thursday in San Francisco," she shrieks into the phone when I pick up.

"Trent loves Ed Sheeran." My face pinches against unexpected tears as I remember all times he sat with his guitar on the edge of my bed and sang "The A Team" to me. I've always thought of that and "Someone, Somehow" as our songs.

"Duh! That's why I got the tickets—and a reservation at the Hyatt. It's going to be a night he'll never forget, culminating in mad animal sex that will rock his world."

I breathe deep. This is what I wanted. Trent and I have an agreement—which means he's going to see other people. "He's going to flip," I tell her. And hope I'm not.

BUT I DO.

I spend the next week obsessing, imagining them together in ways I'd rather not. Friday morning, I sit in class and keep looking at my clock, doing the math. San Francisco is nine hours behind Rome, so right now it's . . . eleven o'clock last night there. The concert is probably breaking up right about now. Are they walking to the hotel? Will they stop for a drink on the way? Maybe a scotch?

Damn. Stop it!

I can't torture myself over this. I'm moving on, building a new life with new friends. It's been six months since

Trent and I slept together. It's ancient history, and he's moving on too. It's all good.

It's all good.

It's all good.

If I say it enough, maybe I'll start to believe it.

The truth is, I'm loving my life here. I love the time I spend with the kids at the Vatican, and I love hanging out in the cafés with my classmates drinking espresso and eating pastries. I love getting lost on purpose in the charmed streets of Rome and making some new and marvelous discovery—a crumbling marble fountain tucked away in a lost alleyway; a hidden catacomb; a quiet, undiscovered flower garden just steps off the beaten path. I love taking a panini and my sketchpad to the bridge and sketching the artists along the Tiber as they sketch their Roman scenes. I sketch the awed tourists stumbling over the cobbles at the sprawling floral market in Piazza Campo Dè Fiori. I sketch the sad, homeless man on the corner next to the tired street musician with his guitar. I love Rome. I love my classes. My professors are great. And I'm even starting to love Abby.

Things are looking really good for that internship at Galleria Nazionale d'Arte Antica too. I was super nervous about it until Alessandro wrote me a letter of recommendation, which I think might help push me over the top of the other candidates.

His ordination is less than two months away and sometimes when we're talking about it, he goes all quiet and contemplative. I guess it's normal that he'd be reflecting on his decision a lot right about now. I mean, this is it. He's promising his life to God. No wiggle room. It's not like he can say a month or two down the road, "Hey, God? Sorry to bag out on You, but I think I changed my mind." Though, he swears the decision was made months ago when the bishop called him, and he took his vow of celibacy. He says it's the vow he's already taken that binds him to the Church.

And I'm happy for him if this is what he wants.

I really am.

I am.

I look at the clock. Ten past eight. How is time moving so slowly? I count on my fingers just to make sure I'm right. Yep, it's ten minutes after eleven last night in San Francisco.

Is he kissing her?

No. I'm not going to think about it.

Our Vatican tour that afternoon keeps my mind off it, for the most part, and Alessandro and I catch a quick bite after. So it's not until I get Sam's text that night: *Your stepbrother is the fucking master of my universe,* that the fist around my chest tightens again.

Does it mean they slept together? Did she rock his world? She sounds pretty rocked.

I can't even text her back. I feel myself implode, and all I can think about is how much I miss him. I miss curling into his arms and telling him about my day. I miss knowing he'll always be mine—that no one will ever know me like he does. I miss his lips and his hands. I miss his heart and his soul. I miss every part of him.

I feel so empty. Can a person die of emptiness?

I GOT ALL my assignments from my professors and turned them in early. I feel moderately guilty about skipping out on class for three days, especially since Alessandro says there's not much historical art to see, but it's Corsica. With Alessandro. For three days. With Alessandro.

It's a beautiful day for February—warmish with a bright blue sky and nary a cloud. I'm breathing in the fresh air, which is only this fresh after it rains like it did last night, when a taxi squeals around the corner, spraying the puddle there onto the side of the building, and careens down my street. I leap back from the curb into my doorway when it jumps the sidewalk before stopping right in front of me.

A tall man in a sapphire blue button-down shirt and jeans steps out of the back, and I wonder what he's doing in my little alley. The bar won't be open for hours, and there's not much else down here.

I stay tucked into my doorway in case the taxi driver decides not to leave any survivors on his way out.

"Do you have your passport and student visa?" I hear Alessandro's unmistakable silk voice ask, and, when I look up, he's standing right in front of me, smiling. "We're going to France, and they won't let you back into Italy without them."

"What are you wearing?" I ask, stepping onto the sidewalk and staring at him.

He looks down at himself, spreading his arms slightly to the side. "I think they are called clothes."

His blue button-down is open at the collar and tints his charcoal eyes, making them look indigo. The shirttails are loose over faded jeans that fit him perfectly. And, God, he's hot. "You look . . . amazing."

He lowers his lashes, but I see a smile twitch his lips as he takes my bag and bangs on the trunk, which the driver pops open. "I'm glad you approve." He slides my beat-up suitcase in next to a black leather duffel, then, with a hand on my back, escorts me to the backseat of the taxi.

"Why the change?" I ask when he opens the door and ushers me in.

"I'm on holiday." He settles in next to me. "I am really looking forward to this."

"Me too," I say, but the too comes out as too*AH* when the cab jerks forward, jumping the curb, and knocks the wind out of me. "So . . . your family . . . they're okay with my coming?" I ask to distract myself from my impending death around every corner.

"Mémé is overjoyed."

I settle deeper into my seat, turning to face him. "Tell me about her."

One shoulder lifts in a shrug, a gesture so casual that it surprises me a little. I don't think I've ever seen Alessandro this relaxed. He wears it well. "She's a typical grandmother. She loves to dote over everyone around her"—he smiles at me—"which you will soon find out includes you."

"You're close?"

His nod is pensive, his lips pursed. "It took some time, but we became close."

I'm thrown against the car door as we fly around a roundabout, knocking the wind out of me again. "You were sixteen when you moved in with them, right?" I realize as I say it that I sound a little hysterical. *Just don't look out the window,* I coach myself.

Alessandro, on the other hand, is cool as a cucumber. He nods.

"How was that . . . moving in with your grandparents?" *Just keep talking and don't look out the window.*

"For me, it meant I didn't have to fend for myself anymore. In all honesty, it was a relief, but Lorenzo didn't see it that way. He was only there a few months before he left."

"Was that hard on you . . . after everything you'd been through together?"

"Mémé took it harder than I did. Lorenzo was angry, and there was nothing anyone could do to change that. I hoped he would find the peace I did in God and the Church, but he didn't."

I lean back into my seat and look at him for a long minute, temporarily forgetting that I'm careening down the narrow, cobbled streets of Rome in Deathcab. "How did he die?"

Alessandro flinches, and I wish I could take the question back. "He was shot by a grocery-store owner in Toulon during a robbery."

"I'm sorry."

He sinks deeper into the seat next to me and squeezes my hand. "I've made my peace with it."

I settle into his side, and he loops an arm over my shoulders, and somehow the rest of the ride doesn't seem quite so scary.

"We're flying in *that*?" I say, digging in my heels and putting on the brakes as soon as we step out of the terminal onto the tarmac. I should have known the deal when there was no jetbridge, but I wasn't really thinking about what *size* plane we were flying in. I was too busy trying not to show Alessandro how freaked-out I was that we were flying at all.

He grasps my hand. "What's wrong?"

"That," I say, pointing at the tiny little plane that everyone else is climbing into without batting an eyelash. "Is there a train . . . or a bus?"

"Corsica is an island, Lexie." His voice is calm, but amusement dances in his eyes.

"Okay, a boat then? There has to be a boat, right?"

"Yes, there is in fact a boat."

I'm starting to hyperventilate and lean my hands on my knees. "Can we take the boat? Please?"

"This is about your fear of heights?"

"And my fear of plummeting from them. Yes."

"Can I coax you onto this very airworthy vessel if I promise to distract you?"

Breathe.

Breathe.

Breathe.

"How?"

"With my quick wit, infinite capacity for engrossing conversation, or if all that fails, with these." He pulls a small white paper bag out of his satchel and hands it down to me, where I'm still stooped over, trying to catch my breath.

I open the end of the bag and hold it over my nose and mouth, watching it inflate and deflate as I hyperventilate into it.

"That wasn't quite what I had in mind," Alessandro muses.

When I can finally breathe, I stand up and look into the bag. Currant croissants. Four of them. "Hope you didn't want any of these because I just loogied all over them."

"Are you ready?" he asks, his eyes flicking to the plane. *OhGodohGodohGod.*

He loops an arm through my elbow, and we shuffle slowly toward the plane. It takes me a few minutes to climb the stairs, and Alessandro puts a hand on my head, reminding me to duck when we get to the door. I step through and look over my surroundings.

On the jetliners I've taken back and forth to San Jose, I've been able to sit far enough from the window that I could pretend outside didn't exist. Not here. There are twelve rows of three seats, two on one side and one on the other. We're last on board, apparently, because the harried-looking flight attendant rushes us up the narrow aisle to our seats, in row five—on the two side, thank

God. Alessandro gestures for me to slide in. I just shake my head and point to the aisle seat. The flight attendant barks something at us in Italian, and Alessandro purrs something back, then slides into the window seat. I sit next to him and buckle up. He twists his arm through mine and grasps my hand, and I don't resist.

When we lurch into the sky a few minutes later, I feel a joint in Alessandro's hand pop under my death grip. "I think I broke you," I mutter, trying to lighten my grip a little. "Sorry."

"I am yours to break." He peels his hand out of mine and circles me in his arms, pulling me tight to his side. I turn my face into his shirt, and he strokes my hair.

"Your wife is afraid of flying?" A woman's voice asks from across the aisle, but I've finally found a spot that works, so I don't move.

"Yes, she is." Alessandro's voice vibrates into me from where my ear is pressed into his chest, and I'm more than a little surprised that he didn't correct the woman—tell her I'm not his wife. But instead, when I burrow tighter into him, he tips his face into crown of my hair, and I feel his warm breath.

I like this Alessandro—the one without the white collar.

Chapter Eighteen

MY NERVES, BY the time we land forty minutes later, have less to do with hurling through space in a tin can and more to do with meeting Alessandro's family. I've found the key to flying. I just need to worry about something else.

We taxi to the terminal, and the pilot parks the plane. After few more minutes, fresh air wafts through the open door, and I know it's okay to peel myself off Alessandro.

"That wasn't so bad, yes?" he asks when I look up at him. I'm sure I've left a Lexie print in his chest.

"If you say so." I breathe a deep, relieved breath as I duck under the door and out of this death trap. Alessandro escorts me down the stairs and into the terminal with a gentle hand on my back.

The airport is small, and our plane seems to be the only one here at the moment, so the bags come up fast. I look at Alessandro as we climb into a taxi on the curb. "Please tell me Corsican taxi drivers aren't suicidal."

He leans into the cab. "Êtes-vous suicidaire?"

The driver, a good-looking man in his thirties with horribly crooked teeth, cracks up. "Non," he says.

Alessandro turns back to me. "Apparently, this one is not."

"That didn't sound Italian," I say.

"This is France, Lexie," he says with an amused smile, urging me into the taxi with a hand on my back. "They speak French here."

I slide in and scoot across, and Alessandro folds himself in next to me. "What about your family? Do they speak English at all?"

"My mother obviously does, but my grandparents don't."

I hadn't thought of that till just now.

"It'll be fine, Lexie," Alessandro says with a squeeze of my hand, reading the anxiety that I'm sure is plastered all over my face. He leans forward. "Cardiglione," he tells the driver, and we're off like a shot.

The taxi driver lied. I know this because we almost died three times before we ever left the city limits and another three as we twisted up the narrow, windy road carved into the hillside rising away from the ocean. My heart is beating in my throat half an hour later when the driver finally skids to a stop. Next to the car, a set of steep marble stairs leads up from the road to a path that wends through a few rows of budding grapevines toward a white, two-story house built into the side of the hill.

Alessandro pays the driver, then climbs out and retrieves our bags from the trunk before the driver fishtails off.

I do a 180. "This is beautiful," I say, taking in the view back toward the expanse of cobalt blue ocean across the street from the house.

"It is," he answers. He loops his bag over his shoulder and takes mine in his hand, then grasps my hand in his other and leads me across the street toward the stairs.

Once we get to the top, I realize the grapevines are just the tip of a huge garden. There are fruit trees to the right, past the vines, which are just starting to flower, and on the left is a large patch of freshly turned earth.

"Who is the gardener?"

"Pépé. My grandfather," he says, leading me past.

An older, pear-shaped woman bursts from the front door, holding up her arms and shaking them at the sky as she spouts French so fast I don't catch anything but, "Alessandro!" Her face is covered in soft wrinkles, and her dark hair, twisted into a bun on the back of her head, is shot through with silver. But she has Alessandro's eyes. She waddles to us before we can reach the door and, after hugging Alessandro, grasps my face in her hands. "Jolie fille, jolie fille! Bienvenue!" She plants a wet kiss on each of my cheeks then takes my hand and tows me toward the house, yelling something at the door. As we step through, a short, stout man with gray hair and a cane steps into the hall. "Alessandro," he says, clapping his grandson on the back and kissing both cheeks.

"Pépé, c'est Lexie," Alessandro says, taking my hand and pulling me closer.

His grandfather grasps my shoulders and kisses both my cheeks. "Bienvenue."

"Merci," I say. And that's all the French I know.

"Lexie," he says to me, "these are my grandparents. You can feel free to call them Mémé and Pépé, as I do."

His grandparents lead us deeper into the house to a living room. Knitting in a chair near the window is a woman who can't be anyone but Alessandro's mother. She's long and slender, in a flowing black skirt and a white top, with dark hair pulled into a tight bun. She has his same high cheekbones and arched brows over charcoal eyes. His same straight nose and full lips. And when she looks up and smiles softly, I see him in that gesture too.

She lays her knitting aside and stands. "It's nice to have you home, son."

He leads me to her and kisses her on both cheeks. "Mom, I'd like you to meet Lexie Banks."

She reaches for my hand and presses it between hers, and I start a little at the scars on her wrist. Ten years later, they're still twisted white knots. It looks like she meant business, and I catch myself wondering how she survived. "Alessandro has told me much about you." Her voice is deeper than I would have expected, and soft, and her words flow smooth and slow as molasses through a musical French accent.

I flash him a glance, wondering exactly what he's told them. "It's nice to meet you."

"Can we offer you a cool drink after your trip?" she asks, releasing me. As she moves past us toward the kitchen in the back, I notice how deliberate her movements are. She's got Alessandro's grace, but it's as if it's in slow motion.

Alessandro takes my hand. "I'm going to show Lexie to her room, then we'll be back down."

His mother nods.

His grandmother says something else I can't understand and pats my arm as Alessandro leads me to the stairs. I smile and nod because I have no idea what else to do, and she smiles back and grabs my face, kissing my cheeks again.

"What did I just agree to?" I mutter as we climb.

"To eat." He grins at me. "She says you're skinny, and she'll fatten you up."

"Great."

At the top of the stairs, he pushes open a door. "This is the bathroom."

I peek in. It's small, not more space than will hold a sink, toilet, a small tub, and maybe a person, but it's clean. "Good to know."

I follow him to another set of stairs, and he points down the hall. "Mémé and Pépé sleep down there, and my mother's room is here," he adds, tapping a knuckle on the door next to the bathroom. We start up the tight spiral staircase to a third floor that I didn't know existed. At the top of the stairs is an open door into a small room with a gabled ceiling—so probably the attic. There are two twin beds with an old wooden chest of drawers in between that take up the entire space.

"This is where you'll stay," Alessandro says, putting my bag on the bed nearest us.

"What about you? Where's your room."

His eyes flit around the bare walls. "This *is* my room. Mine and Lorenzo's."

"Oh." I step between the two beds. "Which one's yours?"

He moves behind me, and I can feel him, so close. "This one," he says, pointing to the one away from the door.

I turn to him. "So, where will you sleep if I'm in your bed?"

"I'll be on the sofa in the family room."

"There are two beds in here," I point out with a tip of my head toward Lorenzo's. "I trust you to be a gentleman."

His eyes go distant for just a second before he breathes deeply and turns away. "Thank you, but I'll be fine on the sofa."

We spend the rest of the afternoon and evening eating and talking . . . or at least Alessandro's grandmother is talking. She's obviously very happy to have him home. I assist her in the kitchen as best I can, with help from Alessandro to translate, and she makes this dish that, even though I have no idea what it is, melts in my mouth.

His grandfather lights a fire in the fireplace after dinner, and his grandmother talks some more as we sit around it drinking something warm and sweet from mugs. Occasionally, Alessandro looks at me when he's talking, and I hear my name, but I don't know what he's saying.

But it's his mother I watch. She sits in her chair near the window, knitting. She hasn't stopped since we got here except to eat dinner, and her eyes never leave her work. At the dinner table, she rocked herself gently as she ate, like the rhythmic motion pacifies her—keeps her focus off bigger things, like life.

It's late when everyone starts looking like they're heading to bed. Alessandro walks me up the two flights of stairs to his attic bedroom.

I turn to face him at my door and hear people shuffling around a floor below. "Your family seems really amazing."

He nods. "My grandparents are extraordinary people."

"And your mom?"

He breathes deep. "She's better."

I think of the things that happened to her to bring her to this place. "I'm glad."

The sadness clears from his eyes, and he rubs his temple as if it hurts. "Tomorrow, I'll take you up the mountain to the Natural Park of Corsica. It's like your national parks. I've told Mémé we won't be back for dinner."

"But it's your last night at home. Shouldn't you spend it here with your family?"

"I'll see them again after the ordination." He takes my hand, and his gaze becomes deeper in the dim light, seeming to search my soul. "I want to share the places I love with you before I don't have you anymore."

I swallow back my hammering heart. "Thank you."

"Is there anything you need?"

"No. I think I'm fine. Unless . . . do you want to . . ."

I lift my fingertips to his temple. "I could massage that."

His eyes darken as they gaze into mine. I push the door open behind me. An invitation.

His fingers brush over my cheek as he leans in and kisses my forehead. "I'm so pleased you came, Lexie, but I can't go in there."

I look up at him, and his hand pauses on my face. His fingers tighten slightly, urging me toward him, but just as he lays his other hand on my hip, someone closes a door downstairs.

He lets me go as if I've burned him and steps away, lowering his smoldering gaze. "Good night." Then he's hurrying down the stairs.

THE SMELL OF espresso and something baking wakes me from a sound sleep, and my stomach growls. Mémé kept shoveling food onto my plate last night, and I kept eating it, so I can't possibly be hungry, but that's not going to stop me from eating anything that smells this good. I roll out of bed and pull jeans on under the black silk sleep shirt I brought as an alternative to what I normally sleep in, which is nothing, then grab the towel Mémé left for me and skip down the stairs to the bathroom. Thankfully, it's unoccupied.

There's no actual shower, just a hand spray attached to a hose from the spigot of the tub, but it will have to do. I sit in the tub and do the quick washup, then dry myself off, brush my teeth, and throw my jeans and sleep shirt back on.

When I open the door, I hear the deep hum of Alessandro's voice speaking French with his grandparents from downstairs. I start my feet toward the spiral stairs to the attic, smiling, but when I turn to look where I'm going, I have a minor heart attack.

Because Alessandro's mother is standing in her doorway, watching me.

"Oh . . . hi. Were you waiting for the . . ." I trail off with a vague gesture at the bathroom door, a little creeped out by her blank stare. "Well, sorry to take so long in there." I start to hurry past her. "It's all yours—"

Her hand darts out as I pass and grabs my arm, scaring the snot out of me. My eyes are about to pop out of my head when I turn to look at her. Her expression is still blank, but her grip is surprisingly strong. "He is in love with you."

Chapter Nineteen

"WHAT?" I'M SO shocked by her words that I don't even move to shake her hand off.

"Alessandro is in love with you."

"No . . . I mean . . ." I'm so rattled I can barely form a coherent thought. "We're just friends."

"I can't help him. He only feels guilt when he sees me."

"I'm . . . he . . ." My head is spinning. What am I supposed to say?

"You can help him see," she tells me, and finally there's some animation to her features. Her brow furrows, and her eyes take on a desperate sheen.

"See what? What does he need to see?"

"He's doing this for me—for his family. Not for himself."

"I'm sorry. I don't understand. What's he doing for his family?"

"Lexie?" I start at the sound of Alessandro's voice on

the stairs, but his mother's only reaction is to drop her hand from my arm. He splits a wary glance between us. "Is everything all right?"

I nod and look back at his mother. "We're fine."

He mounts the last stair in a T-shirt and sweatpants and watches his mother disappear back through her door, then comes to where I am and rubs his warm hands up and down my upper arms. "Are you okay? What did she say?"

I shake my head. "She wasn't really making any sense."

He bites the corner of his lower lip between his teeth. "I'm sorry if she scared you."

"No. It's okay."

He looks at me like he doesn't believe me, which he's probably getting from the fact I'm shaking a little. He pulls me into his arms and rests his chin on the top of my head. "I'm sorry."

We stand here until my shaking slows, then he takes my hands in his. "I just came up to tell you breakfast is ready. Are you hungry?"

After what just happened, no. But I can't tell him that. "Yeah. It smells amazing."

He leads me down the stairs, and the smell gets stronger—yeast and something sweet. "If you think those currant croissants are good, get ready to hold on to your taste buds."

Alessandro's mom doesn't come down for breakfast, so Alessandro and I eat with his grandparents. He translates as Mémé grills me on my family. When she's satisfied I've eaten enough and divulged all my family secrets, she lets us up from the table.

Alessandro walks with me to the stairs. "As soon as we're ready, we should go. There's a lot of island to see."

"Great. Just let me change." I scamper up the stairs, moving quickly past his mother's door, up the spiral stairs to my room, then dig through my bag for the sweater and jeans I'd packed. I slip them on and pull my hair back, then rub a little foundation on, blend in some blush, and brush on mascara. The whole production takes less than ten minutes. On my way back down, I run past his mom's door again and find him waiting in the hall in a pair of jeans and a dark blue hoodie. He looks like half the guys on Notre Dame campus . . . except much hotter.

"We have one stop on our way up the hill," Alessandro tells me as he ushers me to the front door.

Mémé follows behind us, talking in rapid-fire French. I smile and wave because I've discovered that makes her happy.

"Where are we stopping?" I ask as we hop into a small brown sedan in the driveway.

"Father Costa asked me to stop by when I was on the island."

"Oh."

Alessandro navigates down the winding drive to the narrow road and takes a left up the hill. Houses become more frequent as we weave over the switchbacks of the hill until we come to an actual town. "This is the town of Cardiglione," he tells me, slowing as the streets become busier. We wind through town, past markets and cafés, and he rolls to a stop in front of a white church. He steps out of the car, and when I don't move, he holds his hand out to me. "The Father will want to meet you."

"Why?" I ask, getting out.

He gives me the skeptic's eye. "He's a friend. You're a friend. He'll want to know you."

I follow him up the walk to a small house beside the church, and he knocks. We wait for a moment, but when there is no answer, he turns for the church. "He's probably readying for Mass." He lays a hand on my back and ushers me to the front of the church, but we're not even through the door when someone calls out, "Alessandro!"

He smiles and turns as a slender, older man with white hair, wire-rimmed glasses, and a bit of a hunched posture under his cassock skips across the sidewalk toward us.

"Alessandro! C'est votre dernier voyage avant le grand jour!"

"It is," Alessandro answers. "Father Costa, I'd like for you to meet my good friend, Lexie Banks."

Father Costa takes my hand in both of his. "Ah! Lexie!" he says with strong French accent. "Alessandro has told me of the work you have done with the children."

I smile. "I really love it. It's been an amazing opportunity." I glance at Alessandro. "It's probably the thing I will miss most and remember longest when I leave Italy."

"It is a worthwhile mission and one that Alessandro has taken to heart. Children are our most treasured resource."

Alessandro is beaming at me. "Lexie is a natural with

the children. Her love pours out in her work, and it's contagious."

There's a long pause as I flounder for some response to that. Finally, Father Costa breaks the silence. "When will you be returning home?" he asks, and there's a slight edge to his voice that wasn't there a second ago. His eyes move warily between Alessandro and me.

"Um . . . I'm not quite sure yet. I'm hoping for an internship at Galleria Nazionale d'Arte Antica, and if I get it, I'll be in Rome until August. Otherwise, I go home in May."

He nods, then shifts his attention to Alessandro, laying a firm hand on his shoulder. "I will be in Rome for your ordination in six weeks' time."

Alessandro lays his hand on the Father's shoulder so their arms are crossed. "I'm happy you'll be there."

"This is a big day for you—what you've been preparing for since you were a young man." Father Costa's eyes shift to me, then back to Alessandro. "Of course, I will be there for you, as I always have been. If there's anything you need from me, counsel or support, you need only ask."

Alessandro nods, then pulls Father Costa into a hug, kissing both cheeks. "Thank you Father. I've always relied on your guidance." He lets go of the priest and clasps my hand. "À bientôt."

We walk back to the car and climb in, and I can feel Father Costa's eyes on my back.

"I don't think he likes me."

Alessandro looks at me as he turns the key. "Why would you think that?"

I shrug. "Just a feeling."

He pulls onto the road, and we wind away from the church. "I'm sure you couldn't be more wrong."

I watch the scenery as we crawl up the mountain, switching back at sharp angles. Frequently, vast stretches of ocean can be seen off to one side or the other. I'm staring at it out my side window as we crest a hill, and all of a sudden I'm being throw into my seat belt as Alessandro slams on the brakes. When I look out the windshield, there is a herd of . . . something in the road.

"What are they?" I ask.

"U muvrinu. Something like your mountain goats," he answers.

"Will they move . . . ?" I look warily out the windshield at them. ". . . Or attack?"

He breathes a laugh. "They'll move eventually." He revs the engine a little as he inches forward, and they start to scatter, but they're taking their time about it.

"Does this happen a lot?"

"As a matter of fact, no. I haven't seen them in the road like this." He smiles at me. "They're showing off for you."

Eventually, they do move. It's about fifteen minutes later that we're able to pass, and by that time, there are two other cars waiting behind us.

"What I love about Corsica," Alessandro says as we break free, "is that much of it is like this. Unspoiled."

Just ahead, I can see snowcapped mountains. "It's beautiful."

He nods. "It truly is. People come from all over the

world to see it, and yet, so many of the communities are poor. I feel like this is someplace I could make a difference. Coming here saved my life. I'd like to have the opportunity to give something back."

I'm staring at him. I can't help it. "Do you think they'll let you come back?"

"It's still being decided."

For a long time, we wind through trees and mountains and come to where the snow is plowed back from the road.

"Can we get out?" I ask him.

He glances at me. "If you want." He pulls over into the turnout, and as soon as I open the door, I realize my sweater isn't quite enough.

"Brr! It's cold up here."

A corner of his mouth curls into a smile. "Thus the snow."

I make a face at him and go over to the low snowbank at the side of the road, curling my fingers into the snow. Before I realize what's happening, I'm being wrapped in warm cotton. I look at Alessandro, standing next to me in a snug-fitting black T-shirt. He tucks his hoodie tight around me.

"You're going to freeze!" I say.

"Maybe."

I wrap the ends of his hoodie around his waist, so we're both bundled underneath it, and he presses his body against mine. I can feel the cut of his abs, the lines of his pecs through his thin shirt, and I have the sudden urge to slide my hands under and feel them, skin on skin.

I restrain myself, but I do press my cheek into his chest. "Thank you for bringing me up here."

"You haven't seen the best yet. We still have a way to go before dark, so, whenever you're ready . . ."

"It is pretty cold here."

He nods, his chin pressing into the top of my head.

"Okay, enough snow. Let's go."

I pull his hoodie off my shoulders and hand it back. He slips it on, and that fabulous body disappears behind too many layers of brushed cotton. We climb in, and he pulls back onto the road.

"So, where are we going?"

"L'Île-Rousse."

"What's that?"

"You'll see," he says, flicking me a glance as he drives.

It's late afternoon when we wind out of the mountains and into a small costal town. Alessandro navigates the place like he's been here before, and we end up in a sand parking lot across a crumbling road from a shack on the beach. The smell of salt and seaweed seeps into the car even before I open the door.

"Where are we?" I ask as we get out and walk toward the shack.

"L'Île-Rousse."

"Okay, but . . . where are we?"

"This," he says, pointing at the beach, "is the north end of the island. About a 150 kilometers that way is mainland France."

I look out over the endless water. "I wish I had time to see more. I'd love to go to France."

He flicks me a glance and twitches a smile. "You *are* in France." He opens the door and gestures me through ahead of him.

The shack, it turns out, is a very small and nearly abandoned restaurant. The smell of salt from the sea mingles with cigarette smoke and frying food. Behind a decrepit wooded bar that takes up the entire back wall, a bartender gestures with a tip of his enormous head that we should seat ourselves. Alessandro directs me past the only other patrons, two guys sitting at the bar arguing loudly in French, to a small table for two near the windows over the beach.

"This is . . . interesting," I say, looking around at the weather-beaten wood walls and salt-stained wooden floor.

"My favorite restaurant," he answers.

The bartender comes over and says something in French, and Alessandro picks up a laminated piece of paper off the table and says something back in French. The bartender stalks back to the bar, and a few minutes later returns with a bottle of red wine and two smudged glasses.

Alessandro looks at me as the bartender pours. "I should have asked if you like seafood."

"I love it."

He lifts an eyebrow. "Do you mind if I order for you? There are some excellent choices."

"If it saves me having to read a French menu, then I'm all over that."

He smiles and looks up at the bartender, reeling off a list of things.

"So, you're fluent in Italian and French. Did you ever take classes, or was that just from living here?" I ask once he's gone.

Alessandro sips his wine before answering. "I didn't learn French until I came to live here as a teen, but Italian is my first language. We lived in Italy when I was young, and even after we moved to New York, my father spoke only Italian to us."

"He was Italian?"

He nods. "By heritage. His parents moved to New York before he was born, but he grew up speaking Italian in the home."

"So . . . if he's an American from New York, how did you live in Italy when you were young?"

He sets his glass down and runs a finger over the rim. "My father was an Army cook. My parents met when he was stationed at the US air base in Aviano." He looks up at me. "In Italy, not too far from Florence."

I nod.

"He came to Corsica on leave with some friends and happened to stumble into the restaurant where my mother cooked." A wistful smile curves his lips. "The story goes, they got in a huge fight when my father sent something back because it wasn't prepared correctly, and two months later, they were married. Lorenzo and I were born in Italy. I was six, and he was seven when my father left the military and took his family back to New York."

"That's some love story."

He bobs a small nod. "My parents *were* in love. Deeply in love."

"I can't even imagine what it would have been like to lose him that way."

His eyes lower to his wineglass, and he watches his finger trace the rim. "She's never been the same."

"You said you're still American, right?"

He nods.

"Could you have changed when you moved here? Become a French citizen?"

"I could have. For a long time, I thought I would."

"Why didn't you?"

His jaw tightens. "Because my citizenship reminds me of my path, my purpose. My father was American. What happened to him . . . the reason he died, it was because of that. He's the reason I ended up where I am—he and my mother."

I've been trying to make sense of what his mother said to me before we left and what he just said strikes something in that process. "Does your mom want you to become a priest?"

He lifts a hand and scratches the back of his head, grasping a handful of hair. "My mother believes I'm doing this out of guilt. She thinks I blame myself for what happened to her."

"Do you?"

He opens his mouth, then closes it again, and for a long time, he doesn't answer. "I've lost my entire family," he finally says.

"Alessandro, you can't blame yourself for—"

"I understand that I'm not responsible for my father's death," he interrupts, his jaw tight, "but could I have helped my mother? My brother?" He shakes his head slowly, resting his elbows on the table. "I didn't try."

"So this is what you think you have to do to make up for it? Become a priest?"

"I prayed for direction, and this is what the Lord showed me. This community." He gestures out the window. "If I can do for one child what Father Costa did for me . . . if I can make one person see that they're important, it will mean my life wasn't wasted. I can help people here. This is where I hope they send me."

I nod at his determination. He knows what he wants. That's more than a lot of people can say, including me. I sip my wine, and when I look up, I find him staring at me. I don't break his gaze. He reaches across and weaves his fingers into mine, and we sit, looking at each other as, outside the window, the sun sets crimson across the water.

IT'S THE MIDDLE of the night, but I'm mostly awake, watching shadows crawl across the ceiling. Alessandro and I sat at that restaurant for hours, eating course after course and talking. He told me about his favorite memories with his father and things they did together as a family. I told him about the plan I was starting to hatch to stay in Italy for at least another year. He asked if I'd consider Corsica—said if he was here, he could put me to work with the children of his parish.

More and more, the thought of working with children is really starting to appeal to me. My passion has always been art, but when you put art and kids together, they both seem to come alive. And so do I. Could I stay here? Work with Alessandro?

The conversations are still whirring through my head when I hear creaking on the stairs outside my room. I'm the only one up here, and I pull the sheets around me, afraid maybe Pépé is sleepwalking.

When the door cracks open, there's a shape in the dark stairwell. Whoever it is doesn't move for what feels like a small eternity. Finally, I sit up in bed. "Who's there?" I ask in a slightly shaky voice. Still, there's no answer.

But then Alessandro steps through into the moonlight, and suddenly I'm shaking more.

Chapter Twenty

I SIT BACK against the headboard and stare at Alessandro as he steps into the dark room.

"I'm sorry. Did I wake you?" he asks softly, closing the door behind him.

"No. I couldn't sleep."

"Neither could I."

For a long time, we just stare at each other from opposite sides of the room.

"I don't really know why I'm up here," he finally says, looking down at his fingers, which are busy fidgeting with the hem of his T-shirt. "I just felt . . . drawn."

He looks up at me with a question in his eyes, and I scoot over to make room for him on the edge of the bed, both hoping and fearing that he'll take the invitation. "It's okay. I feel bad that I'm in your bed, and you're stuck on the couch."

His eyes drop to the bed, then brush over my sleep

shirt, which I now realize has one too many buttons open
to pass for demure. He breathes deep as his eyes make
their way back to my face, and finally, he comes and sits
next to me. "It's no hardship."

I grasp his hand. "I'm so glad you brought me here.
This has been a really amazing few days. I'm just sorry we
have to go back tomorrow."

He lifts a hand and brushes his fingertips along the
line of my jaw. He lifts it higher and traces my eyebrow
and down my nose with is index finger. "You are truly
exceptional, Lexie Banks."

For a long time, he holds my face and stares into my
eyes. My breathing is ragged, but I don't dare move for
fear of breaking the spell. He leans closer, and my heart
pounds so loudly I'm sure he can hear it, but I still don't
move. His lips brush my down cheek and along my jaw-
line. "You make me question myself . . . my choices," he
says, low in my ear.

I want to turn my head so our lips touch. I want to
pull him to me and feel that warm, hard body against
mine, but I still don't move. "I'm sorry."

His fingers scoop around my neck and thread into my
hair, and when his lips press into mine I can't breathe.
His kiss is soft, so gentle, but I feel it ignite a slow burn
in my belly and curl my toes. His lips leave mine after a
minute, but he stays close, his hand still in my hair, his
breath on my face. "You confuse me, Lexie, more than
anyone has in a long time."

"I'm sorry," I whisper again, then his lips are on mine,
more insistent, pressing deeper into me. I part mine, in-

viting him in, and his tongue slips through and swirls with mine. Our breathing becomes heavier, and the ache in my groin grows until I throb for him.

But I still don't dare move.

Finally, he pulls away. He looks at me a long minute with eyes that burn in the dark, then stands and disappears back into the stairwell without another word.

I STEP OUT of the taxi onto the sidewalk, having defied death once again. Alessandro bangs the trunk, and the driver pops it open. He grabs my bag and carries it to my door.

"I trust you'll be okay from here?"

"Yeah . . . I'll be fine, unless . . . do you want to come up? We could get some dinner and—"

"I don't think that's a good idea, Lexie." That look is back in his eyes, and I long to grab him and kiss him again.

He saves me the trouble.

His arms slip around my waist and he pulls me against his body, crushing his lips to mine. I've been waiting for this—hoping for this since his visit to my bedroom last night, but he's been so careful to keep his distance.

His tongue edges my mouth, and I open wide, pulling him deeper into me. I lose myself in the feel of his body, his warm musk that envelops me, the desperation in his kiss, and my body responds. An ache grows in my heart and my belly. I want this man so badly.

The horn blast shakes me out of my shoes, and my

heart first leaps with the start, then sinks as Alessandro pulls away from me.

"Will you come up?" I ask, breathy but bolder.

He closes his eyes, and his lips press into a line as he fights with himself. "I can't," he finally says before opening them. He steps back and looks at me. "I have to go. I'm sorry."

The next second, he's in the cab, and it's rocketing away.

"What am I doing?" I ask myself out loud.

I hear a clucking noise as I slip my key in the door, and when I turn and look up at the balcony across the street, Grandma Moses is leaning on the rail, tsking me.

I drag my suitcase up the stairs and into my apartment, then pace circles in the small space between the dining-room table and the door, my hands fisted in my hair. "What am I doing?" I ask again.

I plop down in the love seat and pull out my cell phone. It's three in the afternoon, so . . . eight, seven, six . . . it's six in the morning back home. I should wait.

I can't wait.

I dial Trent, sure he's not going to pick up.

He does.

"Hey. What's up?" His voice is full of sleep, blurry and slurred.

"I'm sorry to wake you."

He clears his throat, and I hear sheets rustling. "No, don't be. I'm always awake for you." He's trying really hard to sound awake, so I won't feel bad, I'm sure. Just one more reason I love him.

"I think I might have feelings for Alessandro," I blurt.

"But . . ." throat clear, "you said he's a priest, right?"

"Not yet." I grab a fistful of my hair. "God, Trent. I'm so confused. I don't know what I'm thinking." I'm still in love with Trent. I know that by the way my heart squeezes as I tell him this. But, am I falling in love with Alessandro too? Is it possible to love two men? And Trent and I have an agreement. Our friendship and family are too valuable to risk by following through on my feelings. "We just spent three amazing days together at his family's place in Corsica."

"Wow . . . meeting the family is a big step."

"I know, and it felt like a big deal, you know. I mean, he went out of his way to take me to his favorite places. It's just . . . he's supposed to be ordained in six weeks."

"So, other than taking you to meet his family, has he said anything, you know, about being into you?"

"He's about to become a priest, for God's sake. He's supposed to be into *God*!"

"I get that. I do," he says in that voice that can calm me down even when I'm on the edge of a panic attack. "But has he given you any signals that he might be thinking about walking away?"

"From the Church?"

"Yeah. I mean, if he hasn't been ordained, isn't there still time to change his mind?"

I shake my head, even though he can't see it. "He said he's been called by the bishop and taken his vow of celibacy already."

"And is he?"

"What?"

"Celibate?" he asks with a little bit of an edge. "Have you . . . you know?"

"God, no!"

"Chill, Lexie. I'm just trying to get the lay of the land here. Has he made any kind of move?"

I cringe as I say, "He kissed me."

"On the cheek? On the mouth? Where?"

"On the mouth. French. Twice."

I hear him breathe in and out. For a long second, he doesn't say anything. "You know what you feel, Lexie. I can't tell you that. You know what you feel, and you know if this guy has what it takes to make you happy. I guess you need to decide if that's what you want, and if it is, I think you have to tell him before it's too late. I think you have to go for it. You'll regret it for the rest of your life if you really love him, and you don't at least try, you know?" His voice changes as he says it, the normal vigor vanishing. I can tell he means what he's saying, but he sounds so . . . sad.

"What's wrong?" I ask after a second.

"What do you mean?"

"You just sound . . . did you and Sam fight or something?"

I hear him blow out a sigh. "Lexie . . ."

I wait, but he doesn't finish the thought. I wish so badly I was there with Trent. I want to curl into his arms, where everything is always all right. "I miss you so much," I tell him, and my voice warbles with tears.

There's another long pause. "I miss you too."

My phone beeps in my ear—another incoming call. I look at the screen and my stomach kicks. I breathe deep and stick the phone back to my ear. "I have to go, Trent. But I'll call later?"

"Yeah . . . okay. Love you," he says.

"Love you too," I say back, then click over to Alessandro, my heart pounding in my throat. "Hi."

There's nothing but silence for a long second, and I'm sure I wasn't fast enough picking up and he disconnected. But then he says, "I need to pray, Lexie. I need time away from you to pray for direction."

The bottom drops out of my stomach, and I feel suddenly hollow. "I . . . okay . . . whatever you need."

"Thank you for understanding."

My phone beeps as he disconnects.

So, that's that.

IT'S BEEN THREE weeks since Corsica. In those three weeks, I've seen Alessandro exactly twice. Two weeks ago, for our school tour, and today, for our school tour—which is our last one. After today, he never has to see me again if he chooses.

But that's the problem. He can't choose. I see him struggling. I can see the pain in his eyes every time he looks at me, and I hate that I've done this to him.

We finish the tour in St. Peter's, same as usual, and I turn to follow the students out, but he grabs my arm. "Walk with me." He spins and moves toward the exit, staring straight ahead, and I keep stride.

He's back in his white collar, every inch the soon-to-be-priest, but I see him tugging at it as we walk. It's a beautiful spring day as we step into St. Peter's Square. He takes a left at the sidewalk and moves briskly up the cobbled road until the crowds start to thin. When we're about a block from the Vatican, he turns between two buildings down a narrow alleyway that I didn't even see, then grasps my arms and spins me into an alcove, pressing me against the brick wall.

The next second, he's kissing me. His tongue stabs between my lips, taking possession of my mouth. There's anger and fear and pure need in his kiss, and the roughness of it stirs some animal instinct deep inside me. The length of his firm body pinning me and grinding against mine sends electric currents surging under my skin, and the feel of his erection against my stomach—knowing how much he wants me—makes me want him even more. The muscles in my groin tighten, and a pulsing ache builds in my belly.

His breathing is ragged and his expression agonized when he pulls away a long minute later. "I don't know what the Lord is calling me to do. I thought He wanted me in His service, but . . ." He hangs his head. "I can't stop thinking about you. I've prayed for guidance, and what He keeps showing me is your face." He tips his face to the sky. "I've lost my path."

I collect myself and gently push him back, making more space between us. Every fiber in my body protests, but no matter how much I might want him, he still belongs to the Church. "I can't help you find it, Alessandro.

You're going to have to do that for yourself. What I can tell you is that the Lord sure as hell isn't showing you me. There is nothing godly about me."

His anguished gaze lowers to mine. "I don't know what to do."

I lower my lashes and breathe deep. I won't be able to say this if I'm looking at his beautiful, tortured face. "When you figure it out, you know where to find me."

ABBY AND I wend through the street vendors' brightly colored wares in Piazza Campo Dè Fiori. I've already picked out a pair of earrings for both Katie and Sam, a scarf and a beaded necklace for Julie, a handmade leather wallet for Dad, and a carved wooden guitar pick and few T-shirts for Trent.

It's a Wednesday afternoon, which tends to be quieter than the weekends, but it's spring, so everyone is flocking into the streets again, and tourism is picking back up for the summer. I catch myself smiling when I realize I can pick out the Americans without even hearing them speak. Our sense of style pretty much blows compared to the Italians.

But we're only a block and a half from the rectory. This is the first place Alessandro ever brought me shopping. He said it was the best open-air market in the city and the best place to buy produce.

As we weave our way along the cobbles past the souvenir vendors on the right and the brightly colored and very fragrant floral vendors' tents on the left, every time someone in black passes by, my eyes catch on them until I'm sure it's not Alessandro. It's been two and a half weeks since I left him standing in that alley, and I've heard nothing. His ordination is on Sunday. That's only four days from now. Four days.

That's how long I have to say something.

You'll regret it for the rest of your life if you really love him, and you don't at least try, you know?

Trent's words echo in my head, and my heart squeezes tight. Do I love Alessandro? If I do, can I let him do this without ever telling him?

"These are brill," Abby says, pulling my thoughts back to the crowded piazza. She's running a finger down a row of braided leather bracelets hanging from a cord at a leather vendor's booth. The vendor, an old gray-haired man with gnarled hands, comes over, and she points to one. He pulls it off the cord and hands it to her. She ties it around my wrist. "Do you love it?"

The thick braid of the multiple leather lashes is softer than I thought it'd be. Even though it's in muted tones, it's somehow still eye-catching. I smile up at her. "I do."

She motions for the vendor to pull off another one, then hands it to me, and I tie it on her wrist. She pays the vendor, and we wander toward the next booth. "Have you ever been to England?" she asks, spinning her bracelet and admiring it.

"No."

"You should come for holiday." She grins. "I could get you into so much trouble there."

I grin back. "I have no doubt." As much as I hate to

admit it, I'm really going to miss Abby when I leave. "What's going to happen with Grant?" I ask. He's basically moved into her flat this semester, and she seems really happy. But she's kicked him out every Sunday for our movie marathons.

"He wants to try to keep it going," she says. And there's that smile. Every time she talks about him, it's like she turns into a whole different person. All her typical lewdness melts away, and she becomes this blushing schoolgirl.

"And what do you want?"

Her feet stop, and she looks at me. "I really love the bloke, you know? The thought of going home is bad enough, but without him . . ." Her eyes gleam as her face pinches against tears.

We've talked some during our movie marathons, and I get that home isn't a really happy place for her. I guess there's stuff with her mother and a chain of questionable boyfriends (on both their parts). Even though I have my own issues with going home, it's not because no one loves me. I can't imagine how hard it would be to go home from *this,* where she seems truly happy and has finally found love, to something like that.

I loop my arm around her shoulders and tug her off toward the café on the corner. "Let's get something to eat."

I let Abby have a few more beers than I probably should have, and she was pretty drunk when I left her in

Grant's arms at her apartment. He was so gentle with her as he took her from me and guided her inside. He swept her hair back and kissed her cheek, then promised me he'd take care of her.

I believe he will.

It's after dark when I leave there and, just my luck, it starts to rain in the three blocks between Abby's apartment and mine. I duck my head and run, and plow right into an amorous couple from the bar next door who are going at it in the alcove of my doorway. I shoo them away and head inside. When I get upstairs, I pull my hair out of the clip that was holding it off my face and towel dry it, then change out of my wet clothes into my comfy hoodie and jeans to study. I settle into my love seat with a cup of tea and my laptop and start pecking out an outline for my final paper in my Ancient Rome and Its Monuments class, which is probably my least favorite of everything I took here this year.

My door buzzer shakes me from my concentration and I shove my laptop off and stand, irritated. If that couple doesn't find another spot, I'm going to strangle them.

The buzzer sounds again, long and loud, before I'm even to my door. I rip it open and lope down the stairs, and when I yank open the door to the street, Alessandro is standing in the rain in his clerical shirt and slacks, his white collar slightly askew.

"I am a sinner and I am weak," he says. Before I can say a word, he scoops me into his arms and buries his face in the crown of my hair. "Why can't I stop wanting you?"

I freeze at Trent's words coming out of Alessandro's mouth, and my heart skips up into my throat. After a long minute, when I can finally move, I pull him through the door and up the stairs into my apartment. I lead him around the corner to my love seat, where I move my laptop to the floor so we can sit.

He leans his elbows on his knees and rests his forehead in one hand as if it hurts. His other hand fists hard into the fabric of his clerical slacks. "You walked into my life, and from the first moment I laid eyes on you, you made me feel things I'd thought I'd suppressed—primal urges that needed to be satisfied. At first, I thought you were sent by the Lord to test my devotion." His tormented gaze lifts to mine. "I thought you were my final temptation, and that, if I was strong enough to resist you, I was worthy of serving the Lord." He breathes deep and stands, pacing to the window and looking out at the drizzle falling on my patio. "I have prayed every day for direction, and every day, He brings me closer to you. What He's shown me is that my devotion to Him is not stronger than your hold on me. I'm not strong enough to serve Him faithfully. I think about you and I dream about you and . . ." He lays a palm on the window and leans his forehead into his hand. "I want you every waking minute."

My stomach pulls into a hard knot, and my lungs have turned into bricks. I can't breathe. "You *are* strong, Alessandro. After everything you've been through, I know you are," I finally manage.

He lifts his head and looks at me with tortured eyes. "Do you feel anything for me?"

Now, my knotted insides tingle. I definitely have feelings for him. I can feel them right now: a tightening in my groin at the thought of where this might be headed. If I'm honest, I've wanted him since I met him. Do I tell him the truth and be responsible for possibly ruining his life? Or do I lie? I stand, and my fingers fiddle mindlessly with the zipper of my hoodie. "You are extremely attractive. You must already know that."

He breathes deep and winces as his eyes close. "But beyond the lust? Is there anything deeper?"

I can't speak. Everything in me is totally at odds. He's such a beautiful man. From the very beginning, he's made me a little weak in the knees. But he is four days away from becoming a priest. He's taken a vow of celibacy and pledged himself to the Church.

As if he read my mind, he untucks his white collar, ripping it off and throwing it to the floor. He takes me into his arms again, more possessively this time. "I've fallen hopelessly in love with you, Lexie. I finally realize I desperately want this," he says, his hand gliding down my arm. "I want a wife . . . a family. I know you're in love with your stepbrother, and I'm aware I am not him, but . . . could you be happy with someone like me?"

"I . . ." How do I answer that? Do I love him? My heart aches, but is it aching for him? What I feel for him is intense attraction. He's kind and sophisticated and charming, with a quiet confidence that makes him so goddamn sexy. There's no doubt I want him . . . badly . . . but do I love him? "You are a remarkable man, Alessandro. How am I supposed to resist you when you say things like this to me?"

He presses a kiss to my lips. At first, his kiss is slow and gentle, but as our bodies press harder together, and the friction builds, it becomes deeper and more insistent. Our tongues swirl together in an attempt to somehow blend into one. My pulse pounds through my body so hard that I vibrate with it. After long enough that my lips are swollen, he nips at my lower lip and looks at me with feral eyes, like a starving animal. "If you'll have me, I want nothing more than to be your lover."

This time it's me who initiates the kiss, because I pretty much want to climb right into him. I press up on my tiptoes and pull him down to me. His fingers twist into my hair as the other hand glides down my back and pulls me into the curve of his body.

And, God, this feels good.

I feel like I've slipped into one of my dreams. It's a surreal feeling, because I know this is something that could never be happening in real life.

But it is.

And in case there was any lingering question this is real, it's answered definitively when I feel his erection against my stomach through his black cleric's slacks.

Chapter Twenty-One

FEELING HIS AROUSAL—knowing how much he wants me—starts a slow burn under my skin. As we kiss, I shuffle us past the front door toward my bedroom, and as we inch across the floor, I start on the buttons of his black shirt. I go slowly at first, but before I'm done, I'm tearing at them in frustration. Finally, I give up on the last few and yank his shirt over his head. He grasps the zipper of my hoodie and pulls it down, then slips it off my shoulders. We've only made it as far as the dining-room table when I realize we've stopped moving, too wrapped up in what's happening between us to care where we are.

"You're sure this is what you want?" I ask, and I hear the shake in my voice.

"I've never wanted anything as much as I want you," he replies breathily, his fingertips brushing over my nipple through my bra.

I want this too, don't I? I need to get past Trent. He's moved on with Sam. I know I need to do the same.

As Alessandro leans in to kiss me, and his hand slips behind me and unclasps my bra, I know he's the one person who might be able to help me forget. My bra slides down my arms, and his hands cup the fullness of my breasts, one in each palm. He kisses me harder as his thumbs rub circles over my nipples, and they tighten to rock-hard nubs.

I tip my head back to catch my breath, and his lips glide past the sensitive spot behind my ear, to the hollow of my throat, and down my collarbone. I lean back onto the dining-room table, the closest support I can find, when he takes my right breast into his mouth and sucks.

His teeth and tongue tease my nipple as his hand glides down my ribs and over my hip to the button of my jeans. He pops it open and slides them down. I kick them off, and his fingers trace circles on the sensitive skin at waistband of my thong. I lift one leg and wrap it around him, making room for his hand to slip between my legs. He takes the cue. His long fingers stroke over my thong and he moans into my breast when he feels how wet I am.

His moan shakes me from my lust-induced daze, and I lift his face with a hand. "We can't, Alessandro," I breathe. "You can't."

He stares into my eyes and doesn't even hesitate. "I've made my decision."

His mouth finds mine, and he crushes me in a kiss. My skin burns as his fingertip traces the edge of my thong. "It's been a while since I . . ." He closes his eyes and breathes deep as his hand glides under the elastic onto my tender bare skin.

I can't reconcile the electric excitement dancing through my belly with the heavy dread in my chest. The thought of making love with Alessandro ignites fireworks under my skin and sends lava pumping through my veins with every beat of my racing heart.

But if we do this, it will change everything.

He's giving up everything he's worked for—everything he believes in. And he's doing it for me. Am I ready for that responsibility? Do I want that kind of sacrifice on my conscience?

And Trent.

God, Trent.

I haven't even sorted out what I feel for him. Is it fair that Alessandro should give everything up for this if I can't commit to him? He said he loved me, but do I love him?

He inches my thong over my hips, and it drops to the floor with my jeans as he lifts me onto the edge of the table. I'm naked, on total display for him. He just stares for a long minute. "Lexie," he finally says. "You are one of God's truly spectacular creations."

He lays me back on the table, and his fingertips trail over my breasts, setting my skin on fire. I watch his face as his hands move over me, exploring and setting every nerve ending pulsating with want. They glide over my stomach to my hips and loop under my knees. He lifts them and spreads my legs, then watches his finger trail over the tuft of hair and brush my clit. He's rewarded with a tightening of all the muscles below my waist and my low moan. I wrap my legs around his cut torso and pull him against me. His eyes close for the briefest of seconds, then he opens them and watches his fingers slide inside me. I squirm on the table with his touch, and I can't help rocking my hips with the motion of his hand as his fingers glide in and out.

And the whole time he watches, his gaze flickering from his hand between my legs to my face, which I know is flushed by the way it burns.

"I need to taste you, Lexie," he says, crooking a finger inside me. "Can I kiss you here?"

"God, yes," I moan.

I don't even have time to think about my poor choice of words before his mouth is on me. His tongue presses into my clit, and I cry out. I'm fairly certain my actual words are, "Oh, God!" because that's pretty much my MO, but I can't be sure. His fingers slip inside me, and I buck my hips and cry out again when he sucks. His moan totally unhinges me. He licks me as his wet fingers twist inside me, and I arch up and fight to remember how to breathe. His tongue playing over my clit sends sparks skittering over my skin, lighting me on fire. "Holy God!" I groan. He moans, low and deep, really more of a growl, and I prop up on my elbows so I can see him. His feral gaze connects with mine, and he holds my eyes as he swirls his tongue against my clit. I'm right on the edge of exploding into his mouth when he finally pulls away.

He leans over me, and I feel him hard against me

through his pants. Why the hell didn't I rip those things off when I had the chance?

His hands and mouth move over every inch of my body as if they're trying to memorize me. He sucks my hard nipples—first the right, then the left. When his mouth finds mine, I can taste my arousal on his lips: salty and clean. He hesitates and trails a finger over the tattoo above my left breast as he kisses his way to my ear. "Lexie," he breathes, "please tell me you have protection."

I don't. I've used all of Sam's condoms for self-defense. I never expected . . . this. "I'm sorry."

He pulls back and scowls down at the white collar on the floor. "I can't very well walk into a pharmacy and buy condoms."

I close my eyes, and my face pinches involuntarily. "I'm sorry," I say again, and suddenly I realize it's for more than the condoms.

I can't do this.

My fingers go automatically to my tattoo as my heart under it crumbles. I love Trent. I will always love Trent. I can't deny it, or hide from it, or pretend what happened between us didn't matter. It did matter, and I can't be with anyone else. I can't have sex with Alessandro when I know what it feels like to make love to Trent.

I push Alessandro back and sit up, suddenly uber-conscious that I'm totally naked on my dining-room table with a half-dressed almost-priest hovering over me, his huge erection straining the fabric of his slacks.

"I'm sorry, Alessandro. I can't do this."

I slip off the table and disappear behind my bedroom

door before he even has time to react. I'm afraid he'll knock or call to me through the door.

He doesn't.

A few minutes later, I'm still pressed against the door, holding my breath, when I hear my front door open, then click closed. I hear him on the stairs and hurry to my window. I watch as Alessandro pushes through the door to the street with his head down and strides quickly toward the corner. When he turns and flashes a glance over his shoulder toward my apartment, I catch a glimpse of his starched white collar, snugly in place, before he vanishes onto the main road.

I lean out the window a little farther, still watching after him. A little part of me hopes he'll come back . . . that he'll fight for me. He doesn't, and when I back away from the window and look up, Grandma Moses is watching me from her balcony.

She glances to the corner where Alessandro just disappeared, then back at me, and her clucking sound carries across the street, echoing off the buildings for the whole city to hear as she tsks me. And that's when I realize I'm still buck naked.

On Thursday, I text Abby and tell her I'm sick, so I won't be in class. After class, she texts me my assignments.

On Friday, I text Abby and tell her I'm still sick, so I won't be in class. After class, she texts me my assignments for Monday.

And then it's finally Saturday.

I do the same thing I did on Thursday and Friday. I pull the sheet over my head and pretend my bed is a coffin. Pretending to be dead is a lot easier than living with what I've done.

Alessandro hasn't called. His ordination is tomorrow, at Easter observance. I so want to talk to him . . . to know what he's thinking. He's one of the most incredible people I've ever met, and I'm afraid I just ruined his life.

What if I ruined his life?

I'm terrified to find out, so I don't call him either.

But there is one thing I know for sure. I couldn't be with Alessandro because I'm totally, one hundred percent in love with Trent. So, even though I can't find the nerve to follow up with Alessandro, I finally get up the nerve to send a text I should have sent months ago. I pick up my phone and start typing from memory the speech I'd rehearsed so many times before Christmas.

I'm taking my best friend's advice and telling the man I love how I feel about him. I'm in love with you, Trent. I think I may have always loved you. The way fate brought us together was sort of cruel, but maybe when fate gets its chance, it has to take it. Maybe your becoming my brother was the only way fate could guarantee we'd find each other. All I know is, if there's one person in this world that I was meant to meet and fall in love with, it's you. You are my soul mate. You always have been. When we're apart, it's like a vital piece of me is missing. I can survive without you, but I can't live. I can't be fully alive. I love you with every fiber in my body. I love you with my whole heart. No matter what happens between us from here, I just thought you should know.

I don't even read it over before hitting SEND, afraid that if I do, I'll chicken out.

A minute later, my phone buzzes, and my heart stalls. I cringe, scared to flipped it over and look at the screen. The way I see it, this can only go one of two ways. It's either Trent telling me he loves me too, or telling me that I'm delusional. I mean, when your stepsister confesses her undying love, there's not much middle ground.

I turn the phone slowly in my hand, still cringing, and looking at the screen through slitted eyes. Maybe if I only partially see it, it won't bite so hard. But when I see who it's from, my heart stalls again.

Sam.

Shit.

Was she with him when I sent that? I remember going through Rick's texts when he got out of bed to go to the bathroom. Are they in bed together? Is Trent in the bathroom peeling off his condom?

Stop. Just stop.

I can drive myself crazy wondering, or I can open the damn text. I open the damn text.

Hey gurl! Do you know if Trent likes the beach or the mountains better? Booking a romantic getaway for when we get home for break.

They're not together. But, *shit.*

It's as if she knows I just told her boyfriend I love him. This is her way of making me feel like the girls in Rick's texts—the ones who are just skanky enough to go after someone else's man. That's me, Lexie the skank.

Damn.

I don't answer. I can't.

So: Trent, Alessandro, Sam . . . I'm running out of friends to totally alienate and humiliate. I'm going to die without a friend in this world, then burn in hell for all eternity. Just what I deserve.

Chapter Twenty-Two

I ALMOST WENT to Easter Mass to find out what Alessandro decided, but then I realized that, if he decided to go through with the ordination, the last person he'd want to see there would be me.

But I can't stand not knowing.

It's Tuesday, and the hordes of summer tourists haven't descended on Rome yet, so navigating the streets to the rectory is pretty quick. My feet stall, and my insides quiver harder when it comes into sight, just across from the church where everything started.

I know what I need to tell him if he's there. I need to apologize for leading him on and making him question everything he believes in. I need to tell him it was horrible and selfish, and I hope he can forgive me someday. I need him to know that I was serious when I told him he would make an amazing priest. He has all the qualities of someone who can truly make a difference in this world.

Part of me hopes I get the chance to tell him all this, while another part of me hopes I don't.

I'm shaking as I lift my hand to knock, and a few seconds later, when the door swings open, I'm wound so tight that I nearly jump out of my skin. But it's not Alessandro. Standing there in the doorway is a very round man with a round nose and big, round, blue eyes in the middle of a round face. He's in a full cassock and white collar.

"Can I be of assistance?" he asks with a wide smile, and instantly I recognize the sandpaper voice of Father Reynolds.

I'm afraid to speak, knowing the minute I open my mouth, he'll have a face to go with everything I've confessed. "I'm . . . I'm looking for the Reverend Moretti."

"Ah," he says, and I can tell from the way his eyes change, widen a little, and shine brighter, that he knows who I am. "I'm sorry, but the reverend is no longer at this parish."

"Oh . . . did he—" I'm about to ask if he was ordained on Sunday when I really hear what he just said. He called Alessandro the *reverend*. My stomach knots harder. He didn't go through with it. "Do you know where he went?"

"He needed some more time for reflection. He asked to return to Corsica, to his family parish under Father Costa."

"Father Costa," I repeat with a nod. "Okay . . . good." He went home. This is good. Maybe he'll regroup there. Maybe he'll be okay. "Well, thank you, Father."

"God be with you," he says.

"And also with you." I back away from the rectory and move across the street to the church.

This whole experience has been sobering. The church is Alessandro's conviction. He's pledged his life to it, and now that he's questioning that .... maybe because of me, it makes me realize how little I've truly taken any of it to heart. Isn't the upshot of all this just to be a better person? If I'd tried to be a better person—to live by Alessandro's ideals—would any of this have happened?

I dip my fingers in the holy water and cross myself, then make my way to a pew up front and kneel. The place is nearly empty, a few tourists wandering the frescoes and no one else. The confessionals are roped off today.

I stare up at Jesus on the cross and breathe deep. "Dear Lord, please look after Alessandro. He's a good man. Please help him to find his path again, whatever it is. Please let him find happiness." I bow my head and close my eyes as a tear leaks over my lashes. "More than anyone else I know, he deserves to be happy."

I wipe my face and pull myself up, then turn for home. And the whole way, I picture Alessandro in the restaurant on the beach at L'Île-Rousse. I imagine him looking out over the ocean and remembering why he wanted to be a priest in the first place. I picture him forgetting I ever existed. I can't deny there's a pang in my heart at the thought, but I also know that's what needs to happen.

I feel a little lighter as I walk home, and for the first time in days, food is tempting. I stop at a café and pick up a few currant croissants, one of which I nibble as I stroll over the cobbles. A taxi careens past, and I jump onto the sidewalk to avoid becoming roadkill, but as I watch it go, I can't help remembering my introduction to Rome, in the back of a different careening taxi. That feels like a lifetime ago. I'm really going to miss this place when I leave. Now, I just have to decide when that's going to be.

I got the internship. I found out yesterday. It's what I wanted more than anything, but now I'm not sure what to do. Because of Alessandro, I know I want to work with children. I want that kid-at-Christmas feeling every day. I want to work somewhere I can bring kids and art together. I want to make art fun for them. I want them to love art as much as I do. Nothing else I can imagine would be as awesome as helping build a collection at a children's museum so that kids find art in a way that matters to them. This internship would be great on my resume—give me a leg up.

But without Alessandro, Rome feels a little emptier.

I didn't realize until now how much my desire to stay in Rome was tied to him. I'm not sure my heart is really up for being here for three more months without him. I have a week to decide if I'm going to accept the internship. But if I don't, that means I'm going home.

It's been three days since I sent the text to Trent. Three days that I've been stalking my phone, waiting for something. Anything. A text. A call. So far nothing. I don't want to believe he's so mad or so shocked that, even after I poured my heart out to him, he can't bring himself to respond, but that seems to be the case. Which means I'll probably stay for the internship because I can't go home. Not now.

I can't go home.

The thought sits like a cold stone in my stomach.

When I turn the corner for my apartment, I'm too preoccupied to notice the scooter parked outside my front door. But when I realize it's parked illegally on the sidewalk, I look at the bar to see if it's open early. I catch sight of a foot tapping on the sidewalk in the alcove of my doorway, and my breath catches in my throat.

Because I know that boot.

I round the corner and peer in, not daring to let myself believe it until I see him sitting there.

Trent is leaning back into my door in a black T-shirt and faded jeans, looking every inch as beautiful as he does every night in my dreams. He stands slowly when he sees me, and tugs the earbuds out of his ears, draping the cord around his neck, but he doesn't move closer. The skin around his eyes tightens as he squints a question at me. "I got your text."

I hear Lifehouse's "All In" drifting faintly from Trent's earbuds, and my heart kicks hard in my chest. Is he going all in? Is that why he came? "What are you doing here?" I breathe.

He shrugs and gives me that lazy smile that's always turned me to mush. "I was hoping that was obvious."

My thoughts and feelings are a chaotic jumble that I can't make heads or tails of, but the one emotion that is easily distinguishable in the raging torrent is relief. An involuntary whimper leaves my chest, and I choke back the relieved sob that accompanies it. Trent steps forward and folds me into his arms.

There's no stopping it, the urge to be close to him. I press up on my tiptoes, looping my hand around his neck, and bring him down to kiss me. His kiss is slow and sure, and only now do I realize how much I've longed for it. I was trying to find a substitute in Alessandro—a substitute confidant, a substitute lover, a substitute best friend. But the only person who could ever be all those things is standing right here in front of me.

We don't break our kiss as Trent shrugs his duffel onto his shoulder, and I rifle through my purse for my key, or when I push him through the door. The stairs are a little trickier, but Trent solves the conundrum by lifting me into his arms. I wrap my legs around his waist, and he carries me up and through the door at the top.

He sets me down and looks around. I answer his un-asked question by grabbing his hand and leading him to the bedroom. Our shirts are on the floor before we even make it there. He pauses just a second to drop his duffel on the floor and grab a condom out of the side pocket, and I take that second to admire his amazing, bare chest, but then we're moving toward the bed. One of my flats comes off with my thong, but my skirt is around my waist and his jeans haven't made it below his thighs when we flop sideways across the bed. A second later, we're making love.

It feels like an eternal itch is finally being scratched. No one else could satisfy that itch. No one but Trent.

He teases me, pressing deep inside of me, then pulling his length back to the tip and stopping.

"Please," I beg, pulling him closer.

He smiles into my shoulder. "Patience is a virtue, Lexie."

I sweep my fingers down his back, drawing him deeper into me. "You know damn well I have no virtue."

He grins and kicks off his jeans, then unzips my skirt and slides over my hips. He situates himself on his knees between my legs and looks down at me with pure hunger in his eyes. With every beat of my racing heart, I throb for him. I reach for him and squeeze, and he closes his eyes and moans. He lifts my hips and presses his length slowly inside me and I hear myself purr a moan, but then he withdraws and rubs his tip over my clit, making me gasp. He thrusts into me again, sending pulsating shock waves through my insides, and I cry out.

He teases me more, rubbing circles over my clit with his fingers until I scream with want. "God, *please.*" It comes out as a whimper, and his smile is wicked. But he gives me what I want. He slides into me, thick and hot, and pumps. Each thrust is a little faster and a little deeper, until I'm howling inhumanly with the sensations flooding through my body.

"Christ, Lexie," he groans, all humor gone from his face. His roaming mouth finds mine, and when I open, his tongue slips through my lips. As he kisses me, he hooks his elbows through my knees and pumps against me, each thrust sending a fresh shock wave through my insides.

I cry out, one long "Ahhhh," as the electric tingle in my belly ramps up, and all the muscles in my groin contract around him, holding on, begging for more. Pleasure pulses through me on waves of bliss as the tension builds, and he brings me to climax. I explode around him, over and over, until all coherent thought leaves me, and I dissolve into nothing but sensation. Every touch sets off sparks under my skin, every moan boils my blood, every thrust sends my body into a spin. We're both slick with sweat half an hour later, when he growls with his last thrust and goes still, deadweight on top of me.

But the instant it's over, the guilt hits me like a tidal wave.

As soon as my body stops shaking enough that I have control over it again, I dump him on the mattress and sit on the edge of the bed. My guts tighten into a hard knot when I think about Dad and Julie. I want this more than anything, but how? "What are we doing, Trent?"

He breathes out a long, slow breath and sits next to me. "Listen, Lexie. I'm really sorry I led with sex because that's not what this is about."

"Then what is it about?"

He lifts my hand off the bed and traces the lines of my palm with a fingertip. "Even before I got your text, I'd been thinking a lot about this, and I don't think it has to be one or the other. I think we can be friends *and* lovers."

I bury my face in my hands. "I want that so much, but I'm scared."

His arms circle me, and he pulls me to his shoulder. "I'm scared too, but the one thing I know is I've never loved anyone the way I love you. This feels like forever to me, Lexie. It really does."

I'm not usually swept away by my emotions, but, all

of a sudden, I can't contain them. It's like everything I've been working so hard to suppress erupts out of me. The love, the lust, the fear, the agony, the shame, come heaving out of my soul on sobs that I can't stop.

"I've got you," Trent whispers into my hair, and at that instant, I know he does. And I know he always will.

When my sobs turn to hiccups, I pull my face out of his chest and look at him. "I love you."

He smiles and reaches for his jeans on the floor.

"What are you going to do?" I ask with a sniffle as he pulls his BlackBerry from his pocket. "Post it on Facebook? Dad and Julie would love that."

He pulls me back into his arms and flips through his menu. "That wasn't in my general plan, no." He pokes at the screen a few times with his thumb, then lays the phone on the bed next to us. "I would do this for you real time, but I was kind of in a hurry and trying to pack light," he says as music starts.

It only takes a chord for me to know the guitar in the recording is Trent. It's a tune I haven't heard before. The vocals start low, and I listen as he sings about the person he trusted with his soul, and now the feeling has swallowed him whole. By the time he works up to the chorus, I already feel tears pressing at the corners of my eyes again.

> You picked me up and helped me heal,
> You taught me what it meant to feel.
> Now I can, now I do, and everything I feel is you.
> I would never do you wrong,
> or let you down or lead you on.

*I can't stop now, I'll come unglued, when everything I
feel is you.*

The tears start in the middle of the last verse, about
how we've had each other's backs for so long, and he
knows it won't be easy but that he's lost without me, and I
feel like home to him. By the time the last chord fades out
and Trent shifts off the bed to fish something out of his
duffel, I'm a weepy mess again.

I reach for him to pull him back to me, only knowing
I need his arms around me, but when I wipe my eyes and
look at him, he's on a knee in front of me with a black
velvet box in his palm. When he opens it, the diamond
catches the fading light and sparkles. It's a simple round
solitaire in a thin white gold band. Not big, but it's the
most beautiful thing I've ever seen.

"I came here today because when you finally realize
you want to spend the rest of your life with somebody,
you want the rest of your life to start as soon as possible,"
he says, nearly quoting the line from *When Harry Met
Sally* that always makes me cry.

I can't speak past the hot, pulsing lump in my throat.

"You never seem to run out of ways to blow my
mind, Lexie. You're my best friend, *and* you're the one
woman I can imagine spending the rest of my life with.
Do you know how lucky that makes me? Marry me.
Please."

When I still can't speak, he draws me off the bed, and
I curl into him where he kneels on the floor.

"Please." He cradles my face in his hands, wiping my

tears with his thumbs. "I miss you so much, and I never want us to be apart again."

"I love you," I whisper.

An unsure smile plays over his perfect lips, and his eyebrow quirks. "Is that a yes?"

I sniffle back tears and nod, and he pulls the ring out of the box and slides it onto my finger.

He showers my face with kisses, and pure, unadulterated joy bubbles out of me in laughter, but then his kisses find my mouth, tender and sweet. His fingers thread into my hair as his lips brush softly over mine.

"I love you, Lexie," he whispers. "I always have."

After a brief pause for an equipment change and to relocate to the bed, he loves me again, and this time it's warm and gentle and so tender that it hurts. My heart sings to the slow rhythm, and I never want the feeling to end. I want to lie in this bed forever as he moves on top of me, inside me, through me. I've never felt closer to anyone than I do right this second. And as he brings me slowly and surely to the sweetest, most intense climax I've ever experienced, I know. We were made for this—for each other. Nothing we could have said or done would have changed it.

After, I lay curled in his embrace, drinking in his spicy scent, his strong, sure arms, his warmth, and all else that is Trent, and we fall asleep. When I wake, it's dark, but in the little bit of moonlight filtering through the window, I see by the sparkle of his beautiful brown eyes that he's awake too.

He kisses my cheek. "Are you happy?"

I moan my affirmative and burrow deeper into his warmth.

He sighs, deep and weary, and I pull my face out of his shoulder and look at him, suddenly worried. "Aren't you?"

He bites his lips between his teeth, and I stop breathing for a second, afraid he's changed his mind. "I am," he finally answers. "I just realized why I've never been happy with anyone else. I've been looking for you in every girl I've ever been with."

The second he says it, I feel like I've been kicked in the stomach. "Oh, shit!"

His eyes spring wide. "What?"

"What about Sam?"

He grimaces. "She's a little pissed at me right now."

"At *you*?" I thought it would be *me* she was furious with.

He tucks a strand of my crazy, just-fucked hair behind my ear. "I told her I'm in love with someone else."

"You didn't tell her it was *me*?"

He shakes his head. "I know we have some things to work out before we go public with this, so, no. Mom and Randy don't even know I'm here. They think I'm spending spring break on campus."

My stomach knots at the thought of what "going public" means. I focus on the smaller picture to keep from launching into a full-on panic attack, and for the moment, the smaller picture is Sam. "You were . . . together, right? So, she probably assumed, you know, that you loved *her*."

He sighs. "That first night, when she came by the

house just after you left, we went out and talked"—his gaze lifts to mine—"mostly about you. I wanted to know if you'd maybe said anything . . . told her you were into someone. We sort of connected, and by Thanksgiving, it was obvious you didn't want anything to do with me, so I was just trying to do what you wanted. I was trying to move on, but . . ." He trails off and scratches the top of his head. "I couldn't."

"Why would you think that I didn't want anything to do with you?"

"Well, let's see . . . maybe it was when you texted me you'd confessed everything and hoped you wouldn't . . . how did you put it . . . burn in hell? Yeah, that was it. And then you never texted me again."

He sounds a little angry, which makes me a little defensive. "I did too!"

"Only an occasional picture, or a line or two in response to my texts. I figured you didn't want to hear from me anymore."

He's right. "I was just . . . seriously confused."

"Well, Sam wasn't. I even told her I was on the rebound, and I didn't see anything serious happening between us, but she didn't care."

"So you slept with her."

"Lexie," he says, lifting his fingers to my face and pulling my gaze back to his, "I never slept with her. I haven't slept with anyone since you."

I shake his hand off my face but hold his gaze. "You went out with her the night you got home for Christmas—left me standing there."

"We agreed that nothing could happen between us before you left. I was just trying to honor that. I thought that's what you wanted."

"But the concert . . . the Hyatt."

"We went to the concert and dinner, but I told her I couldn't stay."

"But she . . . she . . ."

"She wanted more. I know that, and I'm sorry. But I was straight up with her from the beginning . . . well, not about you, but about the fact that there was someone else."

"So, at Christmas, if I'd . . . if I'd gotten up the nerve to tell you I was in love with you, you would have said, 'Okay' and not gone out with Sam?"

His eyes darken, and his voice gets quiet. "I would have made love to you all night long."

My heart aches so hard. "Why didn't you tell me?" I whisper.

"I wasn't sure you wanted to hear it . . . how you'd react. I was scared."

I don't get it. "You've always been so confident with girls. Why were you scared?"

His fingertip traces my eyebrow, and I shiver. "It's easy to be confident when there's nothing to lose. When the stakes are everything . . . you . . . it's a little harder."

Even now, there's something a little unsure in his voice. I pull him closer because I need him to know there's nowhere I'd rather be than right here, in his arms. "I should have said it."

His lips brush my forehead, and I close my eyes and

revel in the feeling of Trent this close. "I wanted to tell you how I felt. I planned it, a whole big speech pretty similar to the text you sent me. But then I couldn't read you. Everything was so awkward, and you seemed weird about being around me. We'd never been like that before, and it nearly killed me." He shrugs. "I chickened out, afraid to make it worse, I guess. And, stupidly, I kind of I hoped you might say something to stop me from going with Sam if you'd changed your mind. Then I'd know what you were thinking. But you didn't."

"I want to hear it."

"What?"

I pull back and look into his sincere chocolate eyes. Butterflies tickle my stomach with the sudden realization this is real. He's really here. He came halfway around the world for me. I thumb the diamond on my finger as the love I have for this amazing man swells and overflows, nearly drowning me. "Your speech. The one you had planned. I want to hear it."

The hint of a smile settles over his gorgeous face. "Wow. Talk about putting a guy on the spot. Okay . . . so . . . it went something like this." He blows out a nervous breath and locks his gaze on mine. "Do you know how lucky we are? I think we found each other too soon in life to recognize what we had, but the truth is, I'll never know anyone as well as I know you, and I'll never love anyone so much. I'm sorry I can't be who you thought I was. I can't be the brother you look up to anymore. Not when all I can think about is being more to you. From the first time I met you, you've affected me like no one else ever has. I don't want to hide it from ourselves or the world anymore. I love you and I want to be with you. Some people might think the stepsister/stepbrother thing is a little warped, but they say the most stable relationships are the ones that are based in friendship. We have that."

He kisses me, and I lose myself for a second, but then I remember all the hurdles we still have and what he said about "going public." "So, what happens now?" I ask, parroting back his words from right after the first time we made love.

His fingers stroke down my back, sending goose bumps over my skin. "First this," he says, rolling on top of me and kissing me again, slow and deep.

I smile up at him as an electric tingle ripples through me. "And second?"

He props himself above me on his elbows. "We need to tell our parents."

"What do we say? 'Hey guys, guess what! Trent and I have secretly been sleeping together for months.'"

He brushes my hair off my shoulder and kisses my neck. "I can't speak for you, but I'm going to tell them how I feel. I'm going to tell them I'm in love with you."

I trace my fingertip along the lines of the tattoo over his heart and press my palm into it, feeling his heartbeat. It's slow and steady and calm, and I realize mine is too. All the panic is gone. Our matching kanji tattoos over our hearts—the symbol for knowledge. Our hearts know. They always have. "I am so in love with you."

Chapter Twenty-Three

"MEN ARE DIRTBAGS, that's all there is to it." Sam slouches into the blue vinyl chair in the back of Starbucks clutching her iced mocha to her chest as she finishes her tirade against men in general and Trent in specific.

Katie looks at me with a grimace. "Speaking of which, did you hear about Rick?"

"Rick," I say with a shake of my head. Three and a half years of my life, and it feels like it belonged to someone else. Even though I didn't realize it at the time, Rick was all about going through the motions. There was no intensity. No passion. "No. What about Rick?"

She grimaces. "Stacey's pregnant, and she's saying it's his."

I hang my head. There's no gloating. No one wins here. "Wow. That's tough."

"Like I said, dirtbags," Sam mutters.

I sip my espresso, and my face scrunches involuntarily. It's not nearly as strong or good as Italian espresso. I can't help the mournful emptiness in my chest at the memory of so many afternoons sipping espresso with Alessandro. I hope he's okay. "I don't know if they're *all* dirtbags."

"Well, let's start close to home, shall we?" Sam says, sitting straighter. "Your ex-boyfriend. Dirtbag, yes or no?"

I nod. "I'll concede that one."

"Your brother. Dirtbag or no?" she fires, her eyes narrowing to slits.

"No."

Her mouth drops into an O as her eyes fly wide. "So a guy treats *you* like shit, and he's a dirtbag, but he treats *me* like shit, and he's not?"

"I didn't say that."

Her eyes narrow again, and her fist clenches the plastic cup so hard, I'm expecting it to explode all over her at any second. "Yes you did. I asked point-blank if your stepbrother was a dirtbag, and you said no."

I swallow. I wish I could just tell her. I've been home four weeks, and Trent and I have been waiting for the right time to tell Dad and Julie. We have to tell them first, that much we know. But when I first got home, Julie was all, "Oh my word, Lexie! It's so good to have you home!" and, "Our whole family is finally together again!" I didn't want to ruin all that with our big confession, so I talked Trent into waiting. Then Julie got all weepy for like a week and kept saying how this was going to be the last of our time as a family because Trent had graduated and would be "flying the coop," so I didn't want to make her feel worse. But the longer we wait, the more awkward the whole thing gets.

"I just mean . . . did he ever lie to you?" I ask, remembering what Trent told me.

"Yes," she spits.

"What did he say that wasn't true?"

"He . . ." She bites her cheek for a second as she thinks, but then her eyes widen and shoot to me. "You knew, didn't you? And you didn't tell me? He told you he was into someone else."

I shake my head. "No. That's not what I meant."

She springs out of her chair and glares down at me. "He did! He told you, and you just let me go on about him like some kind of pathetic loser."

"No, Sam. I didn't know he was in love with someone else until just a few weeks ago."

"He's in *love* with her?" she says, exasperated, her free hand flying to her perfect auburn waves and yanking. Her eyes widen even more. "Oh my God! He told you who, didn't he?"

I drop my head into my hand, warding off the headache that's brewing behind my eyes. "Yes. He told me."

She flops into her chair. "Who is it?"

When I lift my head and look up at her, there's murder in her eyes. "Who it is doesn't matter. He said he told you from the start that there was someone else."

She slouches back in her seat and folds her arms across her chest. "He also said she wasn't into him." She glares up at me. "He just told me a few months ago that she'd met someone else. Why would he say that if he didn't want me to try to take his mind off her?"

I shrug. "I don't know, Sam. Maybe he was just trying to be honest. Maybe he just needed to talk to someone." I remember his saying how happy he was that I'd found someone to confide in. He didn't have anyone.

Katie's straw slurps in the bottom of her iced-coffee cup, and I look at her.

"How much weight did you say you lost?" I ask to change the subject before I get myself into serious trouble.

"Thirty-two pounds," she says proudly. Apparently, her roommate at San Diego talked her into joining one of those fat-burning boot camps. It's turned her into a whole new person. Her dark brown hair is pulled back off her face, and she's wearing lip gloss and mascara. Her neckline is a little lower than I ever remember seeing before, and she's in shorts instead of her usual jeans. I've always thought she was pretty, but now she's stunning.

"You look amazing. Maybe I should try your boot camp," I say.

She rolls her eyes but smiles.

When Katie drops me off at home, and her Beetle chugs away, Julie is on her way out.

"I'm running out to the store," she says, giving me a quick hug. "Is there anything you need?"

"I don't think so."

"If you think of anything, text me."

"'Kay, Julie."

"Your dad will be home around seven, so we'll plan on eating then." She closes the door, and when I head up the stairs, I hear Trent singing in the shower. I'm more than a little tempted to join him in there, but I restrain myself. Instead, I head to my laptop at my desk and flip it open. When I see I've got one unread e-mail, I assume it's from Abby. Grant was in London this past weekend. The fact that he made the trip surprised me in a good way, but I'm still worried about her. I spin her leather bracelet on my wrist as I open my in-box.

And my heart stops.

My hand is shaking as I click on Alessandro's e-mail.

Dearest Lexie,

The Galleria Nazionale d'Arte Antica notified me that you'd received the internship offer. I've been in Rome for the past few days and went to the gallery today, expecting to find you there. I was surprised when they told me you'd turned the offer down. Whatever the reason for your choice, I hope you're happy.

I'm writing because I feel the need to apologize for myself. I felt this would be best done in person, but as there is now a continent separating us, I'll have to rely on modern technology to relay my sincere regret for the way I exploited your trust.

I encouraged you to confide in me. I took advantage of my position to earn your trust, then I betrayed it and your friendship by making advances. I knew you didn't love me. I knew your true affections lay elsewhere, and I put you in an impossible position. I will be forever sorry for that.

I am still unsure of my path, but it is becoming more clear. I don't believe I'm well suited for the priesthood, but I believe, through the children's ministry, I can still serve and make a difference. Father Costa's support has been invaluable. I've confessed my shortcomings to him and the Lord, and through his counsel I've begun to sort through how I came to the place I am now and what the proper course is from here. It's been a painful lesson, but I feel stronger knowing the truth. Not everyone is meant for the calling. You helped me see that I am not.

My grandparents ask about you often and send you their warmest regards. I would be grateful for a reply so can I pass your news along to them. Mom asks about you as well. She's doing better now that I've left the priesthood.

I wish you much happiness, Lexie, and I hope there'll come a time you can look back on our months together in Rome fondly. I know I'll never forget you.

  All Warm Wishes,

  Alessandro

I don't hear the door open, which means I must have been truly zoned out because the hinges still squeak.

"Hey," Trent says, sweeping my hair aside and leaning down behind me to kiss the ticklish spot just below my ear. He's in a fresh T-shirt and jeans, and he smells like soap.

I reach up and grab a fistful of his damp brown hair, nuzzling my face into it. "Sam is going to hate us forever."

He turns his head and kisses me properly, hard on the lips. "She'll get over it."

"How are we going to do this?" I ask, my heart twisting in my chest. "People are going to think—"

"We've been over this, Lexie," he interrupts. "We can hide forever, or we can tell people. There aren't many other choices."

"We could move to Machu Picchu," I say with a cringe.

"Americans are getting kidnapped there." I hear the smirk in his voice as he stands behind me and rubs my shoulders, and even though I want to be mad, I feel myself melting into his capable hands.

"We have to tell our parents first," I say, tipping my cheek into the back of his hand as the tension slips out of my shoulders.

"And then I'll talk to Sam," he says.

And the tension is back.

"She thinks we're conspiring." I blow out a breath and roll my neck. "She has no idea."

He leans over my shoulder and kisses me again, then starts to pull me out of my desk chair by the hand. "I'm all for a little conspiring," he says with a wicked smile.

I untwist my fingers from his. "Give me a minute, okay? I have to answer this e-mail."

He looks over my shoulder at the laptop screen. "That the priest?"

I nod. "He's not going through with it, I guess."

He looks at me. "Because of you?"

I've told Trent everything. He knows about what happened with Alessandro on my dining-room table, and he knows I stopped because of him.

I shrug. "Partly. He says what happened with us helped him see that he wasn't meant for the priesthood."

"Take your time." He backs toward my bed and flops onto it. "I'll just be over here."

I smirk over my shoulder at him. "Like your lying on my bed looking all, 'do me, Lexie,' isn't going to distract me."

He clicks on my TV, queuing up Warcraft, then adjusts the pillows and props his head in his free hand. I take a second to ogle the sliver of perfect bronze skin between the hem of his T-shirt and the waistband of his jeans.

"Do me, Lexie," he whispers with a covert smile as Jethro charges headlong into a barrage of orcs. His amused gaze flicks to mine, and he grins.

I roll my eyes, then turn back to my computer screen and hit REPLY.

I breathe deep, trying to remember all the things I was prepared to tell Alessandro if I'd found him at the rectory after Easter.

Dear Alessandro,
    I don't know where to begin. I feel like what happened between us was more because I wasn't respectful of boundaries. I knew nothing could ever happen between us, or at least, that's what I thought, so I flirted with you and led you on. It was horrible

and selfish. I just never thought it all the way through, and I'm so sorry for that. I never realized what I was doing to you.

That night in my apartment, you asked if I had feelings for you. I do. You are probably the best person I will ever know, and you will always hold a special place in my heart. I have always believed that you could make a difference in this world, and I know no matter what path you choose from here, you will do exactly that. But you're right, my true feelings lie with Trent. He's asked me to marry him. We haven't told our parents yet, but we're going to have to. Soon.

Thank you so much for everything you did on my behalf regarding the internship. I'm sorry to have disappointed you. It was a painful decision, but after a lot of soul-searching, I just felt like I needed to come home. And, yes, I'm happy. I hope you find happiness too.

Please say hello to your family for me.

    All warm wishes,

    Lexie

I hit SEND and stare at my screen for another minute before flipping my laptop closed. "So, we're doing this tonight?" I ask as I stand and face Trent.

"I don't want to keep sneaking around, Lexie." Trent pauses Warcraft and hauls himself off the bed, wrapping his arms around me and pulling me into his body.

And, *mmm. . .*

I kiss his Adam's apple. "Me either, but it's not like

they're going to let me move into your bedroom or anything."

He tips his head and looks down at me. "I told you, this isn't about the sex. This is about us spending the rest of our lives together."

"It's a little about the sex," I murmur into his chest.

I feel his chuckle under my cheek.

The truth is, since I've been home, I've become a total nymph. I want Trent all the time. Most nights, I'm in his bed as soon as our parents turn out the lights downstairs. I've gotten pretty good at being quiet when Trent does what he does and makes me feel what he makes me feel, but there are times I just have to bite on a pillow as I scream and hope our parents are sound sleepers.

We haven't been getting much sleep, but I've never felt so alive.

Dad is usually up for work by six, so Trent sets his alarm for five so whoever's not where they belong can go back to their own bed before anyone finds us. He's right. It's been four weeks of sneaking around, and I know it's wrong, but the fact is, if our parents know about us, they're likely to start paying attention to our whereabouts, which wouldn't bode well for my newfound nymphomania.

I slip my fingers under the waistband of Trent's jeans, tracing along the small of his back, around the sides to his cut abs, and end at the button of his jeans, which I flick open.

"Lex," he warns with a glance at the door, but it's half-hearted because his fingers are trailing along the curve of my breast. His thumb finds my hardening nipple and rubs through my clothes, and I want his skin on mine.

Now.

"Julie's shopping." I pull my shirt off as he unhooks my bra, and before I know it, he's lifted me off the ground and carried me the few steps to the bed. He lays me down and tugs his shirt over his head as I kick my jeans and thong to the floor.

He glances back at the door as if he's thinking twice.

"Uh-uh, mister," I say as he starts to balk where he stands at the side of the bed. "Don't even think about quitting now." I sit up on the bed and unzip him, freeing his sizable erection from his navy boxer briefs. I pull him to me with a belt loop, so he's standing between my knees, then grab him with both hands and squeeze as I lean forward. When I take him into my mouth, he tips his head back, and moans. "Christ, Lexie."

I'm not playing fair. He would never ask me for it, but I know he lives for this.

He tastes salty as I sheathe my teeth behind my lips and suck him deep into my mouth. I roll my tongue over him and move slowly, gliding his length in and out. His moans make me want to keep going, to make him feel as good as his mouth on me makes me feel. But his fingers in my hair tighten as his erection grows harder and starts to pulse, and he pulls me back.

"Lexie," he gasps, and I know he's right on the edge of coming.

I look up at him. "You don't have to stop," I say, rolling my tongue over the tip of his thickness. "I'd be okay with it."

He grins wicked and presses me back onto the bed, hooking his hands through my knees and spreading me wide. "Nope," he says, "ladies first." He kneels at the side of the bed, and the next second, his mouth is on me.

"Oh, shit," I gasp when his tongue flicks my clit.

His fingers glide inside me and twist as he sucks, and *shit*! I gasp again as stars flash in my eyes, and I feel dizzy. He has my head spinning and my body aching for him in two seconds flat. How does he do that? With his free hand, he spreads my legs wider and trails his hand between them, pressing a wet finger hard into my clit as his tongue swirls in my belly button. My body has a will of its own, and I writhe with the rhythm of his fingers, gliding in and out. Then his mouth is on me again, and this time, when he flicks his tongue and sucks, the stars I was seeing explode through my body, and every synapse short-circuits as I cry out.

My whole body buzzes like a high-tension electrical wire as Trent reaches into my nightstand drawer. He kicks his jeans off and crawls onto the bed, lying on his side next to me. He kisses my neck and brings me out of the stratosphere and back to the bedroom. My senses start to return, and I take the condom from his hand and tear it open, then push him onto his back and roll it onto my new favorite part of his anatomy. He watches with hungry eyes as I straddle his hips and ease his length inside me.

And that's all it takes to get me going again.

One second, I'm totally spent, and the next I feel the tension build in my belly again as he fills me. My groin pulses with the pounding of my heart as I move on top of him. He pumps from below and rubs his thumb in circles over my clit. "Oh, God," I breathe with every thrust until it all just blends into one long, animal mewl. He presses harder and pumps faster until my body becomes nothing more than a ball of raw nerve endings—all sensation. I feel everything tenfold: the sweat tricking between my breasts, the brush of my hair over my back as I ride him, and Trent, hot and thick inside me. Harder. Faster.

He grasps my hips hard and gives one last upward thrust, so deep that I feel it in my soul, and the fireworks go off in my belly again.

"Ah! Lexie!" he growls, then goes still under me, breathing hard.

I lie on top of him and kiss his shoulder. The salt of his sweat and the spicy scent that's just Trent fill my senses. I close my eyes and just live in him.

His fingertips trail like feathers over my back, raising goose bumps. "I love you," he whispers. "Always."

Two sharp knuckle raps on the door wake me, then Julie's voice. "Lexie, hon?"

I lift my head blearily as the door hinges creak . . . and that's when I realize I'm still draped over Trent.

He jumps at the same instant I do, but it's too late. I hear Julie's gasp.

Chapter Twenty-Four

I PULL THE sheets over me and turn to the door, mortified. "We just . . ." I trail off, knowing there's no explaining this.

"We were playing Warcraft and fell asleep," Trent interjects into the deafening silence.

For a second, Julie's twisted features relax. She obviously wants to believe it because the alternative is just too horrifying. But we're stark naked. There's no way she missed that. She got an eyeful before I was awake enough to yank the sheets up.

She stands frozen in the door. Her gaze turns wary, and her fair skin goes three shades whiter as she works out that Trent must be lying. "What's . . ." She shakes head, still trying to get her mind around what she's seeing. "What's going on?"

Trent's pecs and biceps ripple as he pulls himself up to a sitting position, keeping the sheet draped over the parts he probably hasn't shown his mother since he was five. How is it that even now, when we're so totally and royally screwed, I'm still noticing how hot he is?

He blows out a breath. "I know this is a shock, Mom," he says in his most soothing voice, "and I'm really sorry. This wasn't how we'd planned for you to find out. We were going to tell you and Randy tonight at dinner."

Her wary gaze begins to storm, and her face pulls tight as she regards her son. "Tell us what?" Her voice has gone up a full octave.

Trent's eyes flick to me, and I realize that he might be a little embarrassed, but he's not scared or unsure. Just seeing the confidence in that gaze—knowing he believes in us as much as I do—reassures me. "We didn't plan for this to happen, but just before Lexie left for Rome, something happened between us. Since then, we've realized that we love each other."

Her gaze, somewhere between betrayed and angry, shifts to me. "Lexie?"

I force the cringe off my face. If Trent can be brave, so can I. "It's true, Julie. We're in love." I hold the sheet to cover myself as I wiggle toward the nightstand and pull out the black velvet box, but just then, the garage door opener starts grinding away below us.

Dad.

Julie's expression has gone through so many emotions in the last two minutes, but now it's just blank. I think she's in shock. "That's your father. Dinner's ready." She spins and leaves the room, without closing the door.

"Shit," I hiss when I hear her feet on the tile of the entryway at the bottom of the stairs.

Trent folds me into his arms. "It's going to be okay, Lexie. We were just about to tell them anyway. We're not doing anything wrong."

I bring my knees up to my chest, wrapping my arms tightly around them, and bury my face, trying to make myself as small as possible. "Daddy's going to freak."

Trent pulls the ring box out of my hand and lifts my face. "Is this what you want, Lexie? Do you want me?"

"Hell, yeah. I want you all the time. That's what got us caught."

He shakes his head at me. "I mean for real. Do you really want to marry me?"

I look at him with wide eyes, surprised he'd even question that. "Of course. I love you."

He looks relieved for a second, then opens the box and pulls the ring out, sliding it onto my finger. "Then let's do this." He sweeps my wild hair off my face and kisses me, slow and deep, his tongue twisting slowly into mine, and all of a sudden I know where the term "soul kiss" comes from, because that's where I feel it. My soul aches for him.

He pulls me up, and we get dressed. I straighten myself in the mirror, then we head downstairs.

Julie is banging around in the kitchen, and when I look into the family room, it's obvious she hasn't said anything to Dad. He's in his recliner with his legs up, surfing channels.

"I'll go get Mom," Trent says.

I nod, and he gives my hand a squeeze before heading to the kitchen. I move slowly toward Dad, and I feel as if I'm moving through molasses—everything in slow motion. "Daddy?" I ask, standing at the side of his chair.

He reaches up and gives my hand a tug, smiling up at me with his warm smile. "Hey, kiddo. How was your day?"

How can I do this? He's going to be so disappointed in us. In *me*.

I back away a step, feeling the urge to run, but then Trent comes into the room with Julie, who still looks like she's in shock. He leads her to her recliner next to Dad's and almost physically sits her in it. He ushers me to the couch, where we sit side by side.

I feel like I'm going to pass out. There's a funny ringing in my ears, and I feel cold all over. I can't look at them. But then Trent takes my hand, twisting his fingers into mine, and at least that part of me feels warm again.

The silence has physical weight. It crushes me as I sit, chewing my cheek.

"What's happened?" Dad's voice is edged with alarm, and that forces my eyes to him.

"Nothing bad, Daddy . . ." I glance at Trent for strength. "But Trent and I have something we need to talk to you and Julie about." I dare a glance at Julie, but she's looking straight ahead at some random point on the wall, her jaw tight. Trent squeezes my hand, and I take a deep breath.

Do it fast, like ripping off a Band-Aid.

"Trent and I are in love, and we're getting married." It comes out in a tumble of words that I say, but don't really hear because blood is pounding through my ears, and my mind is a blur of spinning images: Dad throwing Trent and me out, never speaking to me again, yelling, slamming, throwing. It's not like Dad's ever been violent, but the thought of him angry is too much to bear. Before Trent and Julie, it was just us. Dad and me. We've always been together. What if he can't stand the sight of me?

But Julie's gasp catches me and yanks me back to the here and now. "Married?"

She's focused now, her wide eyes fixed on my hand.

Trent lifts my hand and shows them the ring.

"You two are engaged," Dad says slowly, as though he's trying to work it into something that's not totally crazy.

"We realized while Lexie was away that we loved each other . . . as more than family," Trent says. "I think we've always had feelings for each other. We just didn't see our feelings for what they were until now."

Dad's face blanches, and he just stares at us like we have two heads . . . or two heads *each*, I guess, so four heads, really. "I don't even know what to make of this."

"Daddy, please don't be mad," I squeak out through my tight throat.

"So you two have been . . ." He trails off and waves his hand in a circle at us, his face tightening with his discomfort, obviously hoping we'll catch his drift so he doesn't have to say it.

Out of the corner of my eye, I see Julie squirm uncomfortably in her chair.

"Not until recently," Trent says, matter-of-fact.

I know my face is flaming because I feel my cheeks burn.

Dad lowers the legs of his recliner abruptly and stands, yanking a hand through his disheveled hair. He sits, then stands again and stares down at us in disgust before bolting from the room.

I flinch a second later at the sound of the front door slamming behind him.

Julie springs out of her chair without even looking in our direction and flies out the door behind him.

I'm paralyzed in my seat. This is my worst nightmare. Tears prick the corner of my eyes, and, as they run over my lashes, I can't even move to wipe them away.

"They'll come around," Trent says low in my ear, but he sounds as stunned as I feel.

He pulls me into his arms and kisses my forehead when I don't respond, but I wiggle out of his grasp.

I choke out on a sob. Trent is everything to me . . . but what if Dad can't get past this? I stand and walk up the stairs to my room, numb. I flop on my bed with my arm over my face. Tears roll into my ears as I hitch out sobs, realizing I've ruined my family. Our parents will never be able to look at us the same again. I stuff a pillow over my head and hope the Earth will just crash into the sun or something, so I don't have to face Dad again.

"Lex," Trent says from my door. "You okay?"

"No."

I feel the side of the bed dip as Trent sits. "What do you want to do?"

My hitching breath starts to slow, and I toss the pillow aside and climb onto his lap, curling into his arms. "Sing to me."

He kisses my temple, and his voice starts low. He's only a line in when I realize it's a song I've only heard once before, coming out of his BlackBerry as we sat on my bed in Rome. I'm sobbing into his shirt again by the time he gets to the chorus. He lifts my head and thumbs the tears off my face, gazing so far into me that I feel him in my soul. His voice goes all gravel as he sings,

> You picked me up and helped me heal,
> You taught me what it meant to feel.
> Now I can, now I do, and everything I feel is you.
> I would never do you wrong,
> or let you down or lead you on.
> I can't stop now, I'll come unglued, when everything I
>   feel is you.

When he finishes, he kisses me so gently that it makes me cry again. "You are my world, Lexie. If we have to do this without our parents' okay, then that's what it's going to be, but I really think they'll come around." He kisses me again, deeper this time, and the intensity of it crushes my heart.

"I love you so much," I whisper against his lips.

A throat clears from the doorway, and we both look up to find Dad and Julie standing there, staring at us.

Dad's face is pinched. He just looks at us for a long heartbeat before saying, "I'm sorry for my reaction. If you . . ." He clears his throat again as his eyes drift away from us. "If you two wouldn't mind coming back downstairs, we'd like to talk about this." He looks at us for another second, and his expression softens a little before he turns and heads back down the stairs. Julie gives us a wary smile and follows.

Dad motions to the couch when Trent leads me into he family room, his hand firmly in mine. We slide into our seats, and Dad and Julie lower themselves back into their recliners. Dad props his elbows on his knees, tenting his fingers in front of his nose, his chin resting on his thumbs—his thinking position.

"Daddy, I'm so sor—" I start, but he raises his hand, stopping me.

"Every father has dreams for his little girl," he says. His eyes land on Trent. "With any luck, someday you'll know that firsthand." He lowers his hands from his face and presses back in his seat, his gaze finding mine again. "My dream for my little girl has always been that she would grow up to be the strong, capable, beautiful woman she is, and that she would find someone who would make her as happy as she's made me." His eyes start to glisten, and he stops, drawing a deep breath and holding it for a second before blowing it out slowly through pursed lips. "I hoped she would find a good man—someone who would love her as much as I do; someone who would respect her for who she is and support her and encourage her to reach for her dreams." He swallows, and his moist gaze shifts to Trent. "And for my son, I've always hoped he'd grow up to be a good man; someone with morals and solid values. Someone people could look to as a role model. Someone who knows who he is and what he wants and isn't afraid to shoot for the stars." He reaches for Julie's hand and squeezes. "I got everything I ever could have hoped for."

Trent shifts next to me. "So we have your blessing?"

Dad blows out a breath and looks at us for an excruciatingly long time before saying, "This isn't just hormones? You two have seriously thought about this?"

We both nod.

Dad shifts back into thinking position, elbows on knees and his hands tented in front of his face. "You may be done with school, Trent, but Lexie still has a year of college, then maybe grad school. I hope you two aren't planning to rush anything."

"Of course," Trent says. "We won't even think about doing anything until Lexie's done, and we both have jobs."

"Lexie's career path is a narrow one," Dad warns, a deep V forming between his eyebrows. "What if it requires her to relocate?"

"I know she wants to curate a children's museum, and I know those jobs are extremely hard to come by. I'll go wherever she needs me to." Trent squeezes my hand and looks at me. "I'll follow her anywhere."

My love for this beautiful, incredible man swells up and flows over in tears that I quickly wipe away.

"And your music?" Julie asks Trent.

He breathes deep and holds it for a second, his hand twitching in mine. "All I've ever wanted to do was write and perform. I can do that anywhere."

"I thought you were going to teach," she says, looking a little stricken.

Trent pinches his lips between his teeth and rubs his forehead. "That's what *you* want. Randy just got done saying I shouldn't be afraid to shoot for the stars."

I glance at Dad, who inclines his head and lifts an eyebrow. But he doesn't argue.

Julie's expression shifts yet again. She still has that unsure tilt to her mouth, like she's trying to work something out—which could possibly have to do with the fact that she walked in on her buck-naked son and stepdaughter basking in what was quite obviously postcoital glow—but her eyes aren't lifeless pebbles anymore. They're looking us over with the same love I've always seen there.

"Well," Dad finally says with half a smirk, "I guess I know whose family is paying for the wedding."

Trent smiles at Dad, and he smiles back.

"Dinner's getting cold," Julie says, standing from her recliner. "We can talk more about this later."

We get to our feet, and the three of us follow Julie to the kitchen.

Dad shakes his head and looks back at us with a wry smile before passing through the door. "I have to admit, I never saw this coming."

"Neither did we," I say, finally brave enough to open my mouth again.

"Trent, can you get the rolls out of the oven?" Julie says to him, as Dad moves to the cupboard for glasses and starts filling them with ice and water. "And Lexie, if you'll pull some plates down, I've got everything else on the table."

I move to the cupboard and watch as everyone goes about their tasks, like it's just any other night.

Trent and I are out there—official—and the Earth didn't fall off its axis. I have Trent, and Dad and Julie still love us. Alessandro is with his family. He's still sorting things out, but he's going to be okay. Sam will most likely hate me forever, but maybe not. This might just be okay.

Maybe there are happily ever afters. Who knew?

Lexie and Trent may have found
their happily-ever-after,
but Alessandro Moretti's story
is just beginning . . .

Continue reading for a sneak peek at

A Little Too Much

On sale November 2013
from William Morrow

There are ghosts in twenty-two-year-old Hilary McIntyre's past that she'd just as soon forget. But life is finally starting to look up. She's gotten herself straightened out and she's daring to shoot for her childhood dream of becoming a Broadway actress. She's got the voice, she's got the looks, now all she needs is the in, and her boyfriend, who's already scored a major support role, is going to be it. But unfortunately for Hilary, ghosts from your past don't always stay dead.

When Alessandro Moretti shows up on her doorstep, she knows he could ruin everything, but he's got ghosts of his own, and apparently, she's one of them. She hasn't seen him since they were teenagers in the group home, but a week hasn't gone by in the eight years since that she hasn't thought of him or his brother. Even so, there's no way she's going to let his reappearance throw her off her game. And she sure as hell isn't going to tell him her secret—even though there's something about him that makes her want to. When she finds herself falling for him all over again, she has a decision to make. Her future or her past? The truth or the lie?

I STOP AT the ATM and deposit my check, then head home. The drizzle has picked up and by the time I get there, I'm pretty soaked, but I don't really mind. I like walking in the rain. It's one of the few things other than sex that I find really calming. Puddles are starting to form on the sidewalk and I walk right through them, splashing up as much water as I can without full-out stomping like a four-year-old. I'm actually smiling when I get to the door of our apartment and look up.

And then I'm not smiling anymore.

There's a guy standing in my doorway. A tall guy in black cargo pants, army boots, and a blue hoodie. A gorgeous guy. And he's staring at me.

"Hilary?" he asks, and he's got a light accent that I can't identify with just that one word. Something European, maybe?

"It depends," I say backing off a step. He looks familiar, but I can't place him. He's got wavy black hair that's slicked back from his forehead and dark eyes all set in one of the most beautiful man-faces I've ever seen. His skin is olive, no darker than mine, but a totally different shade. He's got to be an actor or something. Maybe I know him from an audition? "Who's asking?"

"It's me, Hilary. Alessandro."

His face blurs and the streetlights above my head spin. I feel myself wobble on my feet before I brace my hand on the building and get my bearings again. "Alessandro?" I've only known one person with that name.

His face scrunches a little. "Alessandro Moretti . . . from the group home?"

The next thing I know I'm on my ass in a puddle, my legs having turned to Jell-O, and Alessandro has my arm. I look up at his concerned face. "What are you doing here?"

He helps me off the sidewalk but stops short of brushing off my ass. "I needed to see you . . . to talk to you."

My stomach plummets to my toes and I think for a second that I should have stayed down. Does he know? How could he have found out?

I lean back against the wall for support. "Where's Lorenzo?" All of a sudden I'm desperate to know if he's coming for me too.

His lips press into a hard line and his charcoal eyes darken. He closes them and breathes deep before opening them again. "Lorenzo has been dead for two years."

About the Author

LISA DESROCHERS is the author of the young adult *Personal Demons* trilogy. She lives in northern California with her husband, two very busy daughters, and Shini the tarantula. If you'd told her five years ago she'd write a book, she'd have laughed in your face. As it turns out, she'd owe you an apology. Writing has become an addiction for Lisa, and *A Little Too Far* is her first novel for adults. When she's not writing, she's reading, and she adores stories that take her to new places, then take her by surprise.

Find her online at www.lisadwrites.com, on Twitter at @LisaDez, and on Facebook at www.facebook.com/lisadwrites.

Visit www.AuthorTracker.com for exclusive information on your favorite HarperCollins authors.